PRAISE FOR WE ARE A HAUNTING

"A gorgeous novel about loss, survival and community. . . . This is a stunningly original and beautiful novel of devotion, a book that gives and gives as it asks us what it means to be part of a family, of a community. Early novels like this don't come around very often; this one brings to mind titles like Toni Morrison's *Song of Solomon* and Louise Erdrich's *Love Medicine*. It's an absolute triumph."

—Michael Schaub, NPR

"Poignant and poetic . . . Each character is acutely aware of the weight of their forebears, which White uses to effectively tell a story that is both intimate and sweeping . . . White works wonders with this inspired story of grief and the struggle for hope." **—*Publishers Weekly* (starred review)**

"The multivoiced novel develops each wounded person in terms of their connections to the city. Their stories are linked by rhapsodic longing . . . There are vigorous details from their lives that evoke deep understanding of their problems. And as Colly is tender in recalling Key in the midst of his own experiences; his bereavement is indelible, and it overlays the book's cityscapes, both rending and buoying him. . . . A Black family's history becomes a salve for its wandering son in the potent novel *We Are a Haunting*."

—Karen Rigby, *Foreword Reviews* (starred review)

"[*We Are a Haunting*'s] wide-ranging, multivocal, quick-shifting style—which incorporates frequent allusions to literature and visual art, brand names and the neighborhood prestige attached to them, and a mixtape element—serves admirably to emphasize the book's ambition, which is to capture and to celebrate not just these characters, this family, but the community and the city they emerge from, serve, and love. An intelligent, gritty, discursive group portrait of working-class New York from the 1980s to now." **—*Kirkus Reviews***

"In this poignant and moving novel, White pulls back the curtain on cycles of violence and reveals the beating heart of tough, working-class individuals. It is somber, harsh, uplifting, shocking, and unforgettable." **—*Debutiful***

"White's work is brave, raw, and tugs at the essence of New York City. As we time travel and bear witness between the living and dead, the past and present, you can't help but fall in love with this cast of characters, worry about them, and ultimately wish them well." **—TC. Mann, PEN America**

"Tyriek White's debut novel, *We Are a Haunting*, strikes me as both a love letter to New York City and a kind of elegy. . . . The writing, on both a sentence and a structural level, is magical." **—Maisy Card in *Poets & Writers***

"What a beautiful, haunting, and hued narrative of American living. I'm in love with this story and the way Tyriek White breathes life into these characters." **—Jacqueline Woodson, author of *Another Brooklyn***

"This is the city. This is beauty, this is harshness. With this magnificent debut, Tyriek White emerges as a seer and necessary voice. " **—Nana Kwame Adjei-Brenyah, author of *Chain-Gang All-Stars***

"Tyriek White did not come to play. He is doing something for New York narratives I've never seen, and really never imagined. This novel is so New York—so, so New York—yet so deeply Southern on lower frequencies. It's astonishing." **—Kiese Laymon, author of *Heavy* and *Long Division***

"This is visionary writing about the lives of visionary people, but they come to us entrenched in the real history of an overwhelmingly real city. Tyriek White's cultural and political erudition is as extraordinary as his lyricism." **—Jonathan Lethem, author of *Motherless Brooklyn***

"*We Are a Haunting* demonstrates the depth and versatility of the family saga as a genre. It's the story of a mother and son whose lives are in conversation with one another through time and death. It's also the story of how Black and brown communities in New York have held each other up and persevered in the face of systematic indifference and deliberate attempts at our obliteration. An impressive debut from a powerful new voice."

—Maisy Card, author of *These Ghosts Are Family*

"It is a wonder to me that a novel so incisive about cycles of violence and generational pain can also be so tender, so generously alive to the pleasures of the body and the ampleness of the spirit. And that sentences so redolent of grief can also be fleet and alert as deer, ready to dart in any direction, or to run up against revelation and be transformed. Tyriek White is the rare, real thing: an astonishment."

—Garth Greenwell, author of *Cleanness* and *What Belongs to You*

WE ARE A HAUNTING

A NOVEL

TYRIEK WHITE

ASTRA
HOUSE
NEW
YORK

For information about permission to reproduce selections from this book,
please contact permissions@astrahouse.com.

Astra House
A Division of Astra Publishing House
astrahouse.com
Printed in the United States of America

Library of Congress Cataloging-in-Publication Data

Names: White, Tyriek, 1991– author.
Title: We are a haunting : a novel / Tyriek White.
Description: New York : Astra House, [2023] | Summary: "We Are a Haunting
is a debut, coming-of-age novel that mixes magical realism and the
Southern Gothic and follows three generations of East New Yorkers
struggling to maintain a connection to their history"-- Provided by publisher.
Identifiers: LCCN 2022049819 | ISBN 9781662601712 (hardcover) |
ISBN 9781662601729 (ebook)
Subjects: LCGFT: Magic realist fiction. |
Novels. Classification: LCC PS3623.H579435 W4 2023 |
DDC 813/.6--dc23/eng/20221122
LC record available at https://lccn.loc.gov/2022049819
ISBN 9781662602665 (pb)

First paperback edition, 2024
10 9 8 7 6 5 4 3 2 1

Design by Richard Oriolo
The text is set in Utopia Std.
The titles are set in Bouchers Sans 2.0.

To my grandmother.

To what end does one conjure the ghost of slavery, if not to incite the hopes of transforming the present?

—SAIDIYA HARTMAN

CONTENTS

BROOKLYN NEW YORK

GREEN COURTS

FLATLANDS AVE

BOULEVARD HOUSES

ASHFORD ST

LINDEN BLVD

AFRICAN BURIAL GROUND SQUARE

SCHENCK AVE

VAN SICLEN AVE

GEORGE GERSHWIN PARK

NEW LOTS AVE

LIVONIA AVE

PENNSYLVANIA AVE

WE ARE A HAUNTING

PROLOGUE

One day, I fell backward into a scar in the world, a fall sudden and lasting. A portal took me whole, sent me traveling across a pulse that could split me down the middle. I tumbled out the other side, a terrible moaning like a hive of meat bees.

I had been pedaling down the block on an unkempt length of road on Flatlands, barreling ahead, ripping along twisted storefronts and storage lots. The smell of hot metal filled the air, lodged itself at the back of my tongue and burned as I tried to catch my breath. I had reached the Belt Parkway and the creek widened, blooming into the bay and into the Atlantic, the dark basin, murky with trash and wildlife, boats twinkling in the distance. The water emptied into a reservoir where it was drained and then treated. There were heating and waste stations, chimneys that gagged out heavy smoke and stray embers into the clouds over the land. A bridge reached over the harbor, kept Far Rockaway at bay, the lights from ferries and small boats parting the darkness. In the distance, I saw the shape of Boulevard through the fog, apartments stacked atop one another, our city in the clouds, embassies of time, crashing dimensions and histories, the cursed, the lost, the all-seeing. No different from Ingersoll Houses, or Marcus Garvey, or Tilden; Chelsea, or Pink Houses, or Brevoort; Farragut, or Walt Whitman Houses, or Baisley Park. No different from Saint Nicholas, or Queensbridge, or Mott Haven.

You died without telling me what it was like to be in two places, without designation, without home, no matter how hard you try to make one for yourself.

When I reach out for you, tipping over, into a slippage of time. I feel my body grow open, my hand wrapped in another. This is Nana, blood rushing to her fingers, her hands the color of pink salt. We are in the doorjamb of a temporary house. I see a shoal of folk near the center of a settlement farther down, along the gray water. I follow the sound. A dirt path like a welt stretching toward the sea. I slip through the cattails and the buttonbushes, under the river birches and needles of the bald cypress. The smell stays with me, on my hands and in my hair. The smoke above the huts on the beach carried spiced meats and greens. Through the bramble, the band of sweet pepperbush, I see the shore open up, the ocean flat. Cloudy. The person standing in front of me didn't look like anyone I knew but felt like you. A ways down the beach I hear a crowd; the smell of fresh food and spices from an open market. High tide sounds like a stampede. My feet are sinking into the loam, the wet paste of sand and dirt. I am barefoot in the duckweed. You see me, the same expression in my dreams, a sad smile.

"Oh, baby, when did it hurt so bad?" you ask. Not why does it hurt, or where does it hurt, but when? I feel like all the times, the time before me, an ache that was precolonial, a Paleolithic expanse of sorrow. You are Cybele carved in Anatolian stone.

"You were just gone one morning," I tell you. "And I know it sounds like I blame you but I don't."

"Yes, you do."

"That's not fair."

"Are love and sacrifice not dark synonyms for one another?"

I turn away, take a few steps up the beach. When all felt lost, being seen through your grief, really seen, was all that mattered. *What if*, I always thought, *if I never met you, never felt you gone because you weren't there in the first place*. In my mind, it was like being without something from birth— sight or a limb—and how it compared to having the thing, losing it, then living the rest of a life without it. Inevitably, the thing dries and crumbles like sand and one is forced to dream away the incessant drum of missing, make themselves anew. When you died, Pop told me I'd only think of life in two phases: life with you and life without you. Said when he lost his own mother, folk could only see him as an unfinished body, what was sundered, removed. Never how he created a new whole, had to reimagine what those parts left could amount to. After he'd finished his stories, I would try to drift to sleep without thinking about the old him, the sawed-through flesh and muscle, the hacking of bone, the dark blood that painted the emergency room. I tried to imagine anything else besides the yellows and browns his body leaked, the pus, the clotting of fluid, a cursive written on his skin and across smocks and sinking through sheets. If I never knew you, perhaps I'd still be who I was before you died. I would never do the hard work of looking beyond myself to see others suffering along with me, that the world and the human condition were threaded around the work of community, our care for one another. I feel my gut stir when I look back at you—remorse. I want you to know the new ways I could love, which I had learned for better or for worse.

"Here," you say, easing me into the current. A cool wind from the ocean had pelted sand into my hair. It stung my eyes, made me shiver down to my toes. There was a hole in the night sky, where it all goes in the end, some giant we've mistaken for sun or light. I have this strange feeling of culmination, what could be made of all those histories, an infinite process—hilltop city of seven waters. "I'll tell you everything."

PART
ONE

BEFORE YOU LEAVE
(2008)

There are mostly women in housing court. It's not like men don't get put out—she had put Virgil out years ago, in the middle of night, and that was her husband. This was just who was left. When a home is emptied out, usually the men take what they can and the women are left to put it all back together again. They were old and young, exhausted, often bounced around buildings, across plazas, directed to addresses across town. You need to go here for a copy of your voucher. The main housing office can verify your proof of address. This form needs to be notarized. Women who worked all kinds of hours to keep a roof over somebody head. *Women like Momma*, Audrey thought, *who would've spent a lifetime in waiting rooms, behind counters or glass windows, filling out paperwork—all to keep it together.*

The central air nipped at the tender parts of her arms, the pinch of flesh above the elbow. The judge listened to the statements her landlord made.

Audrey was sixty-three and fed up with it all: the ring cycle, the taxing of spirit, the cost of forms, subway fare. There was a young woman Audrey kept seeing at the main desk asking questions. She was a nurse at Methodist; Audrey knew because she was still in her scrubs. The woman explained how she had walked from Ingersoll Houses, down the stretch of Myrtle to Jay Street, to get here. Now she had to walk to Atlantic, all the way across the park, to get to work. Audrey asked what she was here for.

"My brother did something stupid," the woman said, almost through closed eyelids. "Now they can evict me and my son 'cause my name is on the lease."

Audrey couldn't afford an attorney, but her cousin, Gloria, had a son who just passed the bar and worked as a public advocate at a nonprofit. Demetrius was a nervous boy, with hands like saucers that seemed too large for his wiry frame. He kept adjusting his cuffs when he spoke to the judge. "Social Security hasn't increased her benefits in years, and with medication, cost of living . . ."

"It's still not up to your client to make that decision," the judge said, which Audrey found peculiar.

She hadn't paid last month's due, nor had she cared to the month before. Not even the month before that. She continued writing her checks for her rent-controlled apartment, all for the same amount as she had before the last increase. The landlord wouldn't even call somebody about the ceiling or the stuff that came up out of the drains every so often, but he asked for extra dollars more each month. In that regard, yes, she was guilty.

When they filed out of the courtroom, Demetrius turned to her to apologize.

"It's all right, baby," Audrey said, and shrugged. "What can you do?"

"If I can get them to give us more time," he said, holding open the door for her.

The sun was hardly over the other side of the East River, laboring over the skyline, peeking through the alleys and streets. She waved the young man away and caught the subway back down toward Flatbush, flipping through the *New York Post*.

Audrey got off at her stop and walked toward her building. There were women her age gathered by the corner, dressed in polished leather flats and church hats, *Watchtower* pamphlets in hand. The ladies who ran the tenant association sat outside on the sidewalk, gossiping in beach chairs. Their husbands played dominos out front the bodegas or tuned their cars up in their driveways. They would be out there until dusk, drinking cold beer across from the park.

When Audrey finally closed the door behind her, she dropped her bags and removed her clothes. Turned the kettle on. Let the silence wash over her, looking out the window as light strained through the blinds. Shadows moved across the apartment walls. She watched them flutter, looked along her shelf—the glass figurines, the decorative plaques from the senior center, wood-sculpted ornaments, picture frames of her grandbabies Satoia and Colly pouting at her, the ceramic succulents, the actual succulents planted in small clay pots.

Audrey had the impulse to call her granddaughter the night before. Key had been gone a year or so. Now she looked down at her from a family portrait done at a shop at the Albee Square mall, those precious babies on either side of their mother in their Sunday clothes. Behind them was Dante, the husband, with those heavy eyes of his.

Where are you going to go? she asked Virgil. He sat in an armchair across the room, grunting at something only he could see.

Are you going to stay here?

Still no answer. He didn't say much when he was alive either.

THE JUNE HEAT set the day in its lap and wrapped the city in its arms as proof. Audrey pulled a weed from the soft soil of the small garden and wondered whether the day had ever wanted room to grow. It sits all day and every day, the world in its lap, watching trees stretch toward its light. Audrey looked up, jealous of the day, wondering, *Is it ever jealous of me?*

As the sun hung over the trees, the mosquitoes would join, a song of blood. Audrey usually worked in the mornings, before the heat, planting green onion and cucumber. Today, she had to begin a little before noon. The soil was dark and rich between her fingers. The garden was a square plot behind her apartment building. When she had found it years ago, abandoned and littered with drug vials, soda cans, and other scraps, she had cleared the plot out and begun putting down a layer of topsoil. She then began working her tiny piece of land, despite her bad knees and lower back that flared up if she bent too long.

Audrey gathered some of what she had been growing. Sweet blueberries, tomatoes across from mustard greens, leeks, and a couple peaches from a slender tree. Being close to the soil cooled her skin under the noon sun. It took her mind away from the fact that it would be gone soon. Her home wouldn't belong to her anymore, as if it ever had.

When she was a young girl, she would spend every summer on her grandfather's farm. She hated it. It was the fifties, and Audrey was more interested in going to the cotillions, the debutante balls, drinking tea with fancy Southern women who offered their homes for plantation tours—than toiling over farmwork. She watched a carrot seed grow and milled around, doing a bunch of yard work when she'd rather just clean the house. You'll thank me later, her father would say. He showed her how to plant the seeds, in rows along the furrows they made, measuring how deep into the earth, how far apart. His big hands kneaded hers into the cool, damp soil. She was more interested in the movie theater that offered tickets for ten cents, the diner so crowded at midnight that folk spilled out onto its back porch, the boys who were wide as the trees that lined her grandfather's property.

Back then every boy in North Carolina had a car and no reasonable curfew. They spoke slowly, more to her body's cadence. Not like Georgia boys or Mississippi boys, too fast with mouths full of rocks or gold. Virgil was no different, talking to her as sweet and slow as growing molasses. He was sun-dried and tall, blocking the sunrays from her eyes when she looked up at him. He was just a boy then, genuine, but with something unquenchable behind his eyes. He drove his car too fast and came home when the sun was just above the hills. Audrey hoped to beat the morning, before the dew set over the land like a spirit, before her grandfather—old as all hell—rolled out of bed to check the farm.

The sun climbing higher and higher, her grandfather would ride into town on the back of his wagon, tumbling among the canvas bags stuffed with the potatoes he'd harvested. He had been a sharecropper as a young man, on the same plantation he had worked as a boy. He always told the story of how he got the farm, how a slave ended up with a few acres for some crops and a mule. Her father forced them to sit around and listen, sprawled across the carpet of Grandpa's den, warming their hands around mugs of lemon juice and honey in boiled water. At the end of one of those summers, as the sun rose later and later, one morning the carrot was fully bloomed. She stared in wonder, this orange stump with roots disappearing into the soil. It was the brightest thing she had ever seen.

Audrey looked up now, sweating, surrounded by fruit flies. Across the street were building fronts, lopsided and too close to one another, packed along the sidewalk like crooked teeth. Nina Simone's live interpretation of "Take My Hand, Precious Lord" played from her stereo, a cheap wireless speaker shoved into the soil, tucked somewhere between the greens and peaches. Key had bought it for her one Christmas, tired of her mother's complaining about cheap earbuds. Above her hung a billboard advertising an old discount at Jack's World from years ago. Car horns blared over the distant buzz of construction and busy halal carts. Her joints throbbed, her knees heavy with water.

"RENT CONTROLLED?" JOYCE EXCLAIMED, from behind the smoke of a cigarette. Her blood was hot and streaked her butterscotch skin, even in the winter. Despite the wrinkles around her eyes, she still looked like a little girl with two missing teeth and ponytail braids. "I'd give anything to hear you say that back in Warren County."

They sat at the kitchen table of Joyce's apartment on the eleventh floor, hollering over the running water and sirens below. The windows were wide open because she was cooking at least three pounds of pork shoulder for a baby shower. She catered; Joyce and her son would show up with a dozen aluminum pans, wire chafers, and some Sterno cans. She even made coquito in the winter and sold it around the neighborhood. "What poor Spanish woman did you scam out of her recipe?" Audrey would tease.

Joyce got up and moved to the stove. Joyce had worn her sureness in her shoulders since she was young, ambling through the world with an ease that may well have been just pure luck. Even though Audrey had looked after her when they were girls, she had always felt Joyce didn't need much of anyone. Audrey had always been jealous of that, she herself an awkward thing tumbling through life, bumping its edges like finding your way through a dark room. It was like everyone else had the light on.

"Where do you even go after forty years?" Audrey asked no one. Her sister put the top back on some collards.

"Maybe we should put you in a home?"

"If you don't quit it," said Audrey.

"You know I'll put you up," Joyce said through a grin. "It'll be like when we used to sleep in the cellar during them hurricane warnings."

"And Momma would let us eat all the sweets we could bring down there."

They laughed, Audrey leaning back before rubbing her knees. Joyce checked the oven once more.

"Don't nobody owe you anything," Joyce was saying. "And you don't owe nobody. If you were to up and leave, no one would complain."

It was simple enough—she could just up and leave. It was so simple, it seemed foolish not to. But people mistake being poor for complacency. Audrey knew she couldn't afford to stay. Even so, she could raise the money. She could go to her church; the pastor was happy raising impromptu offerings for members in need. *They could have a fish fry and raffle*, Audrey thought, *invite the whole neighborhood*. She imagined Joyce with some obscene amount of whiting, hands caked in flour and seasoning. Key, with her kids hanging at her hip, would serve folks who'd wandered by from the smell, the line snaking halfway down the block. When Audrey thought about it, her face grew hot with tears. If she did raise money from other poor people, she wouldn't give it to some landlord. She had worked all her life in Brooklyn and deserved not to be kicked out of her own city. Deserved not be taken advantage of for the rest of her life. Normal people didn't have to transcend their surroundings. Maybe something else was wrong and there was a reason women like her found themselves in courtrooms, in shelters, or on the streets, or dead. Why should she have to transcend a goddamn thing?

AUDREY WAS IN love with Virgil around the summer of 1969, when she had seen him one morning on her way to work. It was a new city, not on fire anymore but still full of smoke. The uprisings had changed the city—not toward a solution for the certain death Black folk felt around them, to which they responded with fire, but toward something more resentful. The glass and debris would be cleaned from the streets. Virgil had moved north a few years ago—to make a real living, he'd told her. That's just what folk did back then. He worked at the navy yard and smelled of seashell and burning metal. He lived with his wife and kid in a lopsided walk-up in Bushwick. He'd come by almost every weekend for Audrey, something she waited for all week. She had grown to be *of* this place, looked like she belonged in New York like subway tokens and Anthora cups. Big hair, gold hoops, and long, knee-length coats. She'd run out when he'd pulled up to her apartment, soca blasting out the windows of his white '68 Corona. Joyce, who lived with her for a while, would kiss her cheek, waving from the front steps as the van pulled off.

Audrey had a studio in Canarsie, above a fish restaurant that left the room heavy and damp from the steam below. Sometimes she'd invite him up. Virgil told her his dreams, how he wanted to tour with a band through a dozen cities. He had his eye on this Fender bass guitar. It had caught his eye through a shopwindow on his way to the docks.

"What about the yard? Ain't you say you might get moved up to the main building?"

"I thought so, too," he said, looking down at her wiry hands. "New shift leader. I could've stayed down south if I wanted to be somebody's boy."

His hair coiled, snapping at the teeth of her comb as she ran it through, black like the shell of a beetle gathering food in the moonlight. Bringing his face up to hers, she saw in his eyes what she'd already felt—an almost painful desire to be washed in some kind of infinite. She slept with him in the middle of her apartment, seeing only the lines of his skin under a silver half-moon and halogen street lamps.

Virgil reminded Audrey of Warren, the back of her grandfather's wagon, the cool balm of morning before the day would break open and sunlight would heat the fields. Virgil had been brought to her because he ran errands with traders in town. Really, it was his eyes, Audrey thought—reflective pools that led down the same endless path she'd grown familiar with. "My mother always said if you were dropped into a well," Virgil would tell her, "you don't find your way out by looking down." They spent that whole summer together, making their way through the city and everything it could offer. The matinees for less than a dollar on Tuesday mornings, sitting under the cherry blossoms in Prospect Park, getting pink sepals in the tight curls of their hair. One night, or a collection of days eased into twilight, she decided she had come to love Virgil. Maybe under the glow of a moving picture, the baroque innards of Kings Theatre on Flatbush Avenue, latched on to some frequency tucked away deep inside them both. Maybe it happened as he became a part of her place; his musk lingered in rooms, stopped her in the middle of door-frames, brought up memories of nights prior, and sent heartbeats to the floor of her belly. He made shelves for walls and nooks, fixed up the legs of coffee tables and a soft, rolled-arm sofa he bargained away from someone he knew leaving town. He built flower boxes out of plywood to satisfy Audrey's green thumb until the apartment was filled with monsteras and umbrella trees; strings of nickels and English ivy tangled from high places and curled toward the light whenever the sun cut across the studio before noon. He bought groceries when he could, would spring up some days with pounds of rice and a few racks of beef, leave one out for Audrey to cook that night, and stack the rest in the freezer. One time, when trying to nail the base of a swing-arm wall lamp above a bookstand, Virgil hammered right through the plaster. Left a hole in the wall about the size of a fist.

"Oh shit," he said, getting down from his stepladder to admire his work.

"My landlord is gonna take my deposit," Audrey scolded.

"We'll get it fixed."

"You really don't care, do you?"

"It's just a wall, that's easy," said Virgil. "Now, if it was this ceiling . . ."

"I'd be in trouble."

"We'd be in trouble."

"Maybe we can get a house one day," Audrey thought aloud, looking up at the foggy lamp stretched above them. "One of those fresh ones they're building in Queens or Long Island. Maybe even move back south. Stretch out."

"We got away from Warren," Virgil said quietly. "Why would we ever go back?"

"Home is good for you," she said, staring out the window. "Peace is good, too."

Audrey would let herself be dragged to the Village or uptown, wherever Black folk could dance and scream in peace, a cavernous hall or backroom— couldn't have been Half Note, maybe even smaller—hoping she looked as pretty and sensual as Eartha Kitt, or the women in *Jet* magazine under "Beauty of the Week." Virgil would lug his bass guitar around in its leather case, sweating through his knit polo, shining like a cinnamon stick in whiskey under the bar lights. He rolled his own tobacco in two quick motions, whipping open an army knife and licking an envelope, kept drinks on the table before they were finished. He'd sneak glances at Audrey between pulls, lean in, and talk into her neck when the music settled, sugar at the bottom of sweet tea before it was stirred. And if the house band played "Jimmy Mack," he'd dance with her in the aisle, let Audrey sing along in his ear, "*When are you coming back?*" She would stroke his cheekbones, high cliffs along the sea, play in his stubble until she wandered upon an ingrown, whisper how she would rub him in castor oil and ease it out. And when the band called him on to fill in around midnight, he'd play cool, hang his head bashfully as he rose to his feet. But Audrey knew just how nervous he was, his anxious heart, had felt its drumming, and counted the cigarettes, and felt his left foot tapping the sticky hardwood all night. Virgil would find his way with only his hands and ears. The bass would make the music a body, full and whole, could trouble the clouds for a rainstorm. He'd find his way blind on that stage, sweat and sweat.

TREBLE OF THE UNIVERSE

COLLY (2007)

Don't forget where you are, you would say. Getting lost in yourself can only lead you to trouble. Summer had been hot, all bleeding heart and no sky. Us kids played under a white, blinding ceiling, happy for days with no school and wet eyes. We slept under the music—pleading sirens and our parents who argued till morning. Soon enough, the smoke and asbestos would clear, Housing would pump stale heat into our apartments, and just like that school would begin. These days I haven't seen myself in a while, standing out front the apartments, waiting for rain, snow, or someone.

I'd see Zaire on the way to school before deciding if I'd go or not. We'd stop at the bodega on Stanley, the shelves stocked high with rows of canned goods and boxes of anything instant; an old head counting out change for a can of Modelo; Ms. Calloway buying two or three Take5s at a time. Merengue

filled the dusty shop, the patron at the counter humming along with a cigarette behind his ear. Every morning, I'd get turkey on a roll, salt, pepper, vine-
gar, yellowed lettuce, and tomato, chips and bright candies I could sneak off
the shelves. I'd splurge on green and blue extra-sour Cry Babys that would
last till lunch if you tucked them away in your cheek just right.

We collected the flat plastic tops off milk gallons or quarter waters,
filled them with candle wax—Zaire's mom stockpiled them from the 99-cent
store—sometimes mixing colors. We had a legion of skully tops between us,
and we would spend hours in and out of school scrubbing the bottoms against
the ground until they were smooth enough to glide across concrete like air
hockey pucks.

The boys played ball at Gersh Park and suicide on the handball courts
until the streetlights came on. It was some twisted incarnation of Chinese
handball, except you were out when you got hit with the ball. Our hands were
red and calloused from the blue rubber ball we'd smack around for hours
on end.

We'd usually have a ball last a couple weeks. They'd split in half or get
lost over the wall into alleys or weeds or some abandoned lot somewhere.
My boy Jose kept his the longest—three months—until Ricky sent it across
the boulevard. Fuck it, had a good run, we'd say. The corner store sold them
for the price of a Charleston Chew, had different colors at the beauty supply a block away, red and green, whatever you could think of. We'd tumble
into the house, filthy, covered in welts, half listening to our mothers, picking
at the dead, splitting skin on our open palms, calluses sprouting like they
might take over our hands.

Me and Zaire fought kids from the neighborhood every day after school,
wiry boys with impatient gaits, with names that were still on all the attendance sheets but who had stopped attending, conceivably of disinterest.
School couldn't quite catch up with those kids. I don't know much about
Joshua, but I saw Tristan at the food-stamp building on Pitkin by P.S. 159. I
was on line with my mother, tried to nod at him, but he was with his mother

and four other kids. And once I peeked inside Joshua's crib and it seemed completely empty.

One time Zaire took Joshua's Braves fitted and hid it in the art cabinet.

"If you boys interrupt my class again," Mrs. Budhris would cut in, "I'll beat the bricks off the both of you." She wasn't allowed to say that, so I took her word for it. Shit, we could've took our show on the road. After school, we'd stroll around Green Courts, or head to Lee's Chinese restaurant up Linden.

There weren't any seats, save a bench up against the wall. The decorative tile from floor to wall a dingy marble, the most consistent thing in the shop. A tacky landscape of a waterfall. A wooden ceiling fan whirred overhead. The cashier spoke to us through a window, sat the food in a large slot that spun in exchange for cash.

We'd buy a bunch of egg rolls, sometimes tender pork-fried rice with thick orange duck sauce in packets that they never gave enough of. We got large containers of iced tea we knew they made with the supermarket brand, but that was perfect every time. We joked around, banging on tables and walls, the woman at the counter peering through the bulletproof Plexiglas to make sure our rowdiness didn't turn to sabotage.

ONE TIME IT went too far.

Zaire and I had climbed the roof of the Parks building, a half-story unisex bathroom that lacked air in the summertime and always smelled like fresh urine, no matter when it was cleaned. It was in the school playground, between the jungle gym and the tall gate that led to the courts. We collected a bunch of beechnuts and started pelting Josh, Tristan, and the girls.

"Come on with that shit," Tristan groaned. He was visibly moody, more moody than usual. But you don't show that. It's a weak spot, a scent that draws grade-school kids to attack. You keep those emotions, those feelings close to you. Don't let anyone see them.

But we had seen and so had everyone else and we laughed.

"You mad?" Zaire teased. Tristan wasted no time and started looking for a way up to where we were. I sat with my legs crossed and threw beechnuts at him down below. When he got to the top, he shoved Zaire and grabbed me by the collar of my coat. From there it all happened too fast. I don't remember what I said but it was terrible and it came pouring out. Then he mentioned you. I was so angry I started to cry—then, my hands around his neck pushing him toward the ledge. He was reaching for my face as if to will it toward him when we tipped over the side; then me, windmilling my arms as if to fly away, a long-limbed bird-thing soaring over the projects in a goose-down coat. I landed hard, the wind knocked out of me. My left side was scraped and aching. A gash on the arm of my bubble coat bled feathers. A glint caught my eye, something hitting the ground, but everyone was running. It looked like a switchblade. I looked at Tristan, already scrambling to his feet, a splash of cool gravel hitting me in the face as he did. I pushed myself off the ground and was out, in a sort of limp-jog, feathers bouncing out of me, peppering the playground turf.

I figured we'd all meet up afterward. But I never made it back for after-school and Josh and Tristan never made it to practice. I didn't go to school the next day either. I left the house with my backpack like nothing had happened and hung out around Green Courts until my house was empty. The school called twice and I deleted both messages. By the time I went back the next day I was sent straight to the office. Apparently a member of faculty had seen the whole ordeal. A full-on investigation had me pinned for the entire thing.

"Your peers seem to feel that you are a danger to their safety," the principal was saying. She was an older white lady from Vermont or something who worked here, dead in the middle of the inner city. She couldn't understand why parents would side with their kids. She once got a chair thrown at her in the gym, in the middle of an assembly. It hit the podium, but she never got over it. She had the police come in and restrain Bobby Ramirez and felt he had a grudge against her. His dad was all but happy about that. She wore starched collars and pleated suits every single day like it was the seventies and wore her hair like Rosalynn Carter. I didn't open my mouth to respond.

"Don't you have anything to say for yourself?"

I said nothing.

"Where'd you get the knife from?" she asked.

"A knife?" I was confused, then remembered the long gash down my coat. She paused, considered me. I stared just to the left of her ear, at a fake ficus tree she had by her coffee machine.

"Do you even want to know who ratted you out?" she asked, and I shook my head. I didn't really care. Blame whomever you need to. Take me out back to the firing wall like Capone would've. Anything to get the fuck out of this ficus-filled office.

"Well, you could very well be expelled for this behavior. I'm going to have to call your mother."

As my mother's child, I dread the times she is proven right. This was something you had always warned about, verbatim. Don't get caught up with the wrong kids, Colly, you'd say. You never know what could happen. If one person has something on them or gets in trouble, you all get in trouble. Except we weren't all in trouble, of course. Just me. I hated to break it to her, but my mother would not be answering that phone. You had gone before the winter was over and I was left with nothing but the seasons.

THESE DAYS I keep looking for myself in books. I can't see anything out my window at night and I choose my friends too wisely. It is easier to talk to you in the early hours, when my timeline is asleep. More beautiful, you feel. The books are the only things that prove to me we've existed before this, that we belong to the treble of the universe. I speak in a broken language from time to time and it drives my sister to throw her slippers at me. I tell her words aren't important. She says all great poems are great because they use words. Great poems aren't really great because the real poems are written with existence, in the hours furthest from light. They are silent accusations against water; direct me to the flood. You were a great poet. You'd drink your dark lager and dance around my father like you had lived forever.

You were proud, as the way books are made, or a binder who has sewn them together, I remember. You sat me on her lap and, like the great poets, made me believe love was the only way I would ever survive. You were lying, though, like all the great poets do.

Pop built you a bookshelf from an old headboard, the one you used as a girl. It had still been at Nana's old studio, and she, up until she lost her apartment, hadn't moved or thrown anything away since the eighties. I was there when he carved the cherry oak in the lobby of our apartment building with a circular saw he snatched up from his brother's garage. He smoothed the edges with sandpaper and polished the surface with a thick wax. He then nailed the wooden slab onto some wall in the kitchen, above your plants and seasonings.

On your shelf was a range of books you were given throughout your life, as far back as when you were a small girl growing up in Brooklyn. For two winters you arranged and rearranged your books, by what order none of us really knew. The Bible went next to your cookbook one week, and *The Salt Eaters* the next. *Letters to a Young Novelist* went next to *Mama Day* and *Sula* next to *The Country Doctor Handbook*.

No one ever really survives, but you had this idea that we all did. "The ancestors speak through us," you had said. I thought the chemo was getting to you, but you insisted. I couldn't understand how any of this was happening and I couldn't understand how you, my mother, of all people, had no answer.

"If God loves me so much," I asked you at your hospital bed one night, "then why would He take you away?"

"We can't think like that." You cried like a baby, uncontrollably, searching for air. You held my hand, pressed hard. "I'll live forever as long as you tell it."

You didn't belong here, really, in this time or this fucking city. You spoke too frankly, laughed too earnestly, and felt too deeply. You opened yourself up to the world like a pomegranate, raw and staining the hands of whoever held it. Sometimes words failed you, like there wasn't enough room in them. You had a language all your own, one that required me to listen with more than my ears.

My sister puts flowers in her hair, yellow and violet, bright enough to bring the bees in. I'd come in from the park, palms red and dried out from handball, yelling at Toya to make me something to eat. I came after curfew, after the streetlights had sprung on. You tore after me, came down with one of Daddy's belts. I limped off, my body stinging where you didn't miss, and laid facedown on my bed, blowing snot into my pillow. Later, you came in to get me ready for bed. To make it up to me, you brought me hot chocolate with extra marshmallows and read to me *I Remember "121"* by Francine Haskins.

"Don't act all sour now," you said in the dark. "You know you deserved it." I sucked my teeth and you laughed, running your long fingers through my hair. That would be the end of our beef. Not like my dad and me, all prolonged silence and threats, that Caribbean male pride of his like the fucking Iron Curtain coming up for no one.

No one but you. Y'all fought, broken plates and ultimatums, you crying wildly and my father, red-eyed and towering, becoming smaller and smaller until he surrendered. Those nights scared me worse than anything. Your voices raked the walls. I'd hide in bed under my sheets, trying to vanish, wanting to sink through the floor, disappear completely. Toya always sat at the edge of her bed, looking straight ahead.

Who knows what y'all argued about anyway? We were shipped to Nana's house one night because of it, and I asked her.

"Being a part of someone for so long can steal something away from you," Nana told me.

My father hates the city, sees no promise in it. He sees the rich dark soils of Barbados when he daydreams. The air is fresh and carries with it the smell of the sea, waters you can see down to your feet, so clear you can see how glass pales in comparison. Then you had the New York winters, which fucked with his sickle cell. He'd spend a whole day at home writhing in pain and you'd rub him down with shea butter, to ease his blood. I couldn't tell if you hated Pop, the way you went on sometimes. You seemed to love him enough. You'd go to the end of the world to take care of him. Yet something got under your skin about him that made you cringe, the way he touched you, made you look away when he spoke. I knew there was a terrible secret we all shared, but no one dared to say it.

When you first got sick, you treated it like a cold. I'd get home and the windows would be shut with the heat so thick my eyes got heavy. You were surrounded by rosemary stalks and peppermint, boiling nettle leaves and camilla petals into tea, pounding dried herbs and beeswax with a mortar and pestle. You used to get us with that stuff too.

"Ma, stop with that mess," I'd whine, with my feet in hot water and Epsom salt. I can't front, though. Your remedies warded off Toya's chronic headaches and my constant colds. Dad's joints would cool under your salves and balms and ointments without the metallic haze his painkiller brought on. You carried these recipes as true, passed along from a time where the land could cure anything. Leave it to the sun. What you give to the earth, it will give back to you.

Soon the land couldn't keep up, couldn't calm the swelling inside, couldn't repair what leaked and bled. Teas and oils became supplements for pills, balms like relief for chemo, a cure for the cure that never seemed to work. You'd take up residency at the hospital for days at a time, shrinking away from us, from the world, like a reverse bloom. After we had that talk about God, you decided to come home.

"How you kids say? I can't go out like that," you had joked.

Toward the end, you were always out of air. I can still hear your cough, a steel organ pipe. Coughing up blood. We would find blood in the strangest places. Sparkling black pools of tar. They seemed like holes in the floor that went down all the way to the basement of our duplex. You wrote your prayers down in a scratchy loop on corners of paper scraps, crying when you thought no one was awake.

You went early one morning, just before the sun rose. We stayed in bed for days, waiting for nothing to happen, praying nothing did. We didn't go to school. Asleep in the corner of your room was Dad, who ran to our room to get us before it could really hit him. Your eyes were closed. Toya touched your hands and gasped at their coldness. I sank into a heap of bones in the corner.

In a flurry of snow at the cemetery near Jamaica Avenue, over by Ridge- wood, we stood in the staunch gray of the breaking February noon holding flowers, yellow and red and violet, the reverend's words scattered among the snowflakes. They lowered you into a plot and buried you in fat soil. It might as well have been concrete. My throat locked on me. Could you breathe, I worried, would you be warm?

After the repast, we all kind of drifted to our own corners of the house. No one remembered to eat until sometime around midnight and my sister heated up plates from earlier. Pops just kinda sat and let the TV wash over him. The next day he took us to Grandma's and disappeared for about a week. One night, Toya was helping Nana with the dishes and asked how he could just leave like that. "Men have the privilege of absence" was all Nana could say.

TOYA AND I began cutting school together, which turned out to be the perfect way to bond in our grief. She was always into her grades; it was nice to have her corrupted in some way. We shared a brooding disposition. You were the perfect counter for her cynicism, Toya being a know-it-all and you being the "for all you know" type.

The second time we skipped went over smoothly. We just had to be there for homeroom. Teachers hardly cross-checked attendance. I took the side entrance and ran for what must've been a block. Toya was waiting for me on Myrtle.

"Did you eat today?" she asked, as she had every day for the past week.

"Yeah," I lied.

"You don't look too good, Colly."

"Neither do you, Satoia," I said, and she cut me a look. She hated that name. Her eyes were puffy and red and I wondered if she even slept through the night anymore.

We took the train into the city, where it was easier to disappear, to fall into anonymity. The last thing you wanted was to end up thrown in the back of a truancy van, sitting in bookings until school was out. I stared at the blankness of the ads with big heads and big smiles looking back. No one on the train car looked like that, save for a suit headed back from lunch, clutching the *Times* like a religious pamphlet. I watched a West Indian woman across from me eating tamarind she'd pulled from a rolling tote bag, the inside of the Ziploc splashed with hot sauce. Next to her, a Korean woman swayed side to side with her eyes closed, threatening sleep. She had the balance of a mother, her arms anchoring paper bags overflowing with groceries, a purse over her shoulder large enough to supply a small campsite. I caught my face in the window behind her—a sunken arrangement of bone and flesh.

A band of mariachi players filled the subway car with music, though they hardly made anything considering the midday lull. At the next stop, they shuffled off, a commotion of bells and clunking hard-soled shoes, extending their hats to us. A couple got on at Marcy Avenue and sat directly across from us. They were both tall, long-limbed—one woman had dark skin with a mane of locs while the other had brown curls and cheeks flushed with blood, her arm and shoulder covered in blue koi fish, sharing kisses between stops. One of your oldest friends from the neighborhood, Minnie, had a girlfriend she couldn't bring home to her family. My father used to talk about her all the time, how she shouldn't kiss the children. Seething, you'd say, "For all that, you shouldn't kiss them either," before plopping his dinner tray into his lap.

We'd talk shit in the schoolyard, all the boys, imagining two women, having two chicks, and how sexy that would be. Seeing it up close, though, the tatted girl smiling into her lover's tight curls, playing with the rings on her fingers—protective, nourishing. It made me think of you and Pop. You had been happy, hadn't you?

Toya was staring at ads, anything to keep from looking straight ahead. I turned to her and she rolled her eyes at me.

"I just hate PDA" was all she said.

THE ONLY MOVIE worth seeing was some rated-R indie feature. Toya knew they wouldn't let us buy tickets and blamed me for being so short. I blamed her for having the body of a twelve-year-old and she shoved my face into the glass door. Eventually, we managed to convince some lady to let us walk in with her so no one would question what we were doing out of school.

"Not sure what's worse," she said while we were getting popcorn. "The fact I'm helping you kids cut school or that I can pass for a mother of two."

We all ended up sitting together and she was young enough to laugh when we cussed at the screen. She did feel obligated to ask why we weren't in school.

"Because school is bullshit," I said.

"You don't really believe that, do you?" she asked, then caught herself. "There's a lot wrong with the schools in this city, but you can't fix it by not showing up."

"You don't really believe that, do you?" Toya countered, nearly under her breath but loud enough for us to hear. The woman flashed a knowing smile.

"What are your names?"

"Toya."

"Meech."

"Come on, Colly—"

I sucked my teeth, "It's Colly."

"My name is Amaal. Nice to meet you," she said, and we shook hands. "I don't mean to lecture you. I just hate to see smart kids get shortchanged."

"We don't do this all the time," Toya reassured her.

"Then what is it? Are you running away from something?"

We both shrugged, still looking straight ahead. Toya spat a popcorn kernel out onto the theater floor.

"I don't know," she said. "Our mother just died."

Her words hung there, emptying out the gravity in the theater. Somehow, I knew this was the first time she had said it out loud. I hadn't even dared. I felt like she had confirmed something for me, almost, just in case I was wondering.

The woman froze, staring into Toya's profile all glassy-eyed with her lips apart. Toya kept going: "And I guess I should want to run away from that but I don't want to. It doesn't hurt like it should, like it needs to."

"You have to figure out how you grieve," Amaal said. "The truth is that loss doesn't go away. You learn to live beside it. And if you end up bawling your eyes out a month or year from now, so be it."

We were quiet for the remaining scenes and I could tell the whole time Amaal was trying to figure out something more to say to us. As people filed out of the theater, she asked Toya for her phone and put her number into the bulky Nokia.

"Stop cutting school," Amaal said again. I smirked and the two of us watched her leave. The lights dimmed. We waited for the next show.

AFTER THE MOVIE, we sat in the park on West Fourth and ate huge pizza slices from a spot across the street, next to the IFC theater. We sat looking toward uptown and chewed with our mouths open to keep from burning our tongues. The sounds from the pick-up game directly behind us were muddy, warbling into the tumble dry of car horns and shop bells, the squeaking bus engines and rolling wheels of halal trucks, conversations melting into the next until everything was covered in a warm, violent murmur. The city has its own accent, clicking and rolling its tongue.

Grease ran down my wrist from between my knuckles, which I licked clean. Toya blotted her slice with napkins.

"Can I help you?" she asked after I stared too long.

"Why do you do that?"

"So I don't have to do that," she said, jeering, motioning to the trail of grease I was trying to get at with my tongue. I sucked my teeth. After a while she started smiling to herself.

"Remember Dad had that old bucket we would drive around in?"

I laughed right away. "That stupid Fleetwood."

"Remember that sound it made? That buckshot?"

"Boy. Was it the engine or something?"

She shrugged. "All I know is Rashad from the next building almost left his sneakers in the street trying to get away from it."

I howled. "I can't. Folk really thought Pop owned a gun those first few years."

"Tell me, you remember the road trip we went on in that thing?" I shook my head and she turned to me, already in story mode. "It was a disaster. We went all the way to Georgia to visit one of Ma's cousins or something. We all had our ears blown out and Daddy was in denial. She made him sleep in the car since that was his baby."

"I might've been too young to remember."

"I barely remember it either," she said, looking up at the large billboard above us. "The only reason I can picture it is Ma. I always had bad dreams when I slept somewhere new. I crawled into bed with her and she said she wouldn't fall asleep until I did. We stayed up till morning. She showed me how to braid lanyards, all different kinds of knots and colors. We had fried ice cream with slices of pound cake that was still warm from the oven. She said to me, you will always be afraid of your dreams if they seem possible.

"I know they're not, I told her, I guess tryna save her the mom spiel. And all she said was, they always will be, and held up a bracelet she'd just finished. Then we sat outside to try and watch the sunrise but fell asleep on this old rocking bench on the porch. Daddy ended up carrying us back to our beds."

We were quiet for a bit. After a while she folded her plate and got up to throw it out. I was still somewhere in Georgia, watching you and a smaller Toya playing with dragonflies in the ever-stretching morning light. You two were writing stories in the crabgrass with your bare feet, each kept in the knots of your lanyards.

WHEN I WALKED in the house, Pops was squarely in his chair, the one he always sat in after work, and if I hadn't known better, everything was normal and my mom was gonna come out of the kitchen now with a tray of deviled eggs. I sat down at his feet and stared off at the TV. There was a game on, might have been the playoffs but I had a hard time keeping track of the months anymore.

"Where's your sister?" he said, the first in what must've been days.

"Nana's." I wouldn't tell him she didn't want nothing to do with him.

"Did you eat?"

I shook my head excitedly. He got to his feet and went to the kitchen. At least he gave me the show of looking around, shuffling through cabinets and slamming things on counters; we both knew there was nothing in that kitchen.

"Well, fuck it then."

He grabbed his coat and left. I stared at the door for a moment, then at some fixed space ahead of me. Un-fuckin-believable.

I waited, trying to imagine him getting us Crown Fried or greasy subs from the deli. Something crawled beneath the floor, clawed at the pipes. I could hear voices from the other side of the walls. Some nights the voices raged and moaned, all I could hear over the television. I stared at my mother's bookshelf; its imperfect finish, the nails in the wall that became loose as the building withered from age. I decided I would read each of them, in no particular order.

By the time I had resolved, fully, within the core of my being, that he was an asshole, he came back with about half a dozen bags of groceries. I started putting things away as he shouted what to leave out. He broiled some chicken breast and fried up potatoes home-style with some garlic, red onions, cayenne, and green peppers. He made cornbread with cinnamon butter and a dollop of whipped cream. We sat and ate with the TV on mute, Dwyane Wade rolling off a pick across our screen.

"I know you and Toya been cutting school," he said suddenly, and I sat completely still. "It's okay, I know you feel some type of way about your mom."

"Don't you?" I asked. Looked at the floor, the edge of my plate, my ashy knees. Pop looked at his own plate, swallowed a bit of gristle.

"More than anything," he started, before trailing off, mumbling into his plate, "I kind of cut out on you guys," then half phrases, "I didn't understand myself" and "I know that ain't no excuse," and more, all tumbling into a pile at my knees.

Then he paused, looking me dead in the eye, deep lines crossing his forehead like a river, just to say, "I can't imagine what you've been thinking." He seemed resolved on that.

And I must've looked like shit because he saved me the answer and put his saucer of a hand behind my neck.

He considered me, like someone new, noted my hair, my eyes—her eyes, they'd say when I could still fit in their arms—my cheeks, my skin, a mix of her cedar complexion and his dark coffee. What could he possibly say to me? Outside, there was a sole cry from the street coming from the light of the bodega on Stanley, lapping over the approaching drone of a crowd. It had to be a cry of mourning; it asked too many questions. Sirens would soon rule the street and the sureness of grief would give way to hysteria. The fever of summer would dry my eyes.

THE KILLING FIELDS

KEY (1989)

Mama would tell me the story of Igbo Landing. She was a sad woman growing up, lost all her family to the sun-worn south and its many afflictions. Here
in New York, her lover died in the street but only after he left her. Anyway,
Igbo Landing is the story of a people who were kidnapped, chained together
to be sold in some strange land, and decided to kill their captors instead,
throwing them overboard. The stolen, who were now free, walked back the
way they came, back through Dunbar Creek and across the freezing Atlantic. It was called a mass suicide. Mama said they were going to march right
back to the shores of West Africa, singing to the water spirits. Years later,
when I moved out for good, I had already tried to kill myself. I still consider
it in the dark, not a creek or shallow in sight. Just like Mama, I am a sad
woman.

In the last years of the eighties, I worked in a department store in the city where my boss often confused me with the other Black girl who worked there.

"Keisha, could you make sure the men's tie display is tidy," she said today, the beginning of May already warm and stiff with overcast. Margie was tall for her jacket and sheath dress, her hair an orange tuft she shoved into a bun.

"It's Key," I blurted out.

"On the first floor, dear."

"It's Key," I said louder. "My name. Just Key."

"Isn't that what I said?"

"No, you said Keisha."

"I'm not seeing the difference?" she said, and walked ahead, the self-importance of a retail manager overseeing a near-evangelical dogma. I hurried along beside her.

"Keisha usually closes."

"This is important to you." Margie could understand.

"Well, it's just, you know, my name."

"I get mixed-up. You understand, don't you? I'm not racist or anything."

"I'm sure," I said. We were by a women's display, dark Ann Taylor suits over willowy mannequins with their toes pointed. "You mix up the two Jewish girls in perfume just the same."

"Marta and Jenny?"

"Jenna and Martha," I corrected her.

Margie's eyebrows knit together, had grown bushy and acicular because she hadn't plucked them in the breakroom like she normally did. She considered me, the display section, and a drop shipment from Warnaco or G.H. Bass that she would tend to later.

"Key?"

"You've got it."

"The ties?"

I hung out at the Strand between shifts, or when I was afraid to go home. Its corner, some cobblestoned blocks away from NYU, was full of punks and addicts, skaters and artists, schoolkids from small towns upstate or out west. Inside were students with thick-rimmed glasses, girls with dirty blond hair or dyed hair, young white boys in stonewashed and bright T-shirts. A white girl in a denim-wash top follows me around the store, as disinterested as I am. I picked out what I liked, hid in a corner surrounded by bookshelves. I set down my bags and sat for what seemed like hours.

On this day, I read a story about a man who, on his dying mother's wish, sets off to find his father in a far-off town somewhere in Mexico. When he goes, he finds that everyone in the town is dead and has been dead for a long time. He sinks into madness, not knowing whether he's been talking to ghosts or illusions within his own mind. I wondered the same thing as I rode the subway to its last stop in Brooklyn, if this town is but a place for the half-living. Actually, I think I've seen ghosts. I have had dreams of meeting people I don't know to exist since I was fourteen. There was this woman I saw around with a young boy, always in front of the strip mall on Pennsylvania and Wortman. She had a scar behind her ear, her nightgown worn at the bottom where it covered her feet. A look of longing had settled across her face, her skin a deep chestnut that cracked at creases. One day she looked up for what seemed like the first time ever, across the parking lot, toward the bus stop, at me. The longing turned to something more, something I thought I recognized.

I always asked about the woman in the nightgown whenever I remembered, yet no one seemed to know her. Everyone I asked claimed to have never seen her before, nor did she sound familiar. Dante shook his head the first time I questioned him.

"You out here all day," I said. "You must've seen her."

"Never."

"Can't be."

"She owe you money or something?" he asked, his voice a tremble from deep behind his chest, between his large shoulders.

"I think I know her from somewhere," I said. It wasn't a lie.

Stories get retold in different ways. Nehemiah led his people back to their home, only to find it in ruins. All I had really known was ruin. The estate was a maze. Towers swept the length of the boulevard, each window home to a different story, some other war. Some glowed with warm light or strung flags along the protective bars. A few were still lined with Christmas decorations. Someone had left them all stranded—it wasn't just me.

One day, as I got off the southbound bus from Broadway Junction, I looked for the woman through a cloud of exhaust. There was smoke from a grill, an older woman burning chicken skewers by the stop. The strip mall was a line of brick shop fronts in faded blues and pinks and greens, dusty windows under wire-frame awnings and blinking neon displays. There was a beauty supply, a liquor store, a choice of quick and greasy food, and a store that sold everything from jewelry to tape players and pagers to basketball shoes. Plastic bottles and food wrappers tumbled around the parking lot, caught on the hook of a light wind.

I went to the beauty supply, an electronic chime buzzing as I opened the door. The Chinese woman at the counter smiled, eyed my purse and the large shopping bag I carried. The aisles were short but crammed with balms, bottles of grease, tubs of pomade, shelves with nail polish and press-ons, walls of lace fronts and packaged hair. A display of floating Styrofoam heads draped in wigs, from bobs to long and wavy, colors like auburn and brown and blonde.

On the Wortman side were older men who hung out every day, tuning their cars and talking shit. They'd offer car advice and check under your hood in exchange for a few Wild Horses. The sun moved through the corridor, shining down on their dark shoulders and balding heads. A lather of grease from the cars ran into the streets, made wheels turn, and water from hoses slipped into the gutters. Some stories are older than time.

"Girl, you didn't get no type of shoes to go with this?" Genesis shouted from the bathroom of our apartment. She came out barefoot, a leather with fur detail over a Tommy halter and tight leather skirt. I wore a Guess denim skirt and a sleeveless fur jacket.

"You have a hundred shoes you can put with that," I told her. "Right in your closet."

"You scary as hell. I know you're not worried?"

"My boss don't even know my name." Since I always returned the clothes I stole, usually the day after, there was no reason Margie would notice something missing.

"You see Dee around?"

"I saw him by the jewelry spot," I said. I moved about the apartment in my jacket, as if I must know how it looked in every room.

"He say anything?"

"I had gone into the beauty supply before he could see me. You know that place gotta be a front—"

"Wait, you went to the beauty supply and didn't tell me?"

"You want me to come get you every time I pick out a wig?"

"Yes, I would like that, but continue."

"Never mind."

"I saw him by the BRC with his daughter," Genesis shouted across the hall. She was on the balls of her feet, trying to see her shoes in the bathroom mirror. "They're way too cute."

"You tryna play house with the man already?"

"Ain't nobody playing," she yelled, and I snorted.

"I don't like the way he treats the mother of his child," I said to her, as I searched for the wire hangers we hoarded from the dry cleaners.

"But you know Tiffany."

"So what? He probably the reason everyone so quick to call her crazy."

I took off the clothes and hung them up before they could begin to wrinkle. The living room had been taken over by Genesis's salon. During the day she did hair for most of the girls in the building. She braided designs with her long nails and could wash and set as good as the Dominican girls on

New Lots. There were hot irons and combs and packets of lush extensions across the counter and table. Just before midnight, when she finished her prep for the next day, I put a tape in the VCR. There were at least six movies on it, all stitched together in different volumes and of varying quality. We settled into our pullouts and whispered over *Cooley High*. Genesis fell asleep just as Preach stands over Cochise's grave with a bottle of brandy. I mouthed the words along with him: *"Don't worry . . . I'm gonna make it. I can lie and steal too good not to survive."* I feel that all the way down to my toes.

I DREAM THAT there are people who meet by the ocean, who sleep and find themselves near bodies of water. The first time the tide is at my ankles, cold and thick. I yell out, fall backward into the sand, the back of my throat raw from the song of my breath. The brush whines, shaking from a chorus of bush crickets. I had made it across the expressway, through a field of wheat and mud, half-conscious, smelling of sweat and exhaust, dirt and cuts on my feet. The bay opens up into an infinite black, the Atlantic murky under the white of the moon. I hear the parkway behind me, the heating plants and boiler stations, chimneys choking up heavy smoke and flashes of ember.

"Is someone there?" I ask but my voice is carried out over the water and drowns under the lapping waves.

I walk toward the sound, behind a bend and broken trees, over a hedge of rock, and I see them. They are still, all lined across the sand a couple feet apart. The harbor is dotted with a couple dozen people, men and women, young and old in water to their ankles, all along the sandy bowl. An older woman walks toward me, the bottom of her tattered nightgown swaying with the tide.

SOMETIMES MY MOTHER stared across the room, at the wall, the bookcase, or the recliner, her face held together in tight knots. I'd make noise so she'd notice me and she'd come back, tightening her hand on the broom or remote. I'd wonder where she went, if she'd return from some faraway world. When she saw me, she smiled, but her eyes were tired. She saw someone who had become soft and defenseless. I wondered if she could see the ocean, hear the water in her dreams, like I did.

It was the middle of May. I was combing my hair in the living room and asked Mama to reach the back for me. She held the comb like a cross when I handed it to her and sat behind me on the couch. I asked her why she never had more children. They had to cut me out, she said, along with part of her; a sacrifice of flesh. She couldn't go through that again. I was enough for her to worry about.

I had no money, no real savings. I dropped out of community college after a year. City College seemed like one big high school, one that cost money we didn't have. There didn't seem to be much else on the other side of this.

"Lord knows I've tried since you," she said. She stopped combing, smoothed grease from my mane along my scalp. "You're my only one."

I thought about the boy outside the strip mall even more, and his mother, who stayed with me like a hangover. I felt a connection to the woman; she could see what I claimed I wanted, and that most days those desires meant nothing. I'd pass a few shelters on my way to work, look at their corkboards in the lobby or search the front desk for a number to call to someone who could help the kid, grabbing flyers for coat drives and housing programs.

At work, I'd wander the floors and, seeing Margie or the other manager, tidy a display or help a customer who didn't need it.

"Everyone steals shit here, I assume?" Jenna said before lunch, and looked at Martha, then me. We were huddled over a glass display case full of perfume, hiding out before we had to work the floor. Jenna's brown hair was frizzy and burned out; she left strands behind whenever she went somewhere. I didn't say anything.

Margie had placed a number of memos in the stock rooms and employee lounge, all regarding proper clock-out procedure and new ways of keeping track of all items on the sales floor. It seemed sudden, though knowing how many folk took advantage of the old rules was a relief.

"I might've misplaced a few jeans in stock," Martha conceded. She was blond and pale, her lipstick like red paint across a white barn. "Some belts."

"Bras."

"Those Donna Karan jumpsuits that just came out," Jenna said, and we all marveled at the thought. "Someone's been sloppy,"

"Or maybe Margie's just being a pain," Martha huffed. "More than usual."

I had my own theories. The holidays were over and there wasn't as much of a need for employees. With all the seasonal folk gone, it left this excuse for Margie to fire someone. It was getting warm and the wind along Sixth Avenue, which bullied our store during the holiday season, was a balm. Rather than fuss over what could happen, I read the paper. A student occupation in Beijing's Tiananmen Square was going on its third week. A groundbreaking labor contract had been worked out between unions and AT&T, including adoption grants and funding childcare on work campuses. President Bush said his proposal of an arms control agreement could transform relations between Western Europe and Soviet bloc nations. Everyone wondered if he could pull a Gorbachev and mend the rift, ease the arms race that threatened mankind. Mostly, however, I daydreamed about the woman in the torn night-gown and her son.

We really had thirty for lunch, but I usually went out to buy something and clocked out when I came back to eat. Everyone did it, as it'd probably take about twenty to stand on a line downtown and wait for your order. I ended up going to the Strand for a sweet bun and reading a book about a young girl in Chile who has visions. After her sister is poisoned, she doesn't speak for nine years. She marries, but her husband becomes possessive and violent, abusing her and their daughter as he tries to suppress the surging socialist ideals of rebels in his country. She begins to see more and more, stretching across generations, the many futures of her children and grandchildren. She speaks to the dead from her perch, from her world of the living, those before her and those after her. She knows her country will be free because she has seen it and has made it so.

I thought about my dreams, the people along the shore, wondered if I could reach them like Clara, the girl from *The House of Spirits*. If I could bring them back home. Even if I could speak past the living or see beyond my time here, I didn't really think I could save anyone. What good were the hotlines and social workers and coat drives? We'd all die before anything changed.

That night, Genesis and I wore what I could haul from work to the basketball game. Gersh Park was crowded from the street all the way to the courts, the park even hotter with the lamps, folk eager to hang around during one of the last games of the tournament. It was mostly players who were college prospects at one point, who either flunked out of school or couldn't afford it. The game was like a graceful chase in a strange wilderness. Folk crowded the bleachers, sat on benches, beach chairs, on top of coolers, the hoods of their cars. Lanky boys hung from the gates, whooping for friends they called their cousins. I liked to look at all of us under the half-moon, the brown of our skin and the way it held light, the dips of muscle under sleeves, fleshy parts that showed under shirts and tops. Girls younger than me were rubbed down in Vaseline, glowing a dulled bronze from the park lamps. Boys left their shirts and jackets in their cars or slung over fences, some covered in dull ink and piercings.

The heavy smoke from the smoldering grills made me tear up, so we did a lap around the court back out toward the street, Genesis popping her gum like fireworks the whole time. Double-parked along the street were MPVs and Land Cruisers, a Lexus coupe with the doors open, the frame rattling, "Eric B. Is President" blaring from the car, the sound of motorbikes like chainsaws barreling down the street. Their front wheels pointed up toward the sky like they could take off into the falling dusk.

"There go Dee," Genesis shouted, straining above the noise.

"Where?"

She pointed toward the street and I saw his broad frame, his cocoa tone almost red in the orange lamp. There were police vans across the park, along the boulevard, white boys in their cruisers or lined up like their own self-fashioned barricade. They spoke to each other and sometimes their Black or Hispanic partner, some guy who was the top of his class at junior college. Some wore T-shirts, black with the words KILLING FIELDS in bold white across the front. That was what they called this place. It was a badge they wore, ironically, while home on their days off in Hempstead or Howard Beach, maybe in the dim light of their favorite bar or while cleaning out their garage. They survived. I guess we survived, too. I didn't feel much pride from it.

The news ran with the moniker, too. I imagined this place a hundred years ago, a field of blood, acres of sun-washed stalks sprayed red at the tips; not this stretch of train yards, empty lots, and walk-ups. A street behind the old theater on Elton sat below sea level, an entire city block of gutted houses and abandoned cars on swampland. Women who lived there hung laundry wires from fence posts and trees. There was the mob, who'd send a guy over here from Bay Ridge or Bensonhurst or wherever to dump a body near the edge of the marshlike fields to be pulled into the ocean by the tide. Steps from where I'd wake up at night, at the crest of the bay, there were shopping carts and tents, the hard sand threaded with bottle tops and needles. Who knew how many dead were beneath that water?

"Find your missing person?" Dante said as we approached his Saab. I shook my head. I was surprised he remembered. "Nothing?"

"I'm about as good as those guys." I gestured at the cops across the boulevard.

"Shit, no good at all."

"Hey, Dee," Genesis sang, and I almost rolled my eyes.

"How's the hair business?" he asked.

"Good. Very busy."

"I might have to come by, Minnie so damn tender-headed."

"She won't even know I'm doing them," she said, and nudged me in my side. "You know I'll take care of her."

"Is that how you can afford all this?" He looked at our outfits, the fur trimmings, the name brands checkered across us like a subway advert.

"You don't know? Key the plug," Genesis told him, and Dante looked at me like, *Is that so?* I shrugged. The game was close to an end and people had started to pool out, headed back down the road or across the boulevard. The courtyards would be full and the restaurant drive-thru at a standstill. I had work in the morning and made to say goodbye before I remembered one last thing.

"You ever see the kid she's with?" I asked Dante, grabbed his arm so he would lean toward me. I meant the woman from the strip mall. "There's usually a boy out there with her."

"What boy?" Genesis cried.

"I do see a boy out there all the time," Dante told her, "by the beauty supply."

"Oh, Charlie?" Genesis said. "His mother died last year. Miss Pat. They say she hurt herself while Charlie was at school. That's her boy. He used to come by my nephew's house all the time. Not anymore, after that. Poor thing. Hasn't been the same since. How could anyone be?"

Of course Genesis would know; why wouldn't she? She did everyone's hair; a woman could be convinced to give her Social Security number, her grandmother's sweet potato pie recipe, the nuclear codes, all under the comforting water of a deep shampoo. At least I could. I treated my hair appointment as a form of therapy. Before I could say anything, I realized Dante was staring at me.

"You said you've seen her around?"

THE DAYS CAKED together, a generic batter that could be anything, a body that could be anyone's. I logged the days by the books I'd read, stories that melted together, like burning metals that held and became a new thing entirely. The only thing I could think of was Ms. Pat's boy out on the strip. Where did he go to sleep at night? How often did he eat a day? Had he been the one to find his mother that day? Seen her up close and realized she wouldn't wake? I called Child Services and felt their judgment through the phone for asking questions and keeping secrets. There wasn't much outside of group homes or shelters or adoption and no one said anything about talking to the kid, making sure he was still all there. And how could he be?

"Key, do you have a moment?" Margie said from behind me, and I almost ripped the tag off a pair of paints. She remembered my name.

"Sure," I said, and followed her across the men's floor, past dozens of aisles and displays, into her makeshift office behind the stockrooms. The surprise wore off and I became aware of Margie's look. A feigned solemnity yet dutifulness. This can't be good.

"Is everything all right?" I asked, and she took a seat behind a lopsided table.

"I wanted to ask you the same."

"What?"

"Well, you've come in late from lunch on several occasions. Things from the woman's floor have gone unaccounted for during the hours of your shift."

"Several people work during the hours of my shift. That could be anyone."

"I really like you, Key, you're a good employee. But I want you to take some time off. Let's call it a probationary period."

"I'm not seasonal, Margie. I can't just come back in three months. I'd have to get another job."

"If you ever need a referral—"

"It sounds like you're firing me."

"No, no," she cooed. "This is more of a ninety-day probation thing—"

"If it was probation, I'd still be working."

The room suddenly became tight. The horns of Sixth Ave., its many taxis and buses, seemed cut off only by the wall behind Margie. I suddenly worried it was in fact my hearing, behind a wall I couldn't see, that shuffled Margie's words, kept them from reaching me in time.

"We'll give you a call soon, my dear," Margie said, and walked back toward the sales floor, leaving me there to stare at the blank wall of the stockroom.

A fucking referral? What if I referred this place to a four-alarm fire? Only then I'd be the disgruntled Black girl who burned down the appliance section in a fit of Black rage. To already have versions of you imagined before you arrive and depart seemed limiting, reductive. I don't know if I knew the version of me who left the department store, into the sun and glass and stone of Thirty-Fourth Street, or if I even cared to know. On the train, a newspaper had been left in the seat next to me. Food uprisings swept Rosario and other parts of Argentina, motivated mainly by hunger, recent elections, and hyperinflation. Israeli civilians shot and killed a Palestinian girl in the occupied West Bank, spilled her blood on land they deemed theirs. Criticism of the New York State health commissioner's regulatory programs and the severity of the hospital crisis throughout the state. The world's news was local. If you were poor, you'd already been indoctrinated into the global community, could see specific problems of a township, favela, or housing project and see yourself like a shard of glass used like a mirror.

I got off the train one stop early, stayed at the bus stop until I saw him. Ms. Pat's boy, a gangly thing, led by a box of candy bigger than him, stood outside the strip mall in winter gear despite it being well into spring. I swore Ms. Pat's face had sprung from her head and righted itself onto the boy's; the same doughy nose, the jaw that protruded the bottom lip, the broad forehead. He wore a combination of patchwork name brands, the factory blunders they sold for cheap at Marshalls, stared out across the flattened grid to somewhere fixed above us. When he came to, he shook his head at no one, pouted his lips. The boy had adapted to loneliness, relied on his own responses to still feel looked after. Maybe he felt Ms. Pat buzzing around him like a gnat but couldn't be sure. Did he know his mother was with him every day? Would he find solace in that?

"Can I hang out here?"

He nodded, pushed his box of candy and basketball cap toward me. I gave him twenty dollars and only took a Sugar Daddy. His eyes widened a bit as he looked up at me. Said "Thank you, ma'am" in a voice he rehearsed throughout the day.

"What's your name?" I asked.

"Charlie," he said.

"I'm Key, I'm a friend of your mother." Charlie looked wary of me, eyed my outfit, the slacks and button-down Margie made us wear. My hair was straight this morning but had curled and floated, a falling victim of the city's aggressive humidity, convenience store fans, and bus exhaust.

"She'd want me to make sure you're okay," I said, but he stared until his eyes drifted to the middle, unfocused. He looked past me, underneath his eyes puffy and dark. I knew the look, wondered if my eyes crossed when it happened. Charlie didn't believe I knew his mother, or that I just wanted to ask him about that day, ask if he'd found his mother hanging or bleeding into the tub or her bed sheets.

We watched people stumble off the bus, mostly old women with bags that rolled and construction workers covered in dried paint. He held out his box of candy and hat for them. There were children home from school crowding the front of the pizza shop next to us. The old men by the auto shop convened under the hood of a Continental, took turns sliding underneath its belly.

"On Saturdays," he began, "she used to clean all day, then drink beer and smoke cigarettes and laugh on the phone all night."

"What do you do now on Saturdays?" I asked. He looked away this time.

"I can't go to a shelter. They'll send me to foster care."

"What's wrong with that?"

"It's awful."

"What if they find you a home?"

"I'm too old. No family wants somebody my age." His independence, the unknown behind his eyes—he was right. The way folk in this city thought, he was halfway to super predator.

"Your mother would want you to be safe," I told him.

"I know," he said, and threw the box down. He was exasperated.

"And if they catch you on the street they could send you to Spofford. That's worse than foster care." He nodded again, grunted, *I know*.

"It's scary," Charlie let out. "Not knowing what hurt her so bad."

I wanted to hug the poor boy. I wanted to shake the poor boy, tell him to look around. You had come out of despair like the cicada that hid away. All he had left to do was follow the natural order of things; to spring from the earth more whole than he had come into it. But some cocoons are graves. Charlie was far away, already bound to implode. When there's nothing left to burn, you set yourself on fire instead. I asked if we could hang out again. I couldn't tell if his reluctance was feigned, but I promised I'd be back.

I could barely look ahead as I climbed the stairs of Mama's walk-up. I crept to the door of her studio, holding the keys tightly, and turned them in the lock as quietly as I could. The door creaked as I pushed it open and I flinched. Nothing stirred in the apartment, only shadows cast from the light of traffic and the falling sun. I hit the lights and no one was there. I screamed until my throat felt like pulp. I washed my hands and face, my eyes red and puffy from frustration. I fried some bologna in a pan already covered in grease and ate it with some white bread. I stared at my mother's wall unit, the picture frames of me and her and Granddad, glass trinkets she got from antique or craft stores. Soon, I heard the door unlock and my mother burst in, among a storm of shopping bags. She didn't stop her path to the kitchen to put down her bags, managed to turn on the oven. Only after did she stop to kiss my wet cheek and saw me anew.

"What's wrong?"

"I got fired today," I confessed to her. I took my fried bologna sandwich and laid along her couch. I expected a hail of questions but was met only with running water. She opened and closed cabinets and pantry doors, putting away her haul from the supermarket across the street.

"What is it, Ma?"

"Are you gonna keep working these shitty-ass jobs?"

"Here we go—"

"—'cause I been doing that for almost thirty years and I can tell you it ain't fun," she said, standing by the kitchen with her hands full of packaged meat.

"I have rent to pay."

"We all got rent to pay." She threw the meat in the sink, under the water. "I just want more for you. More than I had, or your granddad—"

"Well, maybe this is it for me," I said, and I hated myself for it. Mama paused by the sink before she turned the water off and walked over to me.

"Is that what you think?"

"Yes."

"Then maybe I don't know you at all. The girl I raised always saw more for herself. More for everybody." She touched my cheek and went back to the oven. Didn't she ever have that moment? When all that hope went away, a cotton plant in the early winter shredded in the wind. I didn't have a thing to say and it made me bite the inside of my lips, made me slam the door when I went to the bathroom, run the hot water for a few minutes, and plop down in my seat at the table harder than necessary.

"You know anything about foster care?" I asked her suddenly.

"Key, you too old to get adopted," my mother said, and I couldn't help but feel the beginnings of a smile.

"Mama, there's this boy."

"I swear, Key, if you say what I think you saying."

"Mama, stop playing and listen. There's this boy in front the strip mall on Pennsylvania. His mom passed and he's just out there. He needs someone."

"How you know where the mother at?"

"He told me," I said. It wasn't untrue.

"Well, the church is good for that," she said. "I'll ask around."

"Thank you, Mama."

.   .   .

I WAKE UP with my heart racing, like in a panicked dream where all I can do is fall. The clouds roll across the night sky and I reach for what seems to be the length of the bay, the edges of the world tucked deep somewhere on the other side of the horizon. I am hot with fear, my body a fever that threatens to burn everything around me. Looking out at the shore, Black people poised on the jagged shoreline like marble. Ms. Pat stands out, the only head turning in the line unbroken. The same slow gait as when she wanders the strip mall, her skin full of color. This isn't a dream.

"How did I get here?" I ask the woman in the nightgown.

"Why, you walked, child," Ms. Pat says, as if it's the plausible thing.

I'm losing it. Have to be. Why can't I unsee what lies before me in my dream? I want to cry. Water springs from under my arms, my hairline. I'm breathing like I'd been running. I want to run. Want to turn my back to the whole thing, get as far away as I can. I look away from the woman, back down the bay. The stillness of the bodies swaying along the wrack line. The calm of it. I can't think beyond what's in front of me. My feet are raw from being dragged along in my sleep. A wind from the ocean numbs my hands, makes me shiver down to my toes. It was never a dream.

"I want to thank you for trying to help my son," Ms. Pat says. The voice trembles and the tide pulls the wind away from us. Silence. "I miss him so much. He just needs to know someone actually gives a fuck."

It is unfair, but I am afraid. If she could leave her son behind, then I could leave anything. What did I even have to tether me here? "Couldn't you come back to him?"

"No, I'm already—" She stops, considers her words like food between her teeth. "I'm with him the only way I can be."

"Why did you do it?" I breathe. "Why did you end it?"

"Everyone loved me wrong. I watched my mama die every day, cleaning buildings at night that she'd be kicked out of in the daytime, worked herself crazy. Thought she was suffocating on line at the housing office. I've always felt like that, like I could lose everything and I'd always be suffocating. When

I had my son, I was scared I would pass all of that down and he'd be stuck with it, like I am. He's a beautiful boy, like my daddy and his daddy, both of them, but they was cut from stone. Just as cold. I wish he knew this was happening long before him, that I was dying for as long as I could remember, that he kept me alive. I'd come to this shore alone, wanted to just float away. I wanted my body to sink and keep sinking, till I couldn't tell my skin from the dark. I don't know what day I decided. They all gummed together, those days." She turned away from me; the wind swept the hem of her nightgown. "Have you figured out why you're here?"

"I want to come home," I say. "But I don't want to leave anyone behind."

"It isn't your time yet. Sometimes helping others find ways to live can help you find your own ways. Helping others breathe can stop you from suffocating. Maybe. We'll be here when you're ready."

I regard her through the mist, the morning cooking fires of the dead, then stumble toward the shoreline. My eyes and face are wet, along with the gown I wear. Toward the tide, the hard sand gives way to cold, muddy water. I wince from the sharp chill as it springs from my ankles to my thighs to my hips. Soon the shoreline is a dark wall and I have to hop to keep my chin above the waves. I feel alone in the light of the moon, like it only shines on me and I will be forever cradled by it. I walk below the surface, under the waves, and there is no sound and I am suspended like a child in its mother's womb. I wonder if I will die in the Atlantic like my ancestors, like the folk stranded on Igbo Landing, or if I will wake up in the morning on my pullout, completely dry. I decide it is no different than dying slowly in Brooklyn, or any place in America. Jamaica Bay will be our landing and we'll march to a home that doesn't exist.

LEGBA

COLLY (2008)

Miss Betty lived on the same floor as me and may or may not have been the meanest woman in the neighborhood. She was missing a few teeth from all the rock she did (she'd purportedly stopped some years back), and her skin was like coffee, her eyes, nails, and teeth stained. She lolled around the sprawling lawn, the grass thinned by the countless touch football games played across it, down the path to the courtyard where Zaire and I sat. A year had passed since he helped get me suspended but I didn't blame him. Like the one before it, summer dragged on in the worst way, the crescendo where we almost begged for September to roll around and school to start, if only to fill the hours.

"I remember when you were this tall," Miss Betty said to me. Her hand came up to her stomach. "You have a dollar, papa?"

"I don't have a thing, Miss Betty," I lied. "I'm sorry."

She scowled at us, buzzed into the building and shuffled inside. I usually saw her by the laundromat, limping past the faded shop windows. In the middle of the day, a dust head might come to the bodega window, the price of a sandwich and soda in coins inside a paper cup. They patrolled Linden Boulevard between Hendrix Street and Van Siclen, stood by the store fronts during the day asking passersby for change, anything at all. There were a couple shelters in the neighborhood, one that had closed down months ago and sent dozens away to different corners and bus stops and stairwells. The ones who got high marched through the hood all day putting pieces together, running errands for businesses or sweeping the fronts of shops. Miss Betty was the oldest of them all.

Lou, Zaire's older brother, showed us his trey bags once, jagged stones that looked like yellowed teeth in the palm of his hand. He spoke at us but with the conviction of those conspiracy theorists on the subway, so we tended to get swept along anyway. Someone would appear at his side, as sudden as a sparrow might spring from its perch, asking for two with their head down and Lou would vanish with them around a corner.

Today the sun got all over everything, over the boys and girls by the community center, a hot day that brought the bees out, and I could hardly remember time before this. The light stung my eyes, made my shoulders feel as if the skin would break open. August couldn't end sooner. I had to put my hand up to see what Zaire said.

"They threw quarters at her the other day."

"Who?" I asked.

"Some older kids," he told me.

We sat outside my building watching folk, women with strollers or housing workers on their perpetual breaks. The blocks had to be a third of a mile long each, from Schenck to Ashford, Stanley Avenue cutting through them like a gray blister. Tenements like towering space stations wrecked on some forgotten planet, old relics that housed colonies of the disillusioned. I liked to look up at my window, almost expecting to see you, Ma, leaning against the bars with a Newport. You'd lay a towel out, a pink or a baby blue, and rest your elbows along the windowsill.

"Look at Raven," Zaire said.

Raven was our age and led a dance class for kids ages nine and up at the community center. Her kids were mostly girls and a couple of boys, all short and lanky, roasted brown from being out in the sun. Her class followed her to the center, dressed in bright yellow shirts, some tied at the waist. I found them beautiful. Their eyes were open in ways that made you realize how little you knew, a kind of way with the world that made them seem sure, or made them okay with not being sure, or that existence wasn't a thing to be concerned with or questioned. They had weighty pouts for a world that bruised, that made fun of their hair, said they were too loud or too dark-skinned. At school, at home sometimes. Raven wanted to dance through the haze, pull them out like a body on fire. I went to her house last week and sat on the bed while she went through routines.

"I've been adopted like twice," she had told me. "My brother a few times."

I've never lived in a shelter but I tell her I live with no one now. Dad comes and goes, work mostly, but I know he can't sleep in the bed you passed in. I could see Raven drift, dislodged in a memory of another home, somewhere not far, the thought of which had to be pushed away, the air too heavy, too suffocating for anyone to walk around in.

The girls passed and waved and Mr. Frank pushed toward us with a cart full of laundry, the back-right wheel stuck and dragging along the sidewalk as he pushed it. He argued something with Miss Morales and sat on the bench across from us, in front of the building with the seafoam awning, with the ladies from the tenant association. They talked in circles, shook boxes of cigarettes like ritual. After a while Mr. Frank called Zaire over to send him to the store.

"I'm not going," I said, looking up at him.

"Fine, I'll be back." He shoved his hands in his pockets and headed toward Stanley-side, toward the bodega on the corner.

"Not like the boy need the exercise," said Mr. Frank.

"Y'all so skinny nowadays," Miss Moore chimed, looking at me.

"That's 'cause the women don't cook," the old man grunted.

"Or maybe you ate it all, your big ass," Miss Morales said, and they all busted up. Mr. Frank's laugh was like sugarcane, Miss Morales's and Miss Moore's like ginger. They carried their home countries in the shapes of the words in their mouths, in the way their backs straightened. Miss Morales was from Puerto Rico, said she came as a girl when nothing but Polish couples and mothers whose husbands died in wars lived in these buildings. Said she had a schoolteacher with the thickest accent who looked like Myrna Loy and always brought in homemade doughnuts. She didn't want to stay after the war, until her husband had returned missing a hand and couldn't work. She taught here to this day, aged and less inclined to bring in anything homemade. I don't remember anything from when I had her in third grade other than supermarket pound cake. Over the years, those early migrants moved down Flatlands and farther into Brooklyn; the Italians to Bay Ridge; the Polish closer to Manhattan Beach and Coney Island, or into the rest of Long Island, buying up property in Howard Beach along the Shellbank Basin.

Now, as an old woman with bright red hair and glasses she wore to read coupon books, Miss Morales would watch from the third-story window, or from the lobby where the tenant association became a watch group, sitting around a foldout table playing 21. To us she represented parental authority, often knew what our mothers would say before we did, knew us as the faces of our parents. I was Key's boy.

Miss Moore leaned across the bench, her hospital cane like a staff in her hands, crossed in a regal way, one atop the other. "How's your dad holdin' up?"

"Doing what he can," I said.

"You all must be a wreck over there."

"We're doing okay, Miss Moore."

"I lost my mother, too. Felt like my whole world was coming apart. You have to pray, son. Do you pray?"

"Can't you see the boy don't wanna talk about it, Deb," Miss Morales exclaimed.

"We're having a moment here," said Miss Moore. "Could you quiet your old self?"

"I'm old? Sophia from *Golden Girls* here says I'm old."

"Both of y'all old as shit," Mr. Frank said, exacting his revenge.

Zaire came back with a couple of loosies and a lottery ticket for Mr. Frank. He turned to me.

"Wanna come to mine for dinner?"

"Sure," I said. I knew he felt bad for me. Pop was hardly there and Toya spent nights at Nana's. When she was there, she was painting her toes, covered in the blue light of her flip phone, her boyfriend on the other end. The two hardly spoke to each other, more to the people around them, as if letting the other hear the world as they went through it. I missed sneaking out after the heat put everyone to sleep, and Toya, who always threatened to tell, would never say a thing to you or Pop.

Tonight we were reluctant to go inside, to hear the growing choir of crickets from our windows. I knew Zaire from nursery, from when he scraped his knee running from Lea Braithwaite in the middle of the playground. We were neighbors for a while, Zaire and his family on the eighth floor of our apartment block while I lived right below him. They moved when we were in middle school, when five became six in a two-bedroom. Zaire and I went to the same school about two blocks down—where the building pumped brittle heat into the classrooms every other winter and the walls soaked the posters that hung from them every summer. We even shared a pair of sneakers one summer, when Zaire's father lost his job at the construction site. A pair of gray-and-white Jordan 12s that split at the heel after one too many suicides.

Zaire's was a narrow, lopsided house that made the most of its space.

Inside was clean from his mother's constant diligence, but messy because it was too crowded. Even the furniture contended with one another, the TV too close to the sofas, the dining room too close to the living room. The table was already loud and turbulent. Brown stew with beef, brown rice and peas, and plantains sat in large plates and bowls, Zaire's mother regulating portions from her seat at the helm. Over the dinner table was a knit cloth embroidered in the shape of flower bulbs and vines. On top was a thick layer of plastic.

"Boy, you see the other five plates in front of you," Zaire's mom said to the oldest, Lou. "Leave some for the rest of us."

"If you don't leave him," Zaire Sr. said. "Canarsie High needs their star power forward good and strong."

"Yeah, Mama," Lou said. "This beef stew is for the 'greater good.'"

"And you, Miss Thing?" Zaire's older sister emerged from the kitchen. "You clean that closet out like I ask?"

"Yes, Mother. Should I get everyone's orders as well?"

"How did I end up with such smart-mouth children?"

"You raised them," the father said, and she cut him a look.

Throughout dinner I hardly spoke. Sweet plantains were my favorite, soft and sugary with a slightly crispy layer, the way Zaire's mother seemed to make perfectly every time, yet I kept thinking about how empty my apartment was, how I could hear everything through the walls. Thought of Miss Betty walking about minding her business and getting coins thrown at her. Even if she was a bit mean, she hardly deserved that.

"And what's wrong with you two?" Zaire's mom asked.

I had to nudge him before he realized she was talking to him. We looked at each other. Zaire shook his head.

"Speak, boy," his father said.

"Colly's dad hasn't been around lately," Zaire said, and I looked at him in indignation.

"Is he in trouble?" Zaire Sr. asked, turning to me for an answer.

"It's all right," I said. "He's working extra nights to keep up with things."

"Do you need to stay with us, dear?" Zaire's mother spoke first. "A twelve-year-old shouldn't be in a house alone for days on end. Y'all are twelve, right?"

"We're fourteen, Ma," Zaire answered.

"If the boy don't want no help then let him be," the father said. "No room around here . . ."

"What's that, Husband?"

" . . . too crowded in this house as is." He shuffled to the back.

After dinner, Zaire and I retreated to the room he shared with Lou. He lay on his bed talking into a silver flip phone, cradled by his shoulder to his ear as he put up shots into a miniature hoop on the back of the door. The rubber ball squeaked as it hit the plastic backboard, Zaire tossing it back to him as we sat on the carpet and watched music videos. We could go stretches without saying a word to one another, as if the other wasn't there, without being bored or self-conscious about filling the silence. I appreciated this the most, to sit with someone and not be expected to serve their sense of enjoyment. I didn't want to talk about much lately. Sometimes, Lou played his CDs from a stereo at nearly full blast, classic rap albums from the mid to late nineties and early 2000s, DJ Clue tapes with B-side singles and obscure radio freestyles, Nas and Wu-Tang and Foxy Brown and Jay-Z, State Property, Jadakiss and the rest of the Lox, DMX, Buckshot, the Infamous Mobb (Prodigy was Pop's favorite; "You Can Never Feel My Pain," a song about his lifelong battle with sickle cell).

Zaire walked me out to the front, almost lit a cigarette before noticing Zaire Sr. working underneath his old-school. The car sat on an incline from the rusted jack, lopsided, its insides a mess of grease and machinery, knobs and tubes and pipes that seemed to lead deeper, somewhere in the car's pit. We watched him as he seemed to move with ease, going at some large bolt with a wrench.

"Someday you'll need to know how to do this," he said to us. He looked at me a second longer. "If you ever need to stay here for the night, son, you can. I just like to give her a hard time."

"Thank you, sir," I said. Zaire's dad would be on his way to work soon. He'd come home in the morning, and by afternoon he'd be back out hustling what he could. He had started his own sort of taxi service, wasn't certified by the city at all, but neither were half the cabs that lurked around Broadway Junction or Utica Ave., honking their horns or yelling "taxi" as people hesitated at the bus stop. On weekends, he combed the corners for bottles, piles of trash that wouldn't be collected until morning. The old man often dragged Zaire out of his bed to help. They hunched among the garbage bags spilling cans and melted juice cartons, sorting the plastic bottles on the sidewalk, into a shopping cart that couldn't turn because the rubber wheels were peeling away. Zaire couldn't bring himself to be seen. Sometimes he drew himself far away from the open air, the sweet fumes of rotted food. The plastic, struck by light from behind the watchful clouds, cast a strange light on his father, like he was poised above a church window.

Zaire walked me to the gate.

"I could stay over there if you want," he said.

"I'm good."

"You sure?"

"Positive."

"You don't get lonely up there?"

"I like the space."

"I just think it's weird," he admitted.

"Damn, you my babysitter?"

"You're right," he said, looking at his house shoes for a moment and turning back toward the front door. "Tomorrow."

I walked back to my place, through the doorway, the steel frame matted with mud, the concrete awning colored a rusted seafoam green. Miss Betty was in the hall, a cigarette burning in her hand. She lit up when she saw me.

"Wait right here," Miss Betty said, and disappeared into her apartment.

You used to give her clothes, Ma, old dresses and jackets with padding in the shoulders you no longer fit. One time, Miss Betty caught a mouse for us that had scurried around our apartment for weeks, a mother the size of a shoe. She scooped up the sticky trap with ease, the mouse heavy and writhing, half-dead in her hands. You nearly passed out. Back in the hallway, I heard sirens nearing in the distance, barreling down the eight-lane boulevard. Miss Betty emerged with a damp paper bag and held it out to me.

"I shouldn't," I said, eyeing the rising steam, a sour smell filling the hallway. I couldn't help but think there was a mouse inside.

"Please, take it."

I hesitated, but noticed the way her eyebrows pulled at each other, her eyes red and wet, the color of fresh pennies.

Inside was Tupperware, hot and full of what looked like soup.

"Your mum. I called her Ayida-Weddo. She's the Iwa who held up the heavens. When the first rains were born, a rainbow filled the sky and the Father took her as his wife. She stood at the crossroads."

In my apartment, the dark is a closed fist over mine. Pop would hopefully be home in the morning, gone by the time I came home from school. I could see him, lounging on the couch in nothing but his briefs. When Toya and I were younger, he'd let us trace a withered scar that went from his belly button to just below his chest. He'd show us the hole in his mouth, the fleshy opening where the bullet broke his skin and lodged itself in his jaw. It was a friend of his at the time. He wasn't supposed to be here. "So, don't you trust a soul, 'cept your mama and me," he'd say.

It was after midnight. I listened to old albums with my headphones, had to lay a certain way or the left earbud would give out. Took the lyrics to "Suicidal Thoughts" by B.I.G. and wrote them down in a notebook just to feel the verse in my hands, the shape of it on the page, the small but critical process that happens between writing a thing and saying it aloud. My voice plunked around the empty apartment. When Pop left for what seemed like days and days, the whole place could hollow out and every sound I made was way too loud and sudden. Tonight, something crawled beneath the floor, clawed at the pipes. I listened to the walls. Ran my hands along your bookshelf. My body was so cold my jaw ached from the shivering, but I was sweating. From the darkness of the room, I saw your face clearer than day. It had been over a year but it broke me apart just the same.

I had never stopped crying, I just did it quietly.

RAVEN TOLD ME she dreamed of the community center letting her put on a performance with the children on Boulevard Day. Every year, the first Saturday of August, it gave her a few weeks to come up with something.

"Do you know what you might do?" I asked. She shook her head. "It'll be great."

"Don't just say that," she said. "You don't know."

"I'm confident."

"You've seen me dance in my room," she said. "That's not a show."

"Says who?"

Whenever Raven told me about the girls (and the one boy who came every week), her eyes lit up with wonder like the flick of a lighter. I loved the way her joy almost sounded like tears if I looked away, smoky and exasperated.

"I don't think this is the year," Raven decided.

The girls wanted to learn the dances they saw after school on television or YouTube, dances that seemed to speak a language of desire they probably couldn't all the way grasp. Raven came up with routines, stitched together choreography from the favorites on *106 & Park* and *TRL*. She scrawled lyrics that played on the radio, on the corners of composition pages. Something bothered her, made her type furiously on her Sidekick, sliding the screen up and down like a switchblade.

Her brother played Buju Banton, "Driver A," from a CD that skipped. It wafted into the room like the nag champa he burned. Raven preferred to dance and whine, loved Tony Matterhorn and how Serani sang like he may weep at any moment. She watched Passa Passa videos her brother showed her grainy clips of a township in Jamaica on DVD—a party in the streets, a praise dance while balancing clear plastic cups, the deejay leading in ceremony. Raven said Carlene Smith and Bogle were the best dancers ever and I pretended to know enough about them to agree.

By chance, I caught a glimpse of something silver under her nightstand. It was a spiral notebook with a tattered blue cover.

"What's that?" I asked, picking it up before she snatched it away.

"It's . . ." She paused, staring at me to remind herself that I was who I said I was. "I always forget the dreams I have, so I write them down when I wake up."

"Can I see?"

"You're crazy."

"Read one to me."

"I haven't dreamed in awhile," she said, putting the book under her pillow. "Maybe I'm all out of dreams."

We sat in front her building when the streetlamps came on. Zaire came from basketball practice and joined us. The tenant association passed out flyers for an elderly game night, partnered with the center for advertisement in exchange for days out the week to use the movie room. They wore purple T-shirts with BOULEVARD COMMUNITY CENTER across the front. Miss Morales chatted up the ladies who walked by, spoke Spanish with some of them, handed them flyers between gossip. Mr. Frank got started about the lottery and called Zaire over.

"I'm not going," I announced.

"It's technically your turn," said Zaire, but heeded me anyway.

"How you holding up?" Raven asked me.

"I'm fine," I told her. That was the answer I was accustomed to.

"Your dad been back around?"

"It's been a few days."

"When I was in foster care I used to dream my mother would swoop in one day, grab me by the hand, and we'd fly out a window or something."

"How do you deal with that?" I asked.

"Every day I come up short at the deli tryna buy breakfast and papi just lets you have it," she began. "Mr. Frank gives me five dollars a day just to play his numbers. Zaire's mom has one of us over for dinner every night and I know your ass is grateful because you look like you're turning into a bowl of ramen."

"You teach at the center when you don't have to," I added, a slow and muted understanding. Raven nodded.

"We have to be like family," she said. "How would any of us make it without?"

Before I could say much else, Miss Betty walked up the path, dragging her foot behind her like a bag too heavy to lift. The scowl she wore was a deep line that made her chin look separate, a marionette. Miss Morales acted as if she didn't see her.

"Ey, let me hold a dollar," Miss Betty said to me.

"I don't have it, ma'am."

"Where's your papa? He'll give it to me."

"I don't know." She looked at me in a way that assumed one of my answers was a lie; it couldn't be both. She scowled some more, kissing her teeth as she limped toward the door.

"Fucking crackhead," Raven said. "She's always so rude."

All the while, I watched the old woman limp away. Chewed at my nails.

THAT NIGHT I ended up finding Miss Betty in the hall again, surrounded by cigarette butts. Said she had stew this time, told me to come in for a second. Her place was dark, lit only by a kitchen light and candle by the window. A cat brushed by my leg and I leaned down to pet it.

"Legba," Miss Betty said. "His name." The cat was trying to climb higher and I could feel his claws, my legs feeling like they might spout blood. I pulled him off, had to tear his grip from my jeans. When he scurried away, I looked down at my hand covered in dry, crinkled fur.

The living room floor was cluttered with garbage bags of clothes, a yellowed mattress, chewed-through tables and display stands, and a sunken sofa where I was told to sit. Straight ahead was the kitchen, vinyl peeling from the cabinets, the stove leaking dark grease from its insides. A part of the wall was rotten from what seemed like a leak, grew, and took to the floors and corners. She hadn't called Housing for repairs in years. You would say that's right on schedule, Ma.

Miss Betty shuffled from the back room, the shape of an egg, her bad leg twisted and dragging behind her. She sat next to me, putting Legba in her lap even as he tried to claw away.

"I remember when you were this tall," she said again. Her hand came up to her stomach. "Handsome. You look just like your mother."

I nodded. She rocked back and forth, stroking Legba.

"School," she started. "What do you do in school?"

"Math. Chemistry. We read a bunch."

"Smart boy. You won't end up living here all your life."

"What's wrong with here?"

"Bad place."

I thought about the many meanings of that. Was this immediate room bad? Was she in a bad place? Was a place bad inherently or based on the things that happened to you there? The room had no light except the glow from the courtyard. I watched a pocket on the wall behind her, some crease in the decades old paint, realized it was a roach feeling its way ahead, plotting its next move. "How's your son?" I asked.

"Good, good, that wife won't let him see me. I know she's the reason he's all the way down there anyway."

Mark had a wife and three kids down in Florida. I could see his wife, finding a job as far away as possible, needing to save Mark from his own dust head mother.

How did she pay for the apartment? I just didn't know. I thought she must receive a check once a month from the government, welfare or disability. Maybe she mangled her right foot in a freak accident in Times Square or on the subway and the city had to break bread through a lowly settlement.

"Were you and my mother friends?" I asked Ms. Betty.

"I don't have a lot of friends here. I came from a beautiful place where it's all green and everyone carries machetes to cut through grass on their way to the market. Through a miracle, or what I thought was a miracle, I made it here to New York with my kids." She paused, swallowed something above her throat. Messed with her dried fingers. "When their daddy was murdered, your mother was the first one to reach out to me, prayed with me. Even as time went on, your mother always tried to look out for me. I never returned the favor."

She looked at me, Legba in her lap clawing at the arm of her chair. I could spot the quiet wreck of a particular loss, the inability to reach outside yourself and show someone what was inside. One day what matters to you seems different from what matters to everyone else, like losing a parent to cancer, or becoming addicted; either you remain who you are or accept becoming new. Because loss never leaves anything, anyone, as it was found. It is always different, without.

I am without a mother.

Suddenly I heard a lock turn and the front door swung open with a slow moan. The smell of musk and piss. The rattle of a six-pack. I had seen them in front of the shops asking for change, seen them pacing and sweating most days and nights. Miss Betty's daughter was gangly, the color of a Sugar Daddy bar, her face a knot of anxious lines. Next to her was a man, his hand around her waist; the lines of his face flowed red like smoldering coal. Miss Betty introduced us.

"I've seen him around," her daughter said.

"Smart boy," Miss Betty told her.

"Really? I went to NYU," her daughter said, and flashed a toothy grin with hardly a tooth left.

"You never went to no NYU," the man proclaimed.

"How would you know?"

"She ever go there, Betty?"

"No," the old woman said. Cradled her forehead with two hands. She didn't know how to deal with her mistakes but she was surrounded by them, all she could turn to, mistakes strewn about her like leaves in the fall, like the very mess in her home. She mourned for her daughter, for herself.

"I was gonna take off, Miss Betty," I told her as I rose to my feet.

"Wait," the woman exclaimed and limped into the kitchen. I stood by the door as she handed me a bag that steamed out the top, another medium-sized Tupperware. "Don't forget your food."

"Of course not," I said, a bit too eagerly. I wanted her to know how much I appreciated what she did, what she was doing for me. "What is it?"

"Beef and pumpkin stew," she answered, and opened the door.

"Thank you, ma'am."

"Take care."

Back in my apartment I looked up Ayida-Weddo on my desktop. I found an interpretation of her on a user-made Angelfire website. I read the myth, her holding up the stars and sky. She could also go through the doors of life and death. I ate the stew alone, listened through the walls over the sitcoms on television. My mother's shelf rattled as a door outside slammed and footsteps trooped down the steps, out the building.

ALTARS

KEY (1989)

Stephanie Morales had her back hunched over the stove as she flattened the warm corn husks she would pack and fold for the tamales, taken from a pile on the counter next to her. I watched the smoke from her pan curl out the window, wisp away into the cool October afternoon. Outside I heard the bells of the church, the shuffle of children leaving bible study, their hard soles scuttling along the road. The sun was a knife cutting through the dogwood branches, turning the sky the color of bright persimmons. I ran a hand along the hem of my dress, reminded myself of my own skin, tried to smooth out the goose bumps that rose from the slight wind.

Stephanie said she wanted to talk to her mother one last time, and I could hardly turn anyone down these days. I remembered Rosa, half a decade since she passed in that fire. I had seen the smoke all the way from New

Lots station one day on my way home from Liberty and Guy Brew. I followed the fire trucks and EMTs, saw the windows blown out, the outside of the building charred where the fire lapped at the brick and plaster. No one knew how it started. Most called it a freak accident, a candle left burning overnight near her bedside. The closer you got to those around Rosa, though, the more you got the sense of something sinister. In those days, she had become more and more unhinged, let her neighbors tell it. *Maybe the fire was started on purpose.* The woman had taken in a homeless kid named Bito and a lover we all called Betty, a basehead who lived in my building, both somewhat out of the blue. *Her kids shouldn't have left her alone like that,* the neighbors chirped. *Can't trust a junkie, or anyone for that matter.* Rosa was small, yet she had a voice I often heard from her fourth-story window. It could hitch a ride on the wind. I saw her about, bought every kind of fruit and vegetable at the farmers market up on Schenck. She spoke to most of the vendors and patrons in Spanish, prayed or gossiped or both. She smiled whenever I walked by, asked if my mother was cooking for whatever church event was coming up. Her big eyes were bloated with water.

The apartment was painted the bright skin of a tangerine, full of pots of green stalks and dusty appliances and electronics. I let Steph do whatever she needed to. I breathed the sage she burned, the ends of the ash-colored stalks turning to smoke. I sat at the altar, photos of a young Rosa atop an antique chest alongside paintings of saints, Mary and Philomena. The saints had use in all kinds of conjuring and fortification. A framed Saint Peter without a key was hung to bring about success. Joseph with baby Jesus in his arms was hung up when one needed work. There was a shelf below Mary and Philomena that was lined with mason jars full of roots, seeds, dirt, pastes, roasted corn with palm oil, yam powder for protection.

"Can you tell me how she crossed over? As you remember it," I asked her. It made them easier to retrieve, if someone were still trapped in an in-between place, lost and wandering. Everyone in the neighborhood wanted to sit down with me. They called, asked my mother on the street when she went to the grocery for greens and freshly cut meat. She told them not to believe everything they heard, respectfully. But the ones who knew, really *knew*, came to me. They wanted to say goodbye, or ask one last question.

The problem was that the ghosts stayed with me. Each one left a shadow under my eye. They stood where I found them. They looked at me for longer than it took to remember where I'd met them. I couldn't tell sometimes if I'd met them years ago, in passing at the laundromat or at an old job. But more often than not I knew their faces, pulled them from memories that didn't seem to belong to me, relived what they once told me from the other side. What if I stopped being able to tell the difference? What if the ghosts became more real to me than anything and I mistook Ma or Genesis or anyone who belonged to me? What if I was found out, caught talking to someone in front of the corner store who wasn't there, or who was, just not in 1987? I'd have gone crazy, word around the neighborhood would be, or got laced, some bad drugs. What if time rolled away from me and I was haunted forever? At first, it must've been those who had wished for death. Like I once did.

"They had the . . ." Ms. Pat would say, clear her throat, "autonomy and will to do so." I saw the spirits of folk roam the shores at night, looking for a bridge. Now I'm able to see those who have died traumatic deaths.

It made me anxious, pressed on my stomach and insides. Ms. Pat didn't understand what I was worried about. "As long as you know what is, what's the problem?" It was a reminder of each one of these parlor rooms, the stuffiness, the stories I choked on in order to become a translator, a tongue and mouth for the dead who still wandered the hills. I felt the dull edge of all that trauma. I was a part of the history of each trauma, had to speak it to the living until it became mine, ours, all of ours.

"Since when was the truth easy?" Stephanie asked, hands with shoots of green onions that she would sit and chop. She had turned the stove top down, sat across from me at the kitchen table. It was small, so our knees touched for a moment. She didn't look like Rosa except for the same big eyes, lines stretched about her face like she was older than she was. Had to be the kids. Said she shoved them on their dad for the whole day. We had both gone to the same nursery and elementary school. We weren't friends, but there was an intimacy brought on by knowing the embarrassing things we did as children.

"The fire department told us the fire started in the living room," Steph began, and chopped away at the shoots. "My brother, Angel, got here first so I had them repeat it for me. Anyway, the fire started near that closet and spread through the rest of the house. There were sheets and curtains bundled and tied together, which made it easier for the fire to travel. They found my mother asleep in the bedroom with a bruise on her neck. Other than that, the fire didn't touch her. She died from smoke inhalation. They found the damn dog in the next room, dead from smoke inhalation. I talk to our neighbors downstairs all the time. Woman lives right upstairs. Says she and her son heard a knock on the door that night, around three in the morning. Says it was real soft at first, like a tap. Then it got louder and louder. Rap, rap, rap. Her son got the door and there was that homeless kid Bito, telling them of the fire. He lived there for a few months and she had gave him Angel's old cot. Anyway, they try to follow Bito downstairs but the hall is full of smoke. They get to the staircase and it's even worse. Thick black smoke. She says soot was burning their eyes, getting into their hair. Yet Bito had this clean white T-shirt.

"I'm not saying anything foul happened. Actually, fuck it. I am. My mother burned candles, but wouldn't the fire have started in her bedroom and not the living room? Wouldn't she have died of burns instead of smoke? Who was there with her but the drug addict and that crazy, fucked-up kid? I see them all the time with Angel's old clothes, his shoes, like they raided the closet before they burned my mother's house down. Those same neighbors tell me she and her son always go back to that night. Say they heard shuffling and voices into the night.

"My aunt made a scene at the funeral. Claimed we abandoned her sister, said we were only here now for the insurance claim. You could say the same about her. When money's involved, family just forget who you are. What do Proverbs say? The greedy bring ruin to their household?

"But I didn't want Mami to be forgotten. I wanted this city to know who my mother was. I wanted to know why anyone would kill her. I wanted folk to know that she came from dust and root and came here to give me and Angel a life where we could have anything. And I think she realized it's the hardest thing, just like any brown person who has to find a way in this fucking country—I swear it's the onions."

As Stephanie dabbed at her eye with the bottom of her shirt, the key rattled in the door, and moments later a brawny and tall man walked in. The skin around his mouth was dark and his eyes glazed over like he'd been to work in a gas plant somewhere. Angel went into the bathroom and I heard the water run for some time.

"I better get the food ready for that altar," Stephanie told me. She disappeared into the front. When the apartment had been restored, Rosa's room had required the least work, not much structural damage except a section of wall gnawed away by the intense heat. I sat on the bed and looked out the window. A starling bounced across the treetops. There was hardly anything left of Rosa's. The photo albums, the frames, her clothes. Her scent. Even if someone was gone, you could stand in their room and take them in, weep in the overwhelming smell of their sheets, the clothes in their closets full of mothballs. The walls and shelves held ancestors, their great-aunts who passed, frames holding together black and white photos of their great-grandfathers. Stephanie had laid out some of Rosa's things: a dress she loved to wear in the summer when they went to the Botanic Garden after Mass, a bowl made of hammered brass she filled with water and rose petals to wash her face, candles she made at home from oil and wax that smelled like sunflower and baume. There was a rose dipped in a plastic vase, glasses and teacups around it full of water and tonics. Each cup was family who'd gone on, the intermediaries. There was a line of cowrie shells, meant to evoke Yemaya, mother and sea. The sun was a sty that winked behind the living room curtains, fell slow over the autumn day.

The bathroom door opened as Stephanie passed, the siblings shuffling around each other with rolled eyes and sour exhales. She made her way to the front door and closed it behind her, and I heard Angel in the kitchen, the bubbling of a coffee machine. Before long he found me near the back of the apartment. He stopped in the doorway, stared ahead as his thick hands covered a YMCA mug, concerned me in his mother's room as if the air settled differently, was off somehow.

"So you're what, the medium we paid for?" Angel asked.

"You didn't pay me, this is a favor."

"And you can talk to Mami."

"In a way," I said.

"What way?"

"Why don't you sit down with me?" I asked him. Angel looked as if I would pounce. He took off his hat and fully entered the room, consuming its space with body, his smell. He sat across from me, the foldout chair almost too big for him and his hips. He shrugged.

"So?"

"What's that with your sister?" I asked.

"You know she doesn't live here anymore, Steph. She comes by and cooks. Says she's adding to the altar. I think it's guilt. She left and now she wants to make up for it but it's too late." There was redness beneath the brown dust of his skin.

"It's just you?" I asked.

He nodded.

"Do you remember that night?"

He nodded again and I saw his brutal face turn open, soft.

"Can you tell me about it?"

"She wasn't there," he said. "I wasn't but she really wasn't there. Had checked out. She can curse me out for not being there but what about what I needed? Steph could've taken me with her. She left when she had the chance and left me here because she felt guilty, while she was in Long Island with her boyfriend's family and their house with all those rooms and their yard.

"She never had to wait out the bad days. Didn't have to look for the signs, whether Mami even left the bed or not. Whether she made the dough for empanadas from scratch, or just forgot to eat. Was she gonna look at me without turning away or would she ask where in the world did I go today? It was always work. When it was good, she wanted to hear about what I learned in school. We'd go to Athens or the Nordic region during the saga of Njáll, or Mali with the story of Sundiata. She said even though the cultures were different, the stories we tell about our nations, about ourselves, were usually the same.

"The bad day was when she didn't leave her bed. Her room was like a cave. With me to get her cigarettes, and if I didn't, she was shouting at me, to herself. She would become so frustrated with me and I couldn't be what she needed. Just a storm, drawers and cabinets, aimed at me, at herself, until finally I obeyed, pleaded with her. I would do anything. I'd protect you from anyone, I would say. I'd protect who she was, the woman from San Juan with the huge smile, who was playful, who could feed a community center with a day's notice, opened her home to anyone who had a need. I told my friends you were tired all the time but they loved her, made themselves at home, hoped she might fry some fish. Let them drink the 99 Apples they'd snuck from home. But she was in her cave, and when she came out, she was dazed, half-dressed, wanted to start a fight with me. I was so embarrassed I had to pull her into her bedroom while my friends looked away, tried not to make it a big deal—but I had to leave.

"I went to Bushwick. My girlfriend's family had a place out there. The night of the fire. My sister thinks Mami was murdered. I never knew much about the woman she let live here, except she had that limp and had a son I always saw outside. It's weird, but those last months I was . . . relieved. She had somebody. Oddest bunch ever. I'd see Bito all the time. He fought with his dad until the old man put him out. When I came and checked on her, I found him in the staircase, trying to sleep. We'd bring him clothes sometimes, food, extra paella if we had it. I don't think the kid could do something like that. I just thought he was going through something. We don't know people's intentions. Maybe that woman was a scam artist. All I know is Mami's heart, and on the inside, something was killing her.

"My sister claimed something happened so she could never file the insurance claim. I just got tired of arguing. I didn't want to talk to the church or make statements for the news or the paper. I wanted to bring up big fat tears and lie in them, days at a time. I wanted to sit with the photos I had left of my mother; everything got lost in the fire. I wanted to be about eight or nine and run around. Sink into her soft belly. Where was the pastor now? The papers, the news trucks? The politicians? Now that I can't pay rent, or beg for furniture to fill this place. It was like Mami died and she suddenly belonged to everyone but all the bullshit after was mine alone. I'm the only one who carries it everywhere I go."

STEPHANIE HAD PREPARED the food for the Orishas. She chopped up whole, fat plantains and set them down. Then a pomegranate cut in half, its crown red and pulsing. She sat great onions cut open at the top, along with white yams split open. Angel made a red snapper lined with peppers, cooked in palm oil. She lined all this along the base of the altar. In seven days, she would take it in front of the building, perhaps in the middle of twilight, and bury it in the dirt. We cleansed ourselves, passed the Locust beans down our bodies. Then we ate. Stephanie made macaroni salad with tuna and lasagna. "Did you even want flavor in the sauce?" Angel had said over the pot. He had tossed in some more pepper and garlic. "You're so annoying," Stephanie had shouted, over boiling pots and the water she ran. We then sat in front of the altar. The sun had fully dipped below the buildings, peeled the blue from the sky as it went until it was a ripe plum. Stephanie got on her knees before the shrine and spoke, a tongue I didn't know. She offered the food to Yemaya, then she took a coconut and carved it. The chucks fell to the rug, the meat wet and dripping from the shell. Behind her, I walked and filled the room with steam from a pot of boiling water. Nothing came forth and I couldn't see anything.

"Is it working?" Angel asked. I looked at my feet.

"Just chill out," Steph told him.

I was improvising. Usually, the sensation of being revealed to the dead was immediate, a pressure below my throat that felt like anxiety. It was like a boat with a cracked hull, the water rushing in around my ankles. I had to will myself into an overture, had to ask permission. Only then could I invite anyone in. The whorl of a flower that opened itself to the bee. Rosa, where were you? You didn't have to hide. I could almost feel the silk of her house-coat. I felt my blood go hot, a rolling boil that made me nauseous. I had to sit down, closed my eyes. Steph and Angel swayed over me, or I swayed, be-came darkened shapes that spoke inaudibly. I feel myself cracking through ice, or pulled from under a stream, into catatonia. I taste blood. The dark-ness is hard, waxy and thick. I hear water, first the slow wash of a tide, then rushing, as if caught in a heavy stream that keeps pulling me under. There are voices, pulsing from beneath the water, some wall I can't see. It isn't water but smoke. I could smell fire. I move about the house, down the hall, floating, listening to the walls. They rattle, burst into flames, the smoke and ember like chalcedony, rising and falling around me. There is a chill. It grows cold on my brow, my spine, sends a mallet to my chest. I am breathing like I had been running but I hadn't been and I wanted to. Turn my back to the whole thing, get as far away as I could.

I FIND ROSA in the other room, perched at the end of the bed. Around her the fire rages, grows large as the walls could hold, blowing smoke as thick as fabric. She looks so peaceful. Over the fire I disturb her, disrupt a moment that is dislodged from time. I smell the palo santo she burns, the rose water she bathes in before she goes to bed the night she dies. I hold her hand, walking with her the length of the hall. She wakes fully, says something in Spanish. Then, as if recognizing me, speaks in a language that sounds like pieces of Yoruba and Lucumí.

"Are you going to take me away from here?" she asks.

"Your family." I pause. "They want to say goodbye."

"I WON'T TELL you much about the fire," Rosa says through me. In front of us are still the shapes of her children; I had never left the chair. "What I will tell you hopefully can help you understand."

"You see, Abuelita had a home by the sea in Puerto Rico, your grandmother, on land slaves freed themselves on. One time she gave me money for coconuts, to cook with the oil. I had used it to buy a bracelet made from tiger's eye. I met him in town, your father. We decided to climb a coconut tree and just hack some off. It took him all day to climb that tree. Our skin was raw from chafing against the tree's husk. By the time he got up there he was too tired to hold on and fell about twenty feet. At least he got the coconuts, I thought. I walked around that palm for twenty minutes, digging through sand thinking maybe they rolled away. I looked everywhere for those coconuts. Finally, I walked home all dirty and red. I showed Mami the bracelet and told her about the coconut tree. She laughed until tears ran down the lines of her face. Just do what I ask next time. When she was murdered, along with Abuelito, I remember how silent the street was; how the sound of steel dragging along the dirt was the worst sound I had ever heard. I couldn't bring myself to look directly at them. Shadows seemed to slide into the shapes of the street as they walked. They were boogeymen like Abuelita told me long ago, hid me in the attic, cracking the pieces of them with clubs and automatic fire. I thought some kind of lightning had struck.

"I gave up on that place. I gave up trying to figure out why all of this had happened. I thought of your father, his eyes, brown and wide. He didn't write. Finally, my auntie said she knew where he stayed. He lived in Ozone Park, on Seventy-Sixth Street. He lived with a woman. 'He's stupid,' she said. 'A fucking dog.' I cried all night. I found where he lived, the back of a six-family building. A little boy was with him, his eyes brown and wide. I looked at them both, and ran away.

"I was so sad I just slept. Stephanie, you hated me because I was weak. I could see it in your face back then. You had to cook most nights, pick up groceries, pick up Angel, clean, call the bank, pick me up from the floor. I couldn't keep anything down. I'd watch *Breakfast at Tiffany's* praying I could buy or con my way into money, into happiness. I know you saw your friends with new shoes every year, new school clothes to match. I spent Sundays in church and at the swap meet. I'd send Angel anywhere with the stamps, just to get him out of my hair, and when he left I was lonely. That's when I met Betty.

"When I met her we both missed our home. She was from an island, too, joked that she could still feel the sand in her hair. We remembered the hills, how sticky the air was in our mouths. We talked about being outsiders. We were strangers, even to our people. They couldn't get past our tongues, our umbilical cord to our mother country. Perhaps we were too judgmental. Betty took me from orbit. We chain-smoked cigarettes at the kitchen table. She'd be high, telling me stories of her village, rocking to the kompa beat she could hear in her head.

"And one day the boy from downstairs knocked on the door. I gave him food some nights because his father kicked him out. The man was scared of his own son. I couldn't let him go back out there; he slept on a cardboard mat on the roof landing. You know how cold that staircase can get. So I let him sleep in Angel's room that night. Then whenever he needed. I gave him Angel's old clothes. It felt like family again."

"I know what happened that night," Stephanie says from far away, in the fire. "It was Bito, wasn't it? He was upset with you that day. He got angry with you and messed up and tried to cover his tracks. I know now. It's true, isn't it? Just tell me it's true."

"And what will that do?" Rosa says.

"It'll help me. It'll help me let go."

"If I tell you what happened, will it free you from the hell you think you're in? You can't deal with the idea of someone taking me away, not me, not God, not even Oshun herself."

"Mami," Angel says.

"Mijo, I miss you."

"I miss falling asleep in your arms, in your bed 'cause you had the good fan in your room."

"I wish you could . . ." I feel Rosa saying. "I'm right here. Right here with you.

"Stephanie, I used to fit your whole foot in my mouth when you were a baby. You're so brave. I wish I could've been that. Angel, you're the sweetest boy I could've ever hoped for. And I drove you away, made you harder."

"It's not your fault. It's not. It's not. It's not—" Angel kept repeating the words, stretching further and further until I was on the other side of a chamber, could only hear the resonance of the fleeting sound. The room came back to me, the smell of palm oil. Something around me was undone and I could breathe again. I was crying. And not thinking, not knowing what to do, if I was myself again or the voice of her mother, Stephanie hugged me close.

THE EVENING HAD settled in, inciting the lamps along the road to spring on. If you walked close enough to them, leaned toward their metal base and neck that curled toward the sidewalk, you could hear the disruption in the arcing, an electric hum. People were getting off work, on their way home and stopping for food or cigarettes or a six-pack. Kids coming from school had dropped their bags at home, in their parents' front hallways, before rushing back outside to the comfort of their friends. I visualized the hole I would create when I got home, how dark I would make my room just to close my eyes. About halfway down the block, over the charge of the street, I heard Rosa.

"This takes a toll on you, doesn't it?" she asked me.

"You shouldn't worry about me."

"It doesn't take much to worry. It's all we can do for people. And pray for them." This life is so flimsy.

I took her to the shore. I didn't mention that I knew what had happened that night, watched it over and over, through the flames. The truth was gruesome. A mother's love meant she would always protect them. I wouldn't ask why she did what she did because I knew, and there were moments in my life where I understood more than I should. I could tell you what really happened, but what would it mean if I said it aloud? It wasn't my story to tell, and I've already exploited it for my own. I don't know how it would serve you, or whoever reads this. I don't know how it serves Rosa and her children. I'm so afraid of the stories given to me, so protective of the people I've endured with. I could tell you one day, one morning when you find me only to sit with me, with reverence for the lives you wish to uncover. When it is you and I, only then can I tell you.

HEART FOR HEART'S SAKE

COLLY (2009)

It might not feel better to be well.
—TONI CADE BAMBARA

The second time I watched someone die, it was in a crowded field, at the second base of a baseball diamond. Three quick shots. The white lines that made up the diamond had all but completely faded from the worn, ragged blacktop—I only knew because I used to stand outside the gate and watch runners fly from second base, cut slightly through the lines near third, only to take off toward home. I'd cry to my dad, upset that someone would ever cheat in a game. I knew it was second base only because I wasn't far away. I chewed gum until it was tasteless. The hot report of a gun echoed above the playground, reached the beeches, pushed the starlings out from their perch.

No one got down at once. There was a moment, a breath or two, where every-one in the park went on as usual, words still whole in their mouths or laugh-ter still full in their bellies. Then they scattered every which way, along the fence, out onto the sidewalk and the middle of the street. Only when the crowd was thin did anyone notice Joshua kneeling, laying down real slow as if he was tired. His brother put his head in his hands, looked about wildly. Blood had pooled beneath his body. It got into the uneven blacktop, soaked the dirt and faded lines, and, I imagined, flowed down and down until it fed the earth. Someone else screamed for help. I remember the paled mint stuck under my tongue, the blood and iron I could taste from biting into my lip.

A MUSEUM WAS a theater with walls for curtains, where the show was right in front of your eyes and most things happened backstage. That's what impressed me the most, the walls. That a room could become something new, the sliding panels, the portals that appeared, whole spaces undone and put together again different from last time. It gave us possibility: being complete, being whole, was a process. I walked through an L-shaped corridor with old pottery, antique jewelry, and silverware, all sitting in display cases lit from beneath in dramatic lighting. Took the escalator down. A group of men in suits passed by, college students who smelled like cigarettes, couples in dark jeans and Chelsea boots meeting before dinner. The buzz of the crowded gal-lery crept through my headphones, so I jacked the mp3 player I'd gotten from RadioShack up to its highest volume. "Anti-American Graffiti" by J Dilla.

There were about seven of us total, three boys and four girls selected out of a citywide call for applicants. We all seemed to be around the same age, fifteen or sixteen. Ms. Hirsch was the senior curator of photography, and she would "be leading us this spring as we learn more about the curatorial pro-cess," her nose said. A dark-haired woman in her twenties assisted her, with a voice that caught high up in her throat.

The landing was a cavern, a mess of dark rooms and dying light. Deep inside was lit only by a red glow from the other end. It was a panel of pure light. Must've been thirty feet high, almost wide enough to cover a whole museum wall. More light flickered, stutters and burns, the shadows making the shape of a room. An entryway ablaze. I wanted to walk through it, climb through the other side, stand with my eyes closed in a wash of red infinite. I touched the panel.

Flat. It was a light show, and the entryway went nowhere. I came back to my body, felt the tips of my fingers. The label on the wall to the left said *Frontal Passage* (1994).

"Turrell," said a voice behind me. I turned, watched Dominick, one of the other applicants, run his hand along his neck, from which a silver chain with a pair of blank metal dog tags; his nails were almost gnawed to the cuticle, and his hair, while purposefully mismanaged, seemed on the verge of leaving grease marks on his shirt collar.

He was from the Upper East Side and had raved for weeks about the genius of John Cage. I couldn't remember his high school—Calhoun, Dalton, LaGuardia, the goddamn UN school—one of those fancy, liberal types. I wished I could afford to be eccentric. I was forced into Harry Van Arsdale, one of many campuses the city deemed unsalvageable before carving it into a mess of charter schools. The past February, the day I turned fifteen, one of the metal detectors bugged out and there was a line around the block. As I strolled in, halfway through first period, my art teacher cornered me about applying to an internship at MoMA. I had no idea what a curator was, let alone what they did, but the stipend and free MetroCard seemed worth it. And disappearing . . . even if just after school once a week.

"What'd you think this Turrell guy was saying?" I asked.

"Something about nothingness . . . or, I guess, something-ness." Dominick shrugged, the chains of his dog tags bouncing into each other, and he stared at the glowing wall.

"What are you listening to?" Dominick asked.

"Dilla," I said.

"Who's that?"

"Who?" I mocked. "Who's John Cage?"

"He's a pioneer, man. Real experimental. He's like, one of the reasons we make music the way we do." I was anxious to get out of this cavern, to find light somewhere else.

"Who's Dilla?" Dominick asked me again, but I couldn't speak. I caught sight of Naima walking toward the other side of the exhibit. I took off my headphones and put them and my mp3 player in Dominick's unsuspecting hands and skipped toward her direction.

Naima had disappeared around some corner, or, who knows, through some panel. I always saw her staying late to help out Ms. Hirsch. Would haul over materials and books in a pushcart, from the studio we worked out of, back to the older woman's office. Naima was from uptown and her favorite artist was Betye Saar. She had the skin of fruit, a brown that seemed red like the inside of papaya, a peach. Wore her hair close to her face, black curls over gold hoop earrings with her name studded in the middle. I immediately felt an affinity with her. Those hoops reminded me of twinkling storefronts on Jamaica Avenue, the kiosks that sold gold chains and nameplates. Names like Ashley and Keosha and Toya.

I drifted through another dark room, this time with screens on the ceiling and photographs in cutout portions of the wall. Through a labyrinth of images and clips, a full video of a woman combing her hair, I came out the other side of the floor. Nothing, hardly a brown face through the crowd of white folk. As I rounded the last corner of the exhibit, I was struck by a painting that almost knocked me over. It must've been ten feet high, even wider. The colors were like rotting fruit. In the painting, a huge man was laid across a table with something cut out of him. His giant face had slackened, skin peeling and rotten, limbs disfigured. He was being lowered into a makeshift grave as the crowd behind him picked at the body. The slit of mouth slid toward the side, a strange and lifeless smile—it was horrific but I couldn't turn away. I'd seen plenty of people dead. I had known Joshua from Linden side, who had died a couple weeks earlier in the middle of the park. I knew him, but I didn't know him, which felt weird to say, because how was I ever supposed to forget him?

It was like they were devouring him. We devour death. Violence.

"This is fucking amazing," Dominick yelled when he saw me across the hall. He hadn't bothered to take off the headphones.

I RODE HOME that night on a crowded 3 train headed toward New Lots. My mind drifted to empty red rooms, drifted to the dead. I caught myself, forced my body to feel the hum of the train engine, the coldness of the seat, the closeness of the older woman seated next to me. I took in the sour air, caught a whiff of gum, the stale smell of dried sweat and sulfur. I peered out the window, looking out onto miles and miles of mythical land. I hovered over the slackened row houses and backyards, over the treetops and playgrounds, the streets—a grid of bitumen—alive with people and lights. I saw my warped face reflected off the windows along the stone high-rises. They gave way to a railyard, then short stacks of factories and office space. More high-rises. The sun dipped and curled from behind the gray clouds, the sky a shrinking blue and purple underneath the black that spread.

The first thing I'd see when I walked in the house, before you were gone, before the coal in your lungs, would be you surrounded by gutted envelopes and papers with tiny print. Chase or MetLife. The only things visible were numbers with zeros and commas. You sat at the table with your hair up, a scowl beneath your CVS-brand reading glasses.

So, you would've asked. How'd it go?

I wanted to write a response to this, this scene, this piece—I'd call it *Woman with Bills* (2006), ten feet by however wide the dining room table was. It was empty now, covered in a thin layer of dust and lint. Pop had been by, left mail split open and store coupon books tossed about. There wasn't anything to eat. He left money for groceries and rent money he wanted me to deliver. My stomach made a sound of something primal.

I sat a skull made of wood wearing a craven smile with nails jutting out at the scalp on the table. I had stolen it out of an office-slash-workroom after our tours behind the walls. I circled back when we were dismissed, when the museum halls and catwalks were full of people from the other side, the workers who pushed and pulled and scrubbed all day. I swore I heard the voice then, the cigarette-bruised song of my mother, telling me something from far away, behind a wall or from land as I fell into the ocean. I felt I could reach it if I kept heading east, past the shoreline, or kept burrowing into the earth until it split above your casket. I'd hear everything you wanted to say to me. Only me.

I THOUGHT ABOUT the weekends you'd shuttle me into the city, an art class at SVA, a loft with big windows and wood floors splattered with paint. The other kids crowded the workstations, burrowed through watercolors and brushes and acrylic. They were all white; lived only twenty minutes away, their nannies said. Art on the weekends was caught between soccer and yoga for tikes. Their parents, wet and bright scarlet from SoulCycle or the chaos that is Whole Foods, were convinced of how special their child was; how could we be blessed with someone so precious? You were a pragmatist: "You're special to me, Colly—now how are you gonna convince you and everyone else? Put in the time," you said. Simple as that.

We always read on the train—you swept up in a Sister Souljah novel, or those Black independent thrillers they sold on tables along Fulton Street. You'd pick me up on the weekends, let me browse the Barnes and Noble around the corner for what turned into hours. I sat on the floor of an aisle and read from the middle chapters of books, because first chapters were boring and a book that could catch my attention on a random page was always worth it. I'd hide away in corners, the labyrinth of bookshelves running in rows and awkward slants, giving way to new paths, new combinations. I'd felt warm from the smell of roasted coffee and sweet bread, a Starbucks perched on the mezzanine, overlooking the main floor. In a cubby somewhere, some reality I'd put together between mystery and sci-fi, I read *Gone Fishin'* by Walter Mosley. You worked yourself tired all week, so you sat with your latte and sought out coupons for DSW or T.J. Maxx. In turn, we'd do your kind of shopping. You would try on heels in Macy's. I liked to get lost in the aisles, tangled in the coats and long sleeves. Just one more thing you'd say, only for the fifth time. You'd sneak a thing or two in the cart for me. The tailor, with nose hair like a bushel of wheat, starched the shoulders of our suits.

Some days, my favorite days, when I didn't have art class and you slept in until midmorning, we'd venture into the city anyway. Fire escapes like iron nests. We'd ride farther uptown every weekend, the films they showed on giant projectors during the weekends near the northernmost tip of Central Park, the Schomburg on 125th Street, the hills of Morningside Park on the west side, where you could hear the bells from deep inside the basilica of St. John's cathedral. We skipped up the grand steps of the Museum of Natural History, leaving behind Eighty-Sixth Street and its modest bluff looking over the park. We roamed its manicured caverns. We explored up and down, a maze of darkness through prehistoric terrors. A dream, how a corridor reached across time and land, how downstairs was underwater and upstairs were the stars. Through hundreds of people, couples and families and tour guides, I felt a part of a stream, if only a bead of sand, dislodged by the river. I could be a part of a larger story about the world, one that included the very land.

In the large hall with dozens of glass cases full of Native American relics, you told me about my great-great-great-grandmother, Miss Tea, who was Haliwa-Saponi and brown-skinned, with hair down to her back, allegedly.

"Her father was taken in by indigenous folk. Hid him for two years. That's when Miss Tea was born."

"That's cool."

"You hear this, boy? It's not cool, it's incredible. Look at all this. Our art always had a purpose. To eat from, to tell a story, to build cities with. The Haliwa. The Inca. People of the Kongo with a 'K.' You see that?" You pointed deep into a display case with an arrangement of dusty vases and pots. "How they buried their dead. They made those to sit atop the grave. That diamond symbol? The four moments of the sun: dawn, noon, sunset, and midnight. Or birth, life, death, and rebirth. The Ashanti, the Edo."

On the train I read my book to the roar of metal, hot in my bubble coat, shoved between you and an aging woman in a down coat who dozed off occasionally, waking just before her head touched my shoulder. A white woman and the man she was with fawned over my reading ability.

"Why wouldn't he be able to read?" you asked, unsmiling. The couple hardly registered what you'd said.

"He just looks so young," the woman said.

"I bet if it was your kid it wouldn't be very surprising." Your voice was rising and rising, mercury over fire. "It'd be normal."

I felt heat rising to my ears. I was proud for a moment, and then that very knot of heat dropped to my stomach. I was embarrassed. Something about being talked about, yet not being talked to. Worse, I felt myself retreat from you. I thought of excuses that could explain away that white woman's surprise. Still, I wanted to shrink behind the jacketless hardcover, away from the eyes that turned to us, away from the mad Black woman who had surely raised mad Black kids.

"BELIEVE IT OR not," Zaire told me, "That kid's aunt used to babysit us. We were cool, and then we weren't really. You change, go up a grade. By the time you look up you're into different shit, have different jokes you laugh at. But I'd see him. Always nod or say something."

We sat outside my building, spread out along the splintered wood frame of the bench. The ground had dried out, the asphalt an ashen gray that whitened at the corners. Outside was gloomy. Towers shaped like crosses; a curtain wall. The courtyard was busy, felt breathless and restive. Every corner felt the same.

"And they don't tell you how fast it happens," Zaire said. The shooting was just another thing that had us all wound up. The rumors and theories ran wild. Why did it happen? Who could be next?

"I heard they didn't even mean to get him," I said, shrugging. There were a few kids up the block, not a day over twelve, who were pulling stacks of firecrackers out of a trash bag. They lit the wicks with a grill lighter, bunches at a time, scattering as they burst and roared toward the sky. Two of those kids lived in my building, hurried over now with a similar bag stuffed with cherry bombs and sparklers.

"What are y'all even doing?" I asked them.

"We gonna shoot this through Miss Moore's window."

"Why?"

"She been annoying us all week."

"Told my mom about the baby raccoon," the other kid said.

The two had been feeding this thing left nesting in a basement shaft that opened out toward the street. They tossed food through the bars of the vent, cashews and fruit and deli turkey. And even though I was disgusted, there was a compassion in what they did that endeared them to me. Eventually, the mama raccoon came looking and led an escape, closing off the block in the middle of the day as the family scrambled through trash heaps, under cars.

"Put them in front her door," I suggested. "Maybe under the window."

"Huh?" The shortest of them furrowed his little brows.

"You break her window, she might call the cops. "

"Man, fuck twelve," he said, and his friend shouted in agreement. It was something he probably heard his older brother say.

"Y'all bad as hell," Zaire yelled behind them.

The adults kept on about the recession. The economy was all bad, so bad that Black folk and poor folk felt it, acknowledged it as something of note beyond the suffering that crept around daily. Zaire's dad was victim of it. It was usually all bad, all the time, but he'd lost his job for good this go-around.

Just up and disappeared. The company he worked for couldn't pay their bills and went belly-up. Everybody with a job held it close, afraid it'd leave in the middle of the night and be gone by the morning. Labor you'd done for years, sucking your bones dry, gone. They don't need you or your bones anymore. You apply someplace else and it's like, *Position filled? No, this position doesn't exist anymore.* Places shut down. The pizza shop on Van Siclen, the pharmacy next to the Chase. I was heartbroken when they closed down Youngworld.

A police car crept through the pathway but we didn't pay it mind. It was odd not to see them. Windowless vans sat parked days at a time; a cruiser drove through winding trails that connected the complex, chose a shaded spot in the summer by the field or Green Courts. There were NYPD paddy wagons on every other corner, rotated in shifts with the sun, but they never made it in time whenever something bad happened.

Tristan was still a friend to Zaire, though I couldn't stand him since that time he pulled a knife on me. He and his older cousin Rahk always came through in an olive-green Expedition, the hinges and joints of the truck rattling from the music. His full name was Abdirahkman. He wore a gold ring with a matching watch, both crusted at the edges with diamonds as clear as water.

"I heard about your dad," Tristan said. "You know, he always looked out. Even when I was away, he'd check in on my grandmother from time to time."

"Need anything?" Rahk asked.

"Nah, I'm good," Zaire said.

"I told you come by the trap one of these days," Tristan said. Zaire cracked his neck, bristled. Rahk looked at the curb, then reached inside his pocket for a fistful of large bills. I couldn't help but watch.

"Here's fifty," Rahk said. "Just look out."

The two of them headed upstairs, wide in their expensive baseball jackets, embroidered leather slick like hard taffy. I knew Zaire would save the fifty until we happened upon a corner store and buy us both a chopped cheese with provolone and an Arizona before splitting what was left between us. That was how we loved each other.

"You was supposed to meet up?" I asked.

"It was just a thing."

We would not be remembered, but I would bawl my eyes out if you took me away, kept me away from these people, the markets, the crowded handball court. I would go eventually, burned out like the surrounding abandoned lots that were scrapyards or landfill, too tired to keep on. Really it was agony, mourning awash in a coat of sugar, smiling with your neighbors or your parents so you were all right, not saying a word because they had gone through enough and deserved the peace of their own war. It was too sweet, left my stomach aching and in knots, weighed down my ankles after the crash.

A pop from inside the building. Smoke curled out the doorway and the kids ran out the building, laughing until tears came from their eyes. Matchbooks spilling from their pockets. They rounded the corner before Miss Moore could rush out, wielding a mop like staff, wig sliding off so we could see the stocking cap underneath. She turned her head like a robin would from its perch until she saw us.

"Who was it?" Miss Moore asked. I shrugged. Zaire looked stricken. More folk came outside, began to gather in the lobby. The police car pulled up slightly to get a better view. Rahk poked his head down at us from a third-floor window.

"Firecrackers," I answered.

"Who the hell did that?" he yelled back down.

You know Wood's younger brother, I would've said. Except I was looking at Zaire, who was drained of color, his eyes shut tight, eyebrows knitted like moths.

DEEP INSIDE THE Museum of Modern Art felt like I was off to find something lost, buried somewhere underneath the city. That part, the hurried tour, was all Ms. Hirsch. She led us behind the walls, where there were offices, more makeshift classrooms, and workshop stations. There were rooms as cavernous as warehouses, crates and crates of what I guessed was more art. We went down a staircase into another room with high ceilings, rows of towering steel racks, and rusted shelves, extending for what must have been the length of Fifty-Third Street, canvases and instruments wrapped in thick plastic and bubble wrap stacked up against each other.

"The museum isn't what we put on the walls," Ms. Hirsch boomed from in front, "It's a place in which we store memory."

Near the end of the corridor, we passed a room that glowed dimly— different from the white lights that seemed to follow us everywhere. Behind thick glass panes on sliding racks, paintings were seemingly floating above the floor.

"Archival works," Ms. Hirsch told us. "Preserved with specific lighting and temperatures."

She led us down a hall, then into the rush of the main galleries from a door that, when I turned around to look at, dissolved into an outline, a blank panel next to a row of international film posters. *Beat the Devil*, one said. I'd never known anyone who could.

"If you could create your own show, how would it look? What would it be about? One famous piece. Tell me what you'd bring." Ms. Hirsch went around the room and everyone rattled off the titles of the work, the artist, and its resonance, with ease. I had nothing. I mumbled, searched the floor, traced the colors spilled across the floorboards. We filed into another workroom and I fell to the back of the group. Dominick muttered something, and it took a full minute for me to understand before I looked at him.

"At least you didn't say the guy with the soup cans."

ON MY WAY to the bathroom, I saw Naima circling an exhibit. I walked up beside her. She was shorter than me, with almond-shaped eyes. Behind her was a twenty-foot color print of a beautiful woman with an unbelievable shape and valley-like cheekbones and full lips sitting in profile. She was nude and sat behind silhouettes of products that had been whited out. Perfume, a carton of cigarettes, hair conditioner or relaxer. What Naima beheld: three mannequins poised on the platform in front of us. They were tall, looming above us, looking down at us as if they had faces.

They were decked in the kinds of clothes I'd seen in old British movies like *The Importance of Being Earnest*, rich women in layers of skirts that fell to the floor, blouses with ruffled collars and shoulders. The print, however, looked like it was textile from Africa. From where I didn't have a clue but I knew at least four stores on Flatbush Avenue that sold rolls and rolls of fabric like this. I read the placard on the platform where the mannequin's stood. *How Does a Girl Like You Get to Be a Girl Like You?* (1995).

"What do you think it means?" Naima nodded toward the mannequins, which I feared would up and walk away if I didn't answer.

"I think it's asking who we really are," I said. "If someone could just take a thing that represents who we are and fit it into anything they want."

"How we're just parts that barely make a whole," she added. "The exports of the slave trade."

"Do you ever feel like this is a waste of time?"

"What do you mean?"

"We're in this fancy museum looking at art when none of this really matters. This'll never mean anything to the majority of people in the world just trying to get by. And my friend, well, not actually—I knew him and he got killed. Random. But it's hard to believe any of this really matters."

"I'm sorry about your friend," she said, and I suddenly felt justified calling him my friend. "I like to look at art when I feel terrible."

"Not everyone can just do that."

"I know." She looked down at her toes, the Air Maxes. "It's selfish but sometimes that's all we can do. To make sure we're all right."

It broke her heart but she found resolve from somewhere, looked me in the eye. A pause. A toddler managed to shuffle through and slap the edge of white platform before his mother scooped him up.

"All of this matters," she said.

"What?"

"Gordon Parks, *American Gothic*. I look at it when I feel . . . y'know."

"SO WHAT THE hell is it?" I asked. I was in Miss Betty's dive, which was beginning to look more and more like she was squatting. I had brought her the wooden head I stole from the museum. She was alone, with only Legba to curl around, move the shadows as he crept along the walls. He'd grown fat. I sat on a foldout chair; the love seat had collapsed inward somehow. Miss Betty was perched on the windowsill, picked at the mottled skin above her elbow.

"Why you don't come to visit?" she asked me. "Only when you need something do I see you."

"I'm sorry, don't be like that."

"You know I knew you since you were like this," she exclaimed, showing me how tiny I was. "Like this!"

"I know, Miss Betty."

"This looks Central or West African, a nkisi. Reminds me of a Paquet congo. In Haiti, I'd see them in my friend's homes. Their parents would make them with things from the earth, decorate them with sequin, cloth. I've seen them in ceremonies and for altars. It's a powerful object, to bring about an Iwa, the mysteres. They exist in the In-between. They are so close to God yet so close to us."

The In-between. To be close to God was to be close to creation, to be close to the beginning and the end that couldn't be two separate things but one long, infinite thing. That seemed paralyzing to me. I kept my hand in my pocket, around my phone in case it trembled. I hadn't heard from Zaire for a couple days. I texted him earlier.

"What were these ceremonies?" I asked.

"Healing. If there was trauma or shame brought to the community. Bringing health or fortune to a family, the home."

I wasn't satisfied. I couldn't believe what I had resorted to, asking a dopehead about the voices I'm hearing. I might as well go to the G Building and pick a room. Only for you.

"These Iwa folk. Are they spirits?"

"They can walk among the dead," she said, shuffling from the window, pulling her leg straight as she stared down at me. Legba wrapped around her ankle for effect. "What is it, boy? Why you asking all this?"

I didn't plan on saying a thing, ignored the siege of ants that marched from beneath the kitchen cabinet.

WHEN I WOKE up, it was three in the morning. The lights were still on and the computer fan rattled like something was caught inside. The nkisi watched me from the corner of my eye from the end table. I looked at my computer screen, a jpeg of Gordon Parks's *American Gothic*. I'd been barreling through his archive feeling seen, devoured, bones sucked dry. I felt a craven need to burrow deeper into my emptiness, shrink in each room I walked into. You'd pray for a storm, too, in a drought, hollering at the evening news for years and years, always in contention with that very dream, just as Gordon had been. You were shaking with tears as poor people, mostly Black people, were left to drown by the government in the aftermath of Hurricane Katrina. Years before that, Pop pulled me from school before lunch and we went up to the roof of our building. The most impenetrable smoke I'd ever seen spread over Manhattan and toward us, darkened the skies as if it would storm, and filled it with a fiery gray like molten earth. Now we were trying to end a war we had started. The country was in a strange place but it was always perilous, our lives, always with no narrative end other than certain disaster. That was my experience, at least. There was really nothing Blacker than uncertainty.

In front of me, you were wrapped in the coil of a phone cord, the neck of a Heineken in your knuckles, a Newport burning in the ashtray. You could be on the phone with Marilyn, who had a city job and was in a union, took us to the Poconos one year in the early months of winter, her oldest driving a CRV through windy roads to a four-bedroom with a basement and a den and an island kitchen. I remember watching the snow cover the pines, fall until the world was white. We had to stay an extra day until it passed. It may have been Genesis, your earliest friend, the kind you claimed as family for so long I didn't know if she was a cousin or an aunt. She'd lived down south for a while, in one of the Carolinas, in the middle of nowhere with no gas line. It was the first time I smelled the tired metal of an electric stove. She took in a child named Roger, adopted him legally, a white boy older than me, got him braces and took care of him best she could. She wanted to save him. They moved up back to the city, the top floor of a row house in Queens. I didn't really like when he came over. He came with Genesis years ago to Boulevard Day and convinced me to go half with him on stink bombs and toss them into the crowd during a performance. We ran away. I felt horrible after. For the most part, everyone respected when someone put himself or herself out there. I never forgave myself for letting him come in and do that.

We visited them sometimes, took the bus to the A train all the way to Jamaica and then a taxi the rest of the way. We'd stay through dinner, and by dusk, the street would be full of life, people out on their porches, grilling or playing cards or challenging the stereos across the way. Kids rode bikes along the faded yellow lines of the street, hoisted up shots with an overin-flated Spalding into carved-out crates nailed to telephone poles. You and Genesis sat out with the folk who lived in the connected row house. You re-clined in a camping chair, the smoke from your Newport tangled with the gold bangles around your wrist, the gaudy rings on your long fingers. I'd play Dreamcast with Roger for hours, until my eyes teared up from the light of the screen and Roger snored from a tattered vinyl armchair. I'd come back out sometime past midnight, curl around your lap like a cat, purring in my dreary state. You'd run your fingers through my hair, cold from the beer you were drinking. "When are we going home?" I'd whine. "Soon," you'd say, smiling from something a neighbor shouted over a game of spades. I'd melt into the hum of your belly, a laugh rooted from below, your skin like papaya. Your voice is a small theater I find myself wandering in just to feel the walls tremble. It was where you seated those you loved, told them they inspired you, churned an engine inside. You took their heads in your bosom, kissed them atop their heads. We wouldn't end up leaving until the beginning of dawn, blue spotting the night like watercolor. Birds chirped from the top of the linden trees. When we were out of the cab, in front our building, I could hear seagulls squawking, landing in the street, and taking crusts of bread up with their beaks.

PART
TWO

FAMILY TREE
(2009)

On a day like today, Audrey would give her grandbabies the history of her family tree. The short version because these kids stuck to their phones like mosquitos to a bug light.

"Mariah Frank, or Miss Tea, as they called her, my great-grandmother, was born into slavery in Richlands, North Carolina. It's said to have been around 1820 to 1830; they hardly kept track of us back then. She was one of many girls and a boy that got sold to another plantation. One sister we know of was named Etta, who was sold to a plantation in South Carolina. We know nothing of her children.

"Miss Tea had long, straight hair. It was 'cause her father had escaped one night, lay awake in the mud or held off sleep up in the trees. One night he fell asleep and woke up on the fall down, landed wrong on his leg. When he knew it was broken and he'd be found and it would be over, he tucked under the hollow of a tree in swamp water, and he heard the whistle of the

Haliwa. They appeared from behind the logs and trees, a convoy invisible under the Carolina twilight. They took him to their village, where he stayed for months, nursed his now crooked leg. He saw more people like him: runaways, folk who held a certain absence that could only be brought about through chains. There he met a woman with hair down to her hips. The night Miss Tea was born, horses and bloodhounds stormed the village. Slave-catchers snatched up whoever they could, some who looked outright native. The government had made it legal for farmers to retrieve people, or their "property".

"Miss Tea married a Humphrey man while she was enslaved. He didn't know the name he was born with so everyone called him Humphrey, like his master. The couple had a child named Maddock. Mr. Humphrey went down to New Bern to get free from the Yankees. While there, he fell into the river, caught pneumonia, and died. What hurt most was Miss Tea wasn't sure what to believe. He didn't die in her arms. She didn't see a body. Held a little service in the yard with some girls down the road. At night she thought the worst, saw him swollen and blue. She saw thick white boys rounding up the draft dodger, stringing him up in the branches or dragging him along the road or beating him shitless only to throw him in the river. For this she kept to her own, didn't wander past the last black shack on the hill, deemed the edge of town. She filled her bucket to wash at night and cried, a wailing coyote in the desert.

"Miss Tea then got married in August of 1866 to a Mr. Bryant Murrill. He managed to purchase land in Jacksonville, North Carolina, from a white man. To this day it's a mystery how that man got that land. So they moved on down to Jacksonville. Started a little farm, started their big family. From that union she had eleven children. I don't know most of their names, just Hill, another named Albert. But Maddock was my granddad, born in 1865 from that kind Humphrey man who died, or was murdered. He was the oldest of the bunch.

"Granddad Maddock took over the farm when his parents passed. Married a woman named Rochelle of Maple Hill, North Carolina, and resided there. Rochelle had previously been married. They had four children: Minnie, Rena, Nannie, and my mother, Lucy. Lucy was born in 1909 and died in 1975. She married Haywood, born in 1904 and lived forty-eight years. He was from Verona, but they met in Maple Hill and ended up right back in Jacksonville. From this union they had three children, but one died at five weeks. There was Walter, god rest my brother's soul, Joyce, and moi."

Before Audrey became a mother, she had said she would be nothing like hers. Lucy was hard, and she didn't blame her, because she had to be. It took Audrey decades of motherhood to realize what wrongs she would commit in order to keep her child alive. Black mothers have to keep their Black children alive in a different way. There is no other way to explain it. Case in point: Audrey was told, at the honest age of twelve, in a room full of laughing women, that she would get married through a window. Her body, which expanded and flattened in schoolhouse bathroom mirrors, took up too much, too much space.

This was how her mother and aunts would raise her, would raise each other. Lucy, who loved her daughter helplessly, would revise Audrey with her eyes some days, nip and tuck pieces of flesh with her words, found the violence in the way she moved, the way her hips began to swing. Really it is the violence of possibility, of ending up some kind of alone, maimed somehow by the very definition of womanhood as constructed.

Every week since Audrey was born, her family would gather at the dinner table. Back in Jacksonville the house was narrow and sunlit. Grandma Rochelle would cook all day, kneading dough with the strong hands of a sharecropper, chopping peppers and onions and cutlets like cotton stalks. Her forearms stained with flour, hardened in amber by the sun, impervious to hot grease and sizzling butter. Soon the arthritis in her hands shook the knife and soon after then she could hardly steady it, could hardly roll yeast to bread. She needed four metal legs to hold her up, leaned on them to look over the stove. Her daughters cooked like new wives. They were only home when they got time off from work or when their husbands would allow.

Audrey found her mother rolling yeast into bread. Lucy's forearms were solid as if she pulled weeds for a living instead of working in a hospice. They had become impervious to fire. Soon there was no more stove. The women were gone and only Audrey was left. Her eyes were shut. She had become strong, like the daughter of a sharecropper.

Haywood was buried in mud and bands of clay that sank when you walked on it. No hands to knead the soil. Black men covered him in dirt and left the family to cover him in calla lilies. Lucy wept into a silk embroidered handkerchief with Audrey and a tiny Joyce under her arms. A pastor closed his Bible. Their godmother, who practiced Ifá, prayed to the orishas and they answered back with a light rain that turned the ground into mud. The heel of her clogs kept sinking. It had been the first time Audrey looked around and thought nothing would grow here.

There were all these stories that branched out or grew down but were still bound up at one root. To live in service of the next. To be buried by your children, leave them your storehouse of knowledge. We sowed a seed deep into the earth and couldn't accept we'd never see it bloom. When Audrey buried her daughter, she thought she'd take the shovel—the one she used to sow her seed and not the one that covered her baby's white-and-gold casket with cool dirt—and dig a plot for herself. She had burrowed deep into the earth to find light at the other end, only to climb out and find there was nothing worse. There is no light, only the bones buried on the other side. At the funeral she had wept openly. She would bury her child. What light could there be at the other end? Key's children were mute, had curled up next to her in the pew.

Now she watched them distance themselves. They used to run around her studio, then Joyce's apartment, jumping off walls and through portals. Now that they are older, they begin to misunderstand themselves within the shape of the world. And it wasn't as if Audrey didn't worry as much about the girl. She laid eyes on Toya every day and could see the care she took in every-thing, simply listening. She was whatever this new generation was, accepting and strong-willed. Still, Audrey felt the need to worry. Lucy had expected Audrey to show strength, no matter what, and that she did. So much that folk never knew she suffered, all because she never wept openly or remained stoic. We expect our girls to be fine because we have spent generations teaching them to suffer quietly.

Audrey worried about the boy. He fought and skipped school and had sex with some of these fast girls, Audrey was sure. He was impressionable and sensitive, a bruised peach. A man could be as lost as any woman. The difference was that when a man loses himself, he becomes a danger to others, men and mostly women. Instead of fixing his home, he'd set fire to the whole village.

During the funeral, Colly had gone up to the casket and stared and stared, couldn't leave until Audrey took his hand, went to dry his eyes but there was no water there. She could never leave that day either. Across the church organ was a scattered note, the sound of echoes in the hall or down a mountaintop, couldn't be felled. Couldn't be topped, an empire squandered. Trapped between light, shutters letting the outside in. Pastor Youngblood anointed Audrey's forehead with oil, read her favorite passage from Psalms:

> *The Lord is my light and my salvation—*
>   *whom shall I fear?*
> *The Lord is the stronghold of my life—*
>   *of whom shall I be afraid?*

Why should she be afraid?

> *When the wicked advance against me*
>   *to devour me,*
> *it is my enemies and my foes*
>   *who will stumble and fall.*

She thought about what it meant to be devoured, to be overcome.

> *One thing I ask from the Lord,*
> *   this only do I seek:*
> *that I may dwell in the house of the Lord*
> *   all the days of my life,*
> *to gaze on the beauty of the Lord*
> *   and to seek Him in His temple.*

She feared there was no temple that stood, no house left standing for her to dwell during the rest of her days. Only ruin.

> *Then my head will be exalted*
> *   above the enemies who surround me;*
> *at His sacred tent I will sacrifice with shouts of joy;*
> *   I will sing and make music to the Lord.*

SALT EATERS

KEY (1990)

Dante only made a move when I said so, or when I looked up at him under a silver moon, expectantly, like I could be dragged away on a salty wind from the shore at any moment. I took great pleasure in unlocking him, in pushing him to say things he hadn't said to himself, the quiet grip of his nihilism. He was so used to being a locked vault that he became a trapdoor and what was falling out of him was, suddenly, more than he intended. He told me about his last relationship, which ended because of him.

"Maybe I know what happens," he said. "I know what happens so I don't let myself go there."

"You're scared."

"Who can you trust to let all the way in?"

"Yeah, but when you do, it shouldn't dissolve who you are as an individual."

"Exactly."

"Like why can't I belong to myself? And feel good in that?"

"You and me." He motioned between us, drew a line between him and me with his index. I looked up at the ceiling.

"When are we going to fall in love?" I asked him, and I meant it as separate people on separate journeys but realized what I meant wasn't what I said. I thought about how often that happened, even in passing, how easy it was to be failed by words, to knot up your body into a wall, or given away by it. Words could pour out our mouths and look different in the light. For meaning was all people really searched for, even in each other. I saw him in a timeline, a dark cedar tree sprung from earth. There was the reality where our separate journeys continued on as normal, a need to blink, break the stare. I held on a little longer. Another reality sprawled in front of me. Our paths were threaded together, ran side by side. A commotion down the bar forced us to look away. I didn't know what timeline this was, or if it was even the one I belonged in. We decided to close out our tabs and leave. Spent the walk to his car trying to kiss him, trying harder trying not to, it was too painful, already tragic in what it could mean for all of us.

He was a man like all the others. Only quieter, a gentleness about him when he leaned down and spoke to you, held your eyes, the slights of your face. In turn he opened his. He'd share money he kept in knots, in gratitude, a totem of his condolences, to a few of the children he'd seen marching to school every day, the extra he gave to papi at the deli, to his aunts who ran illegal daycares or worked every day for tips, to his uncles and their drinking habit.

The body is a calendar, inhabited by the days and months and years. I don't sleep enough because of work, a series of hospital rooms and clinics or women's homes or shelters. Every day I get closer to God, I feel it settling like salt in my heart, breaking open always. When a woman gives birth, there are only extremes. It is never clean, the insides exposed, a mess. But it is always life changing.

We went to the pier that night and I rolled my jeans up to sit along the tide, Ms. Pat buzzing around my head. It was dusk, lit by the boathouse and the lamps from the parking lot. The last of fishermen took up their rods and tackle boxes, their haul if they were lucky, and headed to their trucks. Folk had packed away strollers or coolers, wrangled kids or took the last of their pictures before winding their disposables. Couples lolled around the shore, chose a bench out of view to touch each other freely. Teenagers sat around a bottle of Easy Jesus, their voices rising over the crashing tide. Tucked against Dante's body, I breathed in. The salt water was a balm, soured by the trash along the sand below. I was mindful of my body, how it moved through the world, the ways I took up space, the ways I didn't. In the world, older men stared at me from the corner of their eyes, on the bus, behind newspapers. They looked at my hips and probably thought of childbearing, other sick shit. Young boys looked at me in the open, brave with desire, hoping I spoke back to them when they gassed me up.

"I have to find a pay phone," Dante said. His beeper was throwing a fit.

I leaned up against his car, its forest-green hull, watched him on a hushed call under the graffiti-bombed phone booth. The tide roared behind me.

I didn't want to be needed. It made me afraid, damn near anxious at the thought. I couldn't pour myself out every day and water others when I had a whole garden to tend, in my home. I couldn't help but refuse him my last drop. Some men need that. Become dependent until they hit the tipping point. Then how would they respond? Could a man see a woman beyond something to possess? We knew how danger could lurk in room corners, in bars and theaters, in the narrow walkways of subways and bus aisles, a hand on our lower back, our arms. On the street. In our families, the uncles and cousins who said, "She gone be right when she get older." In our closets, outfits that showed more skin or less skin, made us more deserving of harm, whatever we had coming to us. I carried with me something that could always be taken, pried from me in an act of barren terrorism. The fact that a man could entrap me, assault me, or rape me was a fear that loomed as much, if not more than the specter of getting killed by the police or lynched by working men and their families. I thought of my mother. I knew her secret, how she could see my father, even though he had been dead for years. I knew she stared at him every day because she didn't know how to make him leave this time. Possessed her space. Even in death, he wanted to have the last say-so.

But this was a different feeling. I felt it now, cold at the center of my spine. The ocean was way too loud and I turned and turned, searching for reprieve, some way out of the very bottom of a church bell, those medieval ones like at Trinity Church or Riverside, the metal bowl ringing from the belfry, deafening. Must've covered my ears at one point. Felt as if they might turn inside out. My feet dragged behind me. People kept ahead, ignored me like a dust head on the side of the road. A fogged space between my eyes and comprehension. Someone rocked me by my shoulders, called me in from afar.

"What is it?"

"Woman." Dante had caught up to me. I was crouched under a park table, beneath a faded orange tablecloth. A man came over and I saw his wife peek out from behind the grill they were packing up. "You almost gave me a heart attack. You all right?"

"Migraine."

"I should take you home."

"No," I objected. "Let's just get some food."

"Get some roti in you?" he said with a grin.

WE WERE QUIET again after dinner. He drove at a steady creep, in no rush to pass anyone. The car was still clouded with smoke, smelled like a fresh Dutch burning. He asked what I was doing lately and I told him I was working as a birth doula. It was almost ten but Van Siclen Ave. was still buzzing, shopkeepers closing their gates and vendors loading their vans.

"That's really important work," Dante said.

"The pay's not the best."

"Do you do it for the money?"

"No."

"All right then, so what do you care?"

"Everything you do is for money," I said. It wasn't malicious. It wasn't like no one knew what he did, how he bought his Range Rover outright, in cash. He kept these things to himself but you know how this goes. Every neighborhood—hell, every block—built their own folklore, existed in their own myths, created a world of heroes and villains that got told at ritual. Around fires we were told of the monsters and demons that roamed the night.

"That's why it's nice to see someone who's not like that," he said. "Do you like what you do?"

"I like the promise of it," I said. We had stopped, had double-parked in front of my building for a few minutes now. I looked at him, his eyes the brightest thing on him, almost like headlights. He was the color malt that turned near black inside the darkness of his Range. I noticed how the lines of his jaw didn't slope but peaked or made a hard turn, and I wondered how it'd feel if I reached out and traced it with my hands. I'd never thought of it before. I shouldn't say that, because I had, though sometimes in the mornings, in the shower, right before I found some random time to sleep. I forced myself to look past him. Our neighbor's light was on and I could see shadows moving across the ceiling of their apartment.

Dante lived in a flop he'd sublet from an older head, a woman I didn't know who needed money and would live with her grandparents in Flatbush in the meantime. Inside was a cave full of smoke, wires all around, amps and a turntable and crates of vinyl collecting dust. He's the type who can peer inside the corners of the breakbeats, search its floors, identify its lineage, the pitched high crooning of the Gap Band, the orchestral strings of Dexter Wansel, Harold Melvin and his blue notes etched, how Bobby Womack's voice was a painful articulation of time and brutal migration. Producers had pilfered James Brown and his discography, and we were thankful for most of what came from it. I knelt by his collection, sifted through the jackets, full of color and dust. Toni Braxton, A Tribe Called Quest, Dionne Warwick's *The Windows of the World*. "Manifest"—built on a breakbeat by James Brown and Joe Tex, pulling artifacts from Miles Davis and Charlie Parker's rendition of "A Night in Tunisia" by Dizzy Gillespie—was in conversation with a tradition, the same way *The Waste Land* was an example of intertextuality. Dante joined me, showed me the cover of what he grabbed first. A Tribe Called Quest's *People's Instinctive Travels and the Paths of Rhythm*. He placed it on the turntable and dropped the needle with a delicateness that made sense now, knowing he touched me like that, soft and with precision. The most august saxophone creeped out of the amp. Dante turned the volume up. Soon the snare and bass came in, shook the floor and my mind was blown.

"What is this?" I asked.

"A Tribe Called Quest. But this where they got it from." When the vinyl stopped there was a stuffiness in the room. He replaced this single with another, holding it up for me to see. "Daylight" by RAMP. There it was, the same dripping melody and, if it were a color, a shade warmer.

"You don't got *The Black Album*?"

"Should be there, it's a bootleg."

"Who's Shirley Murdock?" I showed him the cover.

He took the ten-inch from its sleeve, put it on and walked toward the kitchen. The song was "As We Lay," a ballad Mama loved but said wasn't too Christian.

When he came back out, he carried two cups and a bottle of Crown Royal wrapped in a paper bag. He poured some for us both, with soda and lemon juice, and sat by the window. He looked out over Linden Boulevard; we were fourteen stories up yet the sound of traffic rushing ahead reached us. For miles the buildings are low and flat and we can see the night, the dark sky with gaseous highlights, the sour of orange and green and purple. I leaned against him from behind, ran my hand beneath his shirt, traced his wings, the shoulders that sloped like a dune rising from the sand, a hillside.

We took hungry gulps, first from our glasses and then each other. His lips were sweet from the brandy.

He wanted me on a carnal level, like an animal caught on a scent, a chemical trigger. I think everyone must be this aware, the performance of desire, even when it's genuine, always too much or not enough, are we enough or not enough. It was hard to let your body fall into complete surrender. It was terrifying, even when the sex was good. When it was skin on skin, tender, when it was messy and complete. I was sixteen my first time, in an upstairs room while his mother was home, lying under the bright ceiling fan, the smell of him raw, hanging in the small space like a funk you couldn't beat away. When you're older you find yourself naked in front of a man sucking your stomach in. Afraid he will laugh, look at the body in front of him in disgust. He must notice, must hesitate, must feel my body aware of itself, of the other body up against it. I sometimes tense and his hands move to my neck, he takes my face in his palms with the deep lines, wants me to look at him. A warmness cradles me, makes me search desperately across his dark skin with my hands, under his shirt and along the elastic of his shorts. I could trace my orgasm. It was like biting into a strawberry covered in cream. It could be a breeze up my spine, looking out across Prospect Park with the sun bleeding across the lawn, the petals of the cherry blossoms hitting my skin like pieces of cloud. It could be the hairs that stood up, the bumps that crept up my arms at the moan of my beloved, a guttural pain that brought on tears and release. A rainstorm on the hottest day. This moment and all the others, piled atop each other like the clothes by our bedside.

The pleasure principle. It's what Audre Lorde wrote about. And Janet Jackson. Both seemed terribly important in my throat, the tip of my tongue. I looked down at him, perched on my elbow, said to myself: "how they bang the pages of their wings as they fly to the fields of mustard yellow and orange and plain gold all eternity is in the moment." It was Mary Oliver.

"What is that?" Dante asked. He'd already split open a Dutch Master and was emptying it in a bedside bin.

"It's poetry."

"I like it."

"It's how I feel when I have you." I took his chin in a loose grasp and planted a kiss. I liked to make him blush if he could. My openness made him flustered, humbled in arms.

"Do you know Shakespeare?"

"Uh-huh."

"What else?"

"A bunch of Queen Latifah."

"*Ladies first, ladies first,*" he sang for me, and we rocked the bed with our laughter. I watched him, his solid frame soft in the glow of the street outside. His jaw wide and square. The smallness of the present: the beat before you say a word. The quiet between breathing in and breathing out. That is as large as any turning point in history.

A GRAVE BEHIND
AN ORCHARD

COLLY (2009)

On the train, I carried the old nkisi in my backpack and heard more voices than I counted people. It was making things worse. A flock of older Italian women had dark spots chalked onto their foreheads. They looked to me like X-marks or crosses. I got off at Fifty-Third Street and soon dozens of people were filing into the station, all with the same black cross on their foreheads. I swore I was still asleep, moved about in heavy mud, peered into a nightmare only I could see. Church bells clanged above a fading police siren as I entered the museum, staring at everyone right above the eyes.

At the museum, we were to work together and find three pieces to write about. I wasn't in the mood to talk. I shook my head or nodded when they flashed me a variety of student artwork. Dominick and Naima were in a back-and-forth about theory or whatever. This guy Greenberg wrote a bunch of essays about how social and political stuff didn't have a place in the higher purpose of art. Naima said Greenberg didn't have a clue about Elizabeth Catlett or Alma Thomas.

On break, Naima returned some supplies to the office down the hall. Ms. Hirsch entrusted her with the task after the first month or two. When she came out of the office, she asked if I was doing all right. I seemed out of it more than usual, she said.

"The weirdest thing. I've heard church bells all day and it hasn't stopped."

"It's Ash Wednesday," she said, and I drew a sigh of relief. "What?"

"So you've seen the crosses?"

"That's part of it," she told me.

After school, Naima usually worked at the supermarket, selling candy and lotto tickets behind a counter with a window of Plexiglas covered in scratchiti. I'd catch her drawing on the fleshy part of her hand, between the thumb and forefinger, hearts or diamonds with the pencil of her eyeliner. Sometimes, a dust head would come to the window, ask for change until the manager came out and gave them a broom to sweep the front.

Today was an exhibit called *Day Labor*. The halls were full of photographs, dark corners where projectors lit an entire wall. There was an international scope: Turkey, Israel, France, the United States. The goal was to explore how "cultural identity and bodily perception are driven and socially conditioned by the global economy and the media." What did a world built on money and sweat and blood do to our bodies, how we viewed each other's bodies? Most of the folk in these frames were brown factory workers with clothes frayed, or, if they were white, builders or planters or something—seemed like a different kind of white. Not as white as the other white, the ones who'd donated to the museum or even the parents struggling to pay the tuition of the hipsters by Washington Square. They looked lost, too, split at the ends. I'm sure I saw, buried deep the longing and social paralysis—*At least we ain't brown*. What did my body mean beyond what it could produce, how it could be priced, a medium for transaction? Zaire's dad was another faceless day laborer, a body fated to work until it wore down. But it didn't sound right. He was a loving man, funny when he wasn't trying to be, which was most of the time. He let me into his home, endless nights, fed me when his job was in question and when it was out of the question. His voice was warm and he only wanted to support his family and smoke a cigar every once in a while.

"I need to tell you something," I told Naima, suddenly.

"I know, I know," she said. "Dom must be loaded."

"No, no, I took something." I opened my bag. She was wary at first, but peeked in.

"That's Ms. Hirsch's—"

"Shhh."

"You got to give it back," she said.

"I know."

Would she help me? I walked through another exhibit. In a shipping container made of plywood, a video showed a woman the rich color of a cigar stare blankly ahead, inches away from a bull's eye. Mika Rottenberg, *Tropical Breeze* (2004). A bare man's torso with Nike checks engraved like scars, reminiscent of the ruined flesh of enslaved Africans under a whip or brand. Hank Willis Thomas. The exploitation of labor, particularly Black labor, was terror.

"I need you to leave the door open when you leave," I said.

"That's not gonna work."

"Why not?"

"Ms. Hirsch might think I took that thing."

"She won't."

"But you'd take that risk?" she asked.

"Naima," I said, then stopped myself. "She doesn't even know it's gone."

I wished I could've explained I needed this thing, this wooden head, out of my life, that I was being haunted by something more than voices and visions and dreams. Even more, I wished I could tell what she was thinking.

Naima didn't say a thing but nodded. She brushed past me, retreated back to the office. Something felt different, something in our skin, suddenly, the dust, our atoms, pushed us away like matching ends of a magnet.

Deeper in the cavern were screens displaying what looked like security footage, women alone with men who were their bosses or some authority figure, in the back room of some business. They are still in their work clothes. Subtitles are displayed below. One reads: "It says I'm going to leave." It was Coco Fusco.

When I checked back there was a large barrette caught in the doorjamb. I slipped through, inched my way down the network of hallways until I passed our workroom. Gray and white tones with random paint blotches splattered across the dusty hardwood. There were no windows, only shelves and drafting tables. In the center, around a long work table, a large slab of wood and linoleum under mountains of books, folders, loose paper. I fussed with the headphones around my neck, crept farther down the hall.

Submerged among books and museum prints was that blond hair atop those gold-trimmed frames. Ms. Hirsch. I hadn't seen her when I first came in. She looked young now, except for the corners of her lips, which made her seem twice her age. It wasn't a sneer or anything; typically a mild disinterest. This time, she seemed to pout. Were those tears?

"Colly?" she called out. "What are you doing here?"

"I—" I didn't have anything to say. I inched the head from behind my back. Her eyes went wide.

"You were in my office?"

"I didn't know it was yours." I didn't think this through. She looked around the room frantically. I could see the white woman go off behind her eyes, an alarm, wondered what else this little Black-ass kid might have pilfered through. "It was open and it was right on your desk."

"Why did you take this?"

"I don't know." I couldn't tell her why. I had no idea myself. Could I say I was drawn to it? Would she believe I thought I could listen across worlds, across the very thin scar between the living and nonliving, that I heard my mother's voice like she was behind a wall I couldn't find the door to? "It reminded me of my mother. She showed me a bunch of these. She died a few years ago."

"That's no reason to steal."

"Borrow. But yeah, I hear you."

"It's called a nkisi. I used to work in Toronto at this art museum. Moved there with my husband." She paused, looking down at the head. "Ex-husband, I mean. I've collected a few of them."

"I guess I'm out of the program."

"Maybe. That's letting you off easy," she sighed, suddenly exasperated. "When you come back next week, we'll discuss it. Now go home."

I'd never walked out of a place so fast. I tumbled out of the main doors out of breath, onto the windswept street. Fifth Avenue stretched before me, a stone and crystal corridor. Sirens raged and yellow cabs blew their horns, the sound a part of a strange wilderness. I couldn't help but look up at the buildings, wrapped in silver and glass, the top of one like a saucer holding blue light from the sun creeping down over the Hudson River.

I DIDN'T GIVE Ms. Hirsch the chance to send me home for good. That night, I blasted music for hours. Naima's boyfriend was older, in his twenties, and would pick her up after school with the windows of his car rattling from his music. I went through their pictures on Sconex and Myspace, my computer screen full of glitter from her banner. I'd scroll through posts of encouragement from her friends, pictures of her in Times Square or on the parkway during the Labor Day parade, countless party flyers local promoters sent her, listened to the songs on her page for some sort of sign, a sign that she was unhappy with Darius, and longed, instead, to be with me. I'd only seen the man from the chest up, in his car with the seat so far back I wondered how he could see. Naima seemed older herself, trading a Jansport for a large leather purse from Rainbow. Her books tumbled at its bottom along with her makeup. I thought it was unfair. What could I offer her? I didn't have a job other than playing lookout for local dealers.

I found songs on blogs and message boards like EscoTheory, Nahright, and Fakeshore Drive. My YouTube history had been hijacked by Zaire, full of Gangsta Grillz mixtapes and Wayne features. AOL rang like a busy phone just to sign on. The chat rooms were full of strangers who became familiar, who typed "a/s/l" or invited me to a private message. Sometimes I pretended to be someone else, assumed a role in some fandom, a member of the mob or a side character from an anime, or Harry Potter, wrote out long paragraphs of what I did and how I felt, in role, to specters of people, avatars on a white screen that should mean nothing but amounted to entire lives on the other end. I contributed to a world that was briefly a relief, unlike this one, where I sat in the dark of my living room and thought about what it meant to feel wanted and all that I would do to feel that again. The television crackled, a local station. Brooklyn Community Access Television. *Flex N Brooklyn* was on. Dancers sparred in the cavern of a dancehall, contorted, a syncopated twitch, the body gliding through air, joints out of place then put back into place.

I DECIDED I would stand out in front of the MoMA for shits, dressed in long and boxy jeans, a tall shirt from Jimmy Jazz and a throwback jersey—Carmelo Anthony when he was in Denver, the headband and cornrows, the walking thirty-bucket. Naima was so used to being pressed upon, called out to, "hey ma"-ed to death, and just as quickly dismissed when she tried to ignore it. When she showed up, I saw her almost swollen cheekbones from a distance, her dark eyes the color of a bruise. She'd bite her nails to the beds. Today was the day I would ask her out.

"So you just happen to be in Midtown?" She asked.

"I wanted to see you," I told her. She laughed at me.

"Yeah, right."

"I mean really. Like, I don't know how to deal with not seeing you."

"You should've worked things out at the museum."

"Who cares?"

"Things are complicated for me right now," Naima said. The boyfriend, she meant. This would have to be enough. I almost worried about my own ability to appear indifferent. What was worse, I knew how to feel indifferent. Somehow picked up all of your bad habits.

"Do you have time to chill for a few?" I asked.

"Whatever," she said, cool as ever. But Naima was ice in a frying pan, spice in my blood, looking away from me when she got close, then walking away from me with her shoulders back, bouncing in her Air Maxes like she might tell my secret. You are beholden to a kingdom of gold, I want to tell her, and I urge you to burn it down. To dance on the ashes.

I DRAGGED MY worn Jordan 7s along Fourteenth Street, colliding with curbs and the backs of ankles, almost sending folk out of their shoes. I had been entirely too careful of where I placed my feet, careful of where I placed my body, all my life. Now, in the middle of Union Square, I wanted to expand, take up as much space as possible. There were several rows of a farmer's market, pecks and bushels of wet cucumber and squash and purple cabbage. Conspiracy theorists, women with Seventh Day Adventist pamphlets, Black Hebrew Israelites in all-white trousers and tunics, preachers, and more, all gathered trying to get off their stockpile of CDs and pamphlets. Dancers from across the city gathered, centralized around a speaker one of them had wheeled out. They flexed or got light, would krump or break. Under the music was the wooden crack of a skateboard hitting the pavement. The skaters rode up from the village to jump high off steps made from cement rock, off railings and curbs. In the center of it all of it, a man staggered around with a rolling tote bag, speaking through a megaphone.

"The wealthy elite," the voice on the megaphone said, "represented by the world leaders, pull all the strings they can to keep the world from having diversified, green energy sources. Keep us dependent on oil, coal, and nuclear energy because the rich can 'own' the land and control the technologies only they, by means of wealth and power, will allow. They can put armies and fences around natural resources and nuclear technology and call it theirs. The rest of the world wants clean and diversified energy sources because that would put the means of production into the hands of the many instead of the few. That would mean economic democracy. That would mean socialism. Instead, our world leaders feed us their garbage, much like how Britain forced China to buy its opium back in the nineteenth century, shelling its harbors during the Opium Wars. Ralph Nader said it best: 'If Exxon owned the sun, we'd have solar energy very quickly.'"

The noise was a hum above my ears, a head cold I couldn't get over, thick as sawdust. A soft grip around my arm, I smiled. Naima led me to a restaurant that smelled of semolina. Several horns sounded at once, congestion at the intersection. I looked out the dark-paneled window. Across the park, the country's debt ticker rose anxiously. People around us sat across from each other, bent over their Blackberrys or iPhones, or sat upright with their plates, trying to keep their conversations in the small space between them. Naima ordered us an appetizer, a dish I'd never heard. She said it was just toasted bread with cheese. She had pulled a pen from her purse, etched something in the corner of a napkin. I asked her about her family and she told me her dad was an artist but lectured at a conservatory. Her stepmom was a therapist.

"She just tries to psych me out all day," she said, and we laughed.

"Is it working?" I asked.

"I think so."

Naima ate the olives off her bruschetta before eating the rest. She didn't stare, didn't invite herself into someone's mental space with a hello, or overwhelm them with anything less than necessary. She understood the physical demands of living in the city. Eight million people didn't make you numb but hypersensitive, that constant physical stacking and proximity to people made isolation and relief improbable. The least one could do was provide some kind of social privacy, leave others to their headspace, not let one's eyes linger for too long.

She pushed the napkin toward me. In the bottom-left corner, she wrote a few lines of a poem:

> (after Lucille Clifton)
> what did i see to be except myself?
> i made it up.
> i am given a course name
> a grave behind an orchard

The food arrived and I picked at it. An intricate cheeseburger still red in the center, the bun slick with aioli. Naima had gotten a colorful salad with mint whipped ricotta. The sun was already low, draping the street like tattered silk. Her eyes were the color of slick, dark berries.

"I usually can't eat anything," I said. I never admitted that to anyone. I wanted to keep it inside but felt relief, a deep breath pushing out the tightness behind my chest.

"Maybe you're punishing yourself."

"Instead of other people?"

"Yeah, that's how it goes."

"We could be different."

"We could." She considered this possibility. "But we never are."

SPONTANEITY TAKES SOME rehearsal. The streets were hardly empty, fresh with rainwater. It is an hour of unquenchable darkness. We decided to drop acid in Cobble Hill, past Atlantic, down Court Street, some friend of a friend. On the train ride across the bridge, I watched the neighborhoods un-ravel into one another, feeding each other thread and fabric.

"What did your mom do? Before she passed."

"She was a doula, delivered babies. Worked at a birth center for a while."

"I know what a doula is." She pursed her lips. "That's incredible work."

"It kept her busy."

There was something between us that made me look away; her profile, the hoops of solid gold swaying against her neck, the cart rocking us while it burrowed back underground.

The place was a brownstone; a kid named Nabil's parents were out of town and left him there for the weekend. Three or four stories with high ceil-ings and tall archways, hardwood floors, and a wide kitchen bar with a mar-ble top. There was a fireplace and colored flood lamps, throw rugs and plush couches. The windows opened into a wide fire escape that sat at an odd an-gle. There was furniture shoved to the sides of the room. People hovered about, taking bumps off their pinky fingers or gumming powder. Took a tab in a circle in one of the rooms upstairs. Everyone was drinking out of red cups or teetering over a brew, inaudible under the music, "Heartless" by Kanye West, sinking into their highs or trips. They all swayed like saucers and I could feel the air between my fingers, the blood moving in them. Naima was saying how her heart was knocking, leaning toward me like I should hear it. My own chest pounded, like those other drugs. She went to the Jack and Jill kids from Riverside, the part of Harlem that was still artists and Black elites. There were the Prep for Prep kids who wanted to be like the Jack and Jill kids but didn't have the generational wealth. The white kids from south of the Gowanus, or Williamsburg, or Greenpoint, were a bit more blue-collar, they were skateboarders, or they liked to thrift clothes, or they went to Mets games and ragers in warehouse lofts in Ridgewood. Their tat-toos were plain symbols or quotes by Shel Silverstein in Courier font. There were the ones who stayed on Fire Island, tried to tan along the coast or in the yards of their parents' summer bungalows. They had acceptances from Bard or Wheaton, their parents owned seven-figure homes. I roamed the drawing room, looked at my phone to avoid meeting someone's eye and acknowledge I was alone in this moment, a stranger who had wandered in, a cub abandoned by his pride. On the wall was Kerry James Marshall's *Slow Dance*, its Black atmosphere, and its two lovers' witnesses only to each other, their edges an infinite blot of willowed charcoal. The painting felt too intimate; I'd never let no one see you with your hair up in rollers and your robe from Rainbow, dragging a Newport; or Pop after he'd wrestled out of his work gear and walking around in only his ratty Hanes, dosing warm cognac until dinner was made. Was that art, the inconsolable danger of being seen?

As I walked down the long hallway, I heard the sound of hushed laughter from behind it. I opened the door and peeked in.

"Holy shit," a girl yelled, peeking from a dimly lit room.

"Oh, sorry. I was looking for a place to sit," I said. The smell of weed rushed out into the hall.

"Well, come in. You're letting the smoke out."

I hurried through the door and closed it behind me. I introduced myself to her, nodded at the other two boys, also young enough to be a year or two into undergrad.

"Lana, do you hear this," one of the boys said, arching his eyebrows. I was pretty sure he wanted to sleep with Lana.

"They hate us," the girl was saying. Inhaled. "We're ungrateful."

She passed me the joint, blowing tendrils of smoke out of her nose. I looked at it between her fingers, nails painted plum, then took it from her. After taking a pull, I coughed and coughed until everything was softer, until the lines of all our bodies stained the space around us.

"Who?" I asked her.

"Our parents. Such respectable Black people. They want so much for us. They want whiteness for us. But they're cursed themselves. Scientists say it gets in your genes. Epigenetic trauma. That means pain can get so deep inside you that it's a part of your DNA. Trauma is part of your coding."

"We're all probably just doomed," I said. They played a game of Kings. Smoke clung to the ceiling until it fogged the room. I cashed the tip of the joint onto the plywood coffee table before melting into the worn, leather body of the easy chair. My ears hummed, surrendered to dragonflies. I didn't give a fuck about what they went on about, really. The college kids were eager to use their brand-new words, the talking points gathered from their mandatory humanities course, brought out solely for Reddit and to bed high school girls. Slipping back out into the main room, I found Naima eating pear slices out of a mason jar.

"You good?" I asked her, across the tide.

"I'm fine," she said. "I usually get 'em in the can."

"I think I'm coming down."

"I'm sure this wasn't how you saw your night playing out."

"Nah," I said. "Can't say it was."

"I'm sorry about that. Show must go on, right?"

"This is more like a send-in-the-clowns sort of thing."

"You ever think about what goes through someone's mind while you're talking to them? There's a moment, and it may only last for a second or two, but there's a moment where you feel the space you and this person are trying to fill. You start watching yourself talk instead of just talking."

"Yeah, even if they're looking you dead in the eye."

"People are usually thinking about themselves," Naima said. "What they'll say next. The best is when that fades and you're left creating the space between you and the other person. You create what that language can be." A pause: she was studying my reaction. I was unflinching. My neck and armpits were hot with sweat tracing my shoulders. Under the vintage bulbs and half-moon she was inevitable, her stare a thing you might misname, and I imagined she would lean over and kiss me and I would smell the hops on her breath from her beer, the argan oil in her hair.

Instead, she retreated to the thick forest of her island. Nabil found us and sat between our bodies, and the heat was turned off. I felt a disconnect, like our rhythm had been thrown. After a minute I excused myself, got up from that sofa. We had formed a quiet allegiance to each other and had somehow broken it. She decided I wasn't willing or able to reveal myself, even for a moment, within the space between us. But who wanted to see that? Having to undress a wound in front of her?

I walked through sliding doors onto a landing, toward its edge. There were kids who had coupled up or had come together and sought refuge in the cold. I was above it, the smoldering land dying and being reborn. The sky was unmoving, a body of water dead and still. White lights snaked around window frames, balcony railings; all I could do was look up at the rolling neon, winking, a few dying only to be reborn. The rail was cold under my hands. When I looked down, I felt a desire somewhere deep behind my throat to soak myself in it, of the stone and bedrock. I swore I saw you in the lights below, a ghost that called out to me from below.

I bruised from every moment, raw from a scrape or abrasion. My body hated the way it was used, how it was forced to move and be. It made me sore, made me wince at the thought of the next day, the one after that. My memories didn't follow a timeline. It was all around me, suffocating me. Got my tenses all scattered. They don't matter, anyway. Nothing has begun and nothing is over.

NAIMA AND HER purse looked odd in my apartment, unfamiliar, but I felt like I was undressing slowly instead of quickly in the dark. I wanted to keep her smell in these rooms for days, the homemade shea butter she bought and the soft burn of vodka.

"Did you read all these books?" she asked me, a hand delicate on my mother's shelf.

"My mom did," I said. "I'm not even halfway."

"Tell me one of them. One you've read."

I told her the one my mother loved, about this town in a valley and these two girls who lived there. In the hills with the good land are the white folk, and the valley is for Black people. Their families are really different but they grow up together. One day, they're playing with one of the younger boys down by the river. They swing him around. He slips out of one of the girl's hands and falls into the river and drowns. They keep it a secret between them. The same girl is with her mother one day and watches her burn to death. Her mother lights a fire outside and her dress catches fire. People think she just stood and watched.

"Her friend gets married and she ends up leaving town for years. Went all over the country. The town hates her because she sleeps with white guys. And Black guys. But I think mainly because she's different from them. She sees life as her own. When she comes back, she ends up sleeping with her friend's husband. So now her friend hates her, too. Just before she dies, they kind of reconcile, but it's a lot. When she passes, the people of the town bury her and folk arrive near the end to sing 'Shall We Gather at the River.' There's this moment at the end, when the woman feels her friend in the wind, the treetops. And she cries."

"Why does she have to die alone?" Naima asked me. I thought for a moment, heard the turn of traffic outside my window.

"I don't know."

"I guess it's common. All the women I know . . ." She trailed off, found herself in her reflection of the window. "Otherwise, I love it."

"'My lonely is mine.'"

"What?"

"It's a thing she says."

"My lonely is mine," she repeated between us. "At least I have something."

Naima sat by the window in sweatpants low enough that I could see the stitching of her Pink underwear, rolled a blunt in what looked like a fresh, hanging leaf she had cut from a tree. It was nearly as dark as the creases of her hands, smelled just as sweet. When I gave her the oversized clothes, she laughed as she slid them on. She was drawn to Toya's side of the bedroom, covered in magazine spreads, Missy Elliott with paisley bandanas and baggy jean vests, and Lil' Kim crouched in front of bubblegum backdrops, cutouts from *Vibe* or *The Source*, glossy profiles of Trina, a shirtless 50 Cent. Photos from her twenty-dollar wind-up camera, her stacked mattresses with dozens of pillows, the colors stained marigold from the lamps of the courtyard below.

I ran the shower on hot with the door closed and a towel underneath as we smoked. Through the fog, I couldn't help but touch her skin, the light hair on her arms soft against my fingers. Naima rested her head on my shoulder and I tried to match her breathing. She touched my arms, kept looking up at me, then away, laughing. All alone the world was ours. It belonged at her feet and in my hair. When I kissed her, she tasted like the land, the salt of the very marsh we lived on. I had never seen her so nervous before. I'd feel her drumming, a pulse somewhere beneath a body of water. In my head was the sound of thunder, a blood frequency tucked away inside us.

"Am I the first girl you've been with?" she asked later, falling asleep next to me in bed. This wasn't our first time together, but I knew what she meant. I lied and said no. Then I didn't want to lie and said yes.

I would ease into sleep listening to far-off sirens, would dream until I grew cold. In the dark, it felt like the high beams of a truck or a spacecraft. I'd get this sensation where I felt myself wake but couldn't move. My mind cried out desperately. You were standing over me like you wanted to tell me something, Ma. I felt like I could never seek you out yet there you were, hiding right in front of me. You came to me and I swore I could smell sweetened cornmeal. There was no nkisi in sight. I panicked, my body tangled between my dream and a cold realm where all I could do was watch. You smiled at me and the sound of waves rolled into my ears. It was a sad smile, one that worried for me, which knew my fate but worried anyway. You wanted to straighten my tie, starch my suit, feed me before my demise.

THE OYSTER WOMAN

KEY (1990)

It rained in New York all September, made the city slip from under your feet, made the buildings that hid behind a warm fog look like wandering giants peering over us. When the sun came out, as it did today, it bounced off all the glass and metal and made the city brighter, made the sky a creamy blue you'd want to scoop a spoonful out of. Treasure would be my first home birth, and my first birth as Carrie's sole assistant. When Carrie delivered the baby, whatever happened would be solely on us and the Lord. We were deep into fall and kids in bright Starter jackets played in the leaves that piled near the walkways. We had first met Treasure and her husband nine months ago, at a breakfast and coffee shop run by a Dominican family. They lived just above the place, a walk-up that had to be as shabby as the entire store front. The couple had been on a run of interviews, pulled up Carrie and her accreditation before sitting down with us. They bonded over differing takes on Caribbean dishes.

"Is pepper pot just a Guyanese way to say oxtail?" Carrie asked, winking at me.

"Guyanese pepper pot is a blend of different meats," Treasure explained, "including oxtail, cooked to perfection with cassareep and other things."

"Is that right?"

"I'm just saying if Jamaicans had to cook it, it would be too much. Ruined at the hands of ginger."

"Watch it," Carrie warned, teased with a slight smile.

"Okay, I'm done," she laughed.

Treasure said she liked us, mainly because Carrie wasn't fazed by her idiosyncrasies. The couple knew what they wanted, were very straightforward, had raised a kid in a two-bedroom row house in Flatbush. She wanted what most people thought of as a natural birth, didn't want to be shot up with drugs that felt like rising mercury, forced to make decisions about another life as well as her own while high as a kite. She had said after her first child she'd been traumatized by her experience, said it made the space between her hips feel flooded, a phantom chill.

"And I know it's tricky," Treasure had admitted. "Some girls end up really needing it. But I'm not sure if I did. I felt differently, like Junior would come out on his own when he was good and ready."

I met Carrie at an event a year ago, somewhere downtown where she spoke on a panel. She was intense, her face a kneaded bronze, a midwife who also held a doula certification. The distinction was in accreditation; the midwife was given more legal responsibility in actually delivering the baby. She listed terrible facts: Black women experience the most complications during labor, the most health risks, and the most deaths. I asked her why.

"I'll put it to you like this. General health. Proximity to abuse and what can come with that. We aren't exactly given the best the healthcare business has to offer. Reason why most hospitals in our neighborhoods look worse than the one from that Jack Nicholson movie. I'd rather do what I can so some poor girl doesn't have to go to Brookdale."

"Oh God," I moaned.

"I've lived in this city for years," Carrie had declared. "Everything's changed but the emergency rooms."

Our job was to listen. To be sensitive to habits and women's bodies and try to be preventative, even though they're surrounded by this systemic bull-shit. I had told her I was interested in doing more, the kind of work that served others more than stocking merchandise. For months I shadowed Car-rie, helped her out when I could, though she had another girl with her who had more experience. I had promised Mama I'd find something to do that wasn't wasting my talents, whatever those turned out to be. It wasn't in a department store, or part-time someplace that could keep me forever.

Only in Treasure's apartment on the narrow end of Linden Boulevard, which crashed into Flatbush Ave. like a wave of tar crashing into a concrete pier, did I realize only I had seen it. We were only a few blocks away from the park, but I could smell the forsythia, heard the birds flock to the dogwood trees. Treasure lay across her love seat, her pregnant belly like the mounds in Cahokia or SunWatch, an altar. We all stood around, her mother and her partner and a ghost-child, as well as Carrie and me. Her smile hummed and I could feel the tangle of knots in her hips, her shoulders. She was a teller at a credit union and stood for hours at a window. Her skin was a russet be-neath my fingers, her hair wrapped up in a scarf like a beehive. From the walls she hung mud cloths from Mali and batik, the vinyl case of *A Salt with a Deadly Pepa*, cheaply framed paintings she found at the swap meet near the aqueduct, powerful Black men ascending from chains or holding up curvy Black women among the stars or the middle of the Earth.

Carrie had brought in the ultrasound today. It whirred and whipped as it came to life. I swabbed the inside of Treasure's mouth in the meantime, placed it somewhere in her kit. It would show if her glucose and TSH levels were normal, helping dictate the remainder of her birth plan. Also, it would alert us of any altering dietary concerns and how active she could be as her son prepared his arrival. I covered her belly in clear gel before Carrie began to move the machine's transducer, gliding it across her stomach as if trying to pick up a signal.

"There he is," Carrie said, a smile behind her thick-rimmed glasses, her natural hair coiled and almost silver. The machine squawked and blinked. The screen displayed a cavern and in the center was something like a cashew, wanting to stretch out.

"He's the most beautiful thing I seen," the father marveled. He was boyish, long and pretty like a grasshopper. Treasure squinted at the screen.

"You can't really see nothing," she said.

"Are you kidding? There's your eyes." He pointed at a shape in the giant cashew. "And that's my nose. He's perfect."

"You're right."

"He big," her mother pointed out. "Look like he can't wait to get outta you."

"That's what he been telling me," Treasure said, glancing down at her belly.

I TOOK THE train home, to the outskirts of the richest city, a glass tower of Babel sitting on bedrock and bones. Through blocks of empty lots and scrapyards, fields of junk or auto parts divided by rusted fences, ribbons of barbed wire. For miles were waste facilities so the streets would smell soured around dawn, heat plants that chugged smoke out of their towering chimneys. Bundled in brick were halfway houses, drugstores with bulletproof windows, hospices or shelters where folk had gone crazy, blanked from depressives the state approved, sat in the sun with their damp cigarettes with a look of a stonewall. Farther down were motels that bustled after one a.m., girls I'd seen around or from school in short dresses and heels lined up in the parking lot of the White Castle next door, winking at cars and checking their beepers. There were nursing homes next to salvage yards next to lots of landfill. The animal control center failed to wrangle the stray pit bulls that wandered the lots. They did manage to capture possums and raccoons, sometimes bludgeoned already from cars or shop owners who'd caught them hanging under their store awnings.

Genesis had been supportive, especially since I could keep paying my share of the rent. I remember when I first told her, months ago in our fourth-floor, one-bedroom apartment.

"I want to become a doula," I shouted over the roar of her blow-dryer.

"A what now?" she asked. I told her it was like a midwife but not really. "Is the pay good?"

"Not in the beginning. But neither was sales associate at Macy's."

"You know I support anything you do, girl," she reassured me, but I could tell she would miss the furs and DKNY heels we'd go through, how she'd model the new pieces in front of Dee, who laughed at our enterprise whenever he could. I missed it too. I missed carrying a backpack through Manhattan on Saturday nights, changing outfits between the Roxy or Fun House or Studio 61, jumping between looks at a moment's notice. In the tight, crooked aisles of the Strand, I read about professional midwives and birth attendants. I read about births at home and birthing centers and when none of the plans went right and you had to give birth in a Laundromat or in a car speeding toward the hospital.

Most of the women Carrie and I saw were alone, cradled by their mothers or aunts, their sisters or best friends, women from their church or their community center. Some had men who hurt them, who let them down in every way, could not provide but only take, could not protect but only take cover behind the closest thing to them. Some women belonged to men who loved them with all they had, and not to would mean an existence they fought hard to escape from. You could tell the histories of a community in how they give birth and the ways in which they bury their dead. We ourselves are markers. We have been just like this for centuries, boiling water, laying out rags, soothing a young girl with coos and whispers, all the while at the helm of a war being waged against their existence. We had been mothers of our own, midwives and birth workers, at the threshold, the tall and wet portal of generations.

I WAS TETHERED between both sides of a journey, the cries of being born and the echoes of the dead. I was trying to trace the hundreds of years it took for the shore to recede, only to be stuffed with landfill, to plug the brittle bedrock beneath them. I saw the woodlands and farms become a messy grid of tenements and factories burning metal on the inside. This land was scabbing flesh that would break and bleed like new. I come across the end of it, the land and its broken edges, the shore green and rocky in places. The beach was cracked sand, the water was dark from the sewage treatment plant that, when it rained too hard, spilled its contents into the Atlantic. Do the dead still have a right to this world? Is it fair that I can see them, or hear their near absent padding across dirt, displacing grass and earth like a wind across the inlet? I try to catch my breath but the wind keeps pushing it back down my throat.

"Sit down, you look flushed," Ms. Pat told me, and I sat against a log by a fire made on this slab of gray beach. She looked full of blood, not like someone who had died a few years ago, my guide through this shore. My mother and I helped out her son, who is no longer sleeping outside the strip mall. We spoke to the church and they helped with their connections in shelters and the foster care system. I bought clothes for him, toiletries and money for haircuts or whatever. Ms. Pat really appreciated me for that.

"There's someone I want you to meet," she said. There are other people, all black and silver from the moon. One woman looked all of thirty, younger than Ms. Pat, but in a long, colonial-style dress with a tattered apron. A boy who looked to be around twelve or thirteen wore a tattered wool suit and beat leather loafers. A young woman fed the fire more wood, wore faded Converse.

"You're like this girl I knew way back when," the woman with the apron said.

"I'm scared to know what 'way back when' means for you," I sighed, eyeing her dress.

"Memories are a gift for the living. For me, time is a field and I can look all around it, squint my eyes and walk to where I need to be." Dragonflies hover about the sand with heavy wings, darting through the cherubs and brush.

"This bay was a salt marsh," the woman went on. "Miles and miles of hay." I look out along the estuary, the shore, the Black folk, still waiting along the wrack line. The night is a soothing balm, the sound of water easing into the rocky beach. I forget the freeway was beyond the bend, dozens of yards behind me. "But just north of here, there were once woods. Acres of farms. Fresh soil, the kind sometimes you'd dig into and think water might spring out, how cool and damp it was."

"North," I wondered aloud, hearing my voice drum and echo. An aquarium. "Like New Lots?"

"That church there with the black pointed roof," she said. "Built twice over. Before that we use to walk miles and miles to the next town, just for service. Finally, the farmers and us church folk got together and up and made a town. Well, not us." She glanced at her clothes, at her swollen hands.

"You were a slave."

"We call that kidnapped. The greatest ruse of 'em all."

"Do you remember your home?"

"I was way too young, but my mother . . . She died only a few years after I was born. I remember she sang to me in a language from home and when I'd be ready to be done with all of this, I'd close my eyes and hear the song in her voice. I remember the boys would herd sheep and goat, slice them open and cut 'em up for Mr. Hendrix. The farmers made a killing, ate these huge oysters, left them for us girls to toss out. The boys would till the crop, do odd fixings around the farm. Us girls were up in the house. We would clean the crop for the market or for dinner. Clean the manor, the grounds, some fieldwork. Mr. Lott let us build our own quarters. It was small, built it with the ceiling low to keep it warm. We all stayed there, about a dozen of us.

"There was a girl who was older than me, Cara. She cooked for us after service, when that church gave Black folk time to worship every month or so. She cooked a stew so good, knew how to get all the flavor from the neck bones she threw in. And she'd make these delicious cakes with caraway seed. Would always collect the oysters the big men ate. Up in the house they called her the Oyster Woman. She'd make an altar to her ancestors out of bone and hemp and the best oyster shell. She remembered her village. Could still speak her tongue. Strangest thing, every night she'd get up and leave and be back as soon as the dew hit the grass. Turns out she'd walk the half mile to this here shore. Her husband had told me, 'Think she up and run away.' I asked her why did she go to the shore every night and she said the ancestors called to her in a dream. They called her home."

I stayed quiet, let her words hang out over the bay like clothes to dry, flowing in the ocean wind. It was comforting to hear. I wasn't alone. History would comfort me, could tell me what to do.

"So what does that mean? What you found. What happened to Cara."

"This"—she drew a line in the sand—"is the space between the two worlds. The living world and the world of the dead. This"—she drew another line with her finger, this time through the other like a cross or an X—"is the bridge that connects them both. A crossroads. It's a powerful connection."

"So?"

"It's not a mistake that the living and the dead run into each other. It isn't coincidence you can see both. Maybe your answers come way before you, which is always the case."

BABIES DO SO much in the womb. They urinate, feel pleasure. They cry. You don't hear it because so much is going on, but they cry. It makes me sad. To know that you will never have peace.

• • •

TREASURE LAY TO the side as I kneaded the muscles of her lower back. Last minute checkup for preeclampsia. The aides took blood and urine from her, made us wait for what felt like hours. "This is what the doctor recommends," the same nurse reiterated. There was hierarchy in the way she said "doctor," tugged at the end of the word with her teeth almost. Around us were folk left unattended on hospital beds in hallways, rooms with plastic curtains giving false sense of privacy, crowded waiting rooms with benches full of people who looked just like me. The ebb of equipment, the murmur of doctors, the groans of the sick, the bated breaths of the loved ones waiting along benches and walls, near half-lit vending machines. Grit collected at the corners of the walls, the ceiling edges, yellowed the machines and counters and beds. Treasure's man brought a small boom box and played meditation music, drowned by the frenzy of the maternity ward. Finally, he headed down to the lobby in search of headphones.

We call our hospitals what they are known for. I was born in Killer County. Everyone dies at Crookdale. When the Post reported a death in East New York and mentioned Brookdale Medical Center, we kissed our teeth. We knew all along. How they patched up folk with gauze or tools still in them, misdiagnosed for convenience or expense, often broke people worse than when they got them. This is what the state gives us. After a while, a doctor came over and pulled Carrie and the husband aside.

"We're so happy when girls have somebody who knows what they're doing," an older nurse said to me, one we'd seen most frequently. "Makes our job easier."

There were different doctors than the one we had met with for months. I was irritated, more than usual. My ears kept going in and out, like water was stuck in them. Med students flowed in and out, taking notes in folders and clipboards, watching patients as if behind the glass panel of a display case. I felt a murmuring swelling beneath the quiet, beneath the sweating, the uncovering, and the expanding.

When Treasure began to cry out I could barely hear her. The nurses crowded her but I heard another wailing, a scream so sharp I cowered before it. It wasn't Treasure. It wasn't the hundreds of women in the ward, all in various stages of birthing and degrees of pain. It was a sound that seemed to come from everywhere, drowning out the machines, the nurses' station, the med students and the crumpling of their scrubs. It sounded like a scream from a woman, or maybe a child, fighting over who would be heard. The sound a lick of pain, I covered my ears, jerked into a service cart, heard the clanging of equipment falling from a delivery tray. The same nurse who had been slowed by the swollenness in her feet grew sick of me in her way. She hurried me out the door and into the hallway.

I sulked past a series of triage rooms, kept away from the nurse's station. Something passed through me, a chill or sinking, like I'd seen something I shouldn't have. Carrie probably thought I wasn't cut out for any of this. As soon as the pressure was on, I crumbled and a room full of health professionals could attest to it. They hardly thought I deserved to be in that room anyway. Treasure wouldn't be alone, just with one less advocate whose motive was her wellbeing, not what was best for hospital business.

An obstetrician stood nearby with a younger resident. I could make out a conversation about labor-inducing medication; the young one wondered if it had something to do with the sudden strength of his patient's contractions. I finally got myself to sit, ignoring the itch of the shredded vinyl.

"What happened to you in there?" Carrie asked me, barreling out the double doors.

"I thought—" No, what had I thought? I wasn't sure anymore.

"A lot going on, it can get overwhelming. I thought you had a panic attack."

"No I'm fine, I'm sorry. I had a moment."

"Treasure is in labor. We need to get her out of here and begin prep."

"So we're leaving the hospital with our girl in labor?"

"Well, she ain't having her baby here—that's a quote, by the way," she said, snorted. I ran my hands through my hair. Carrie placed her hand on my shoulder and I smelled the sharp antibacterial soap she used continuously.

"Look, go home and sleep," Carrie said to me. "I'll get Treasure set up at her house."

I nodded and she squeezed the nook of my neck and shoulder. I realized I didn't know much about her, hardly knew where she came from or if she went home to a family at night. A few nurse's aides and a doctor wheeled out an empty bed and Carrie slipped through the double doors as they closed.

WITH A BUNDLE of sage I held in one hand like a scepter, I sat up in my pullout. Ms. Pat stood by the window. She was with me more often than not, it seemed, appearing at her own volition. She fussed about, looking for the ghost-child in every room in one big gust. It was still with Treasure.

"It's gone, Ms. Pat," I cried.

"Explain it to me again."

"I lost it at work. In the middle of the delivery room. Had to be escorted out like a kid. What if this isn't for me? Any of it? I heard this scream, but it couldn't've been any one person, or thing, that could let out a sound like that. I couldn't tell if it was one of the mother's giving birth and her baby, or if somebody was dying."

"Could've been both," Ms. Pat insisted. "Could've been all the births and all the dying. You're putting yourself smack between life and death, you're gonna get some feedback."

"All this should really come with a handbook."

"You need another perspective."

"That oyster lady," I thought aloud, and the older woman nodded.

"Look for her, you both can see the crossroads. You share a gift."

"Not a curse?"

"You wouldn't have me if that was the case."

"You might be right," I said. Smiled at the idea of her keeping me company. Then: "She did say something about that church. She cooked there or something."

Ms. Pat shrugged. She kept me company, smiled from the window as I tried to drift off to sleep, the lights from passing cars passing through her. Finally, I shoved the jade-colored sheets aside and put on my boots.

I SAT IN the park across the church, the old Dutch two-story with the pointed roof. It seemed out of place, a thorn of oak among brick towers and a grid of concrete. There was a man who seemed to be pacing near the bus stop. He made me nervous; I wasn't sure if the bus ran this late. Yet here I was, in the darkest hours, in a playground looking across at a church and cemetery full of scattered headstones and knotted grass. The cemetery was small, hadn't been used in the centuries since. It stretched the length of the block, toward Barbey Street. You could tell who owned land or died with money, could tell the white folk who could only afford the barest tombstone. Then, in the back part of the enclosure, maybe once in a while, there was a Black man or woman interred under what might be just a stone, buried in the middle of the night away from white, prying eyes.

The bus did run this time of night. This paranoia had been my own doing. There was no moon in sight, the sky a bitter plum. There was the acid glow of the lamps on the streets, building windows lit at random. This was stupid. I was hoping to find a woman who had died over a century ago, praying she could tell me how I could see the things I did. The playground was all discolored railings and chains, steel frames showing under chipping paint like a cut that went down to the bone. The dry wind pushed the swings softly and they groaned, their rubber seats rocking back and forth. The man at the bus stop looked at me again, this time stared, knew we'd made eye contact. His eyes were flat, didn't glow in the light, black with a sheen of static. I held my breath. Like a camera out of focus, a dull glow from the church doorway. One near a headstone. Two by the library steps. They held the same flat eyes, were dressed in garb hundreds of years old like the woman from the shore.

"I'm looking for the Oyster Lady," I said to the empty street. "Um, or woman. Whichever she prefers."

The man didn't look surprised, merely nodded. If he knew her at all, he knew what she could do.

"You share a curse," he replied, his voice a timbre that settled at the base of her neck.

"Not a gift?" I offered. He was silent. I got up from the bench and walked slowly toward the gate. He stood his ground.

"She was my wife," he said, looking down at the dust of the road between us. "I saw what it did."

"Why'd she go to the ocean at night?"

"Cara was—" he said, but the words got caught in his throat. "Cara is, Cara was, Cara will. I never knew why. She was so much more than she believed. I thought maybe the ocean reminded her of that. When we got away from that fucking farm, I thought she'd come out of it. You can't really shake a thing like that, not belonging to yourself. It's like sand or mining, it stays with you, in your hair, your ears, between your toes. When we had our son, it helped her. Life mattered."

"She never told you what she saw?"

"When I came home, she sat on the other side of the house, her hands over her ears. Our son must've been dead a few hours. When I asked her if she knew she nodded but said she heard him crying for all those hours. She still hears him crying.

"We couldn't bury him in the cemetery so we did right here. What you're sitting on was dust. We said a few words but I could tell it was off. When I put my arm around her, I could feel her become stone. She walked around here like a shell. Soul gone. One day, she'd gone, too. No one had seen her. She didn't know what to do with the living. Didn't wanna have anything to do with it. I think she went down to that shore there. It called to her one day and she just up and went."

I crept around the gate of the park, into the middle of the street. I realized the dead surrounded me now. They regarded me curiously, held me in the silver of their gaze, their brown eyes alive like tears would spring loose.

"And where is she now?"

The husband looked around, eyed his comrade near the church door. He nodded and the door flung itself open. He then turned to me.

"She's expecting you."

The chapel sat within a single landing that was as tall as two, below its belfry and roof, its clapboard siding a faded white painted over and over for centuries. There were tall, arched windows, stained glass that seemed like an addition within the last decade. There were pamphlets left in pews, bibles tucked in the backs of chairs. The place still held some sort of service in its chapel on Sundays. There was a staircase near the pew. The basement seemed like a shelter, a few men who looked wiped out leaned out of a side door that led to some stone steps, up to the street. They bummed cigarettes, tucked their hands away, jerked and trembled. They stared at me as I passed, didn't know if I was real or not. Everything haunted them.

THERE WAS A door at the other end of the basement and when I went inside it seemed the room went back farther than the church could hold. Even though I was below ground and it was about three or four in the morning, the sun shone through a window. A woman cooked by a stove somewhere in the distance. Soon the sun was in full embrace and the room opened up into the neighborhood. I could see it, marshland stretching for miles. Soft topsoil, fields of wet earth, wooded area. Over the tenements and housing complexes, the factories and burning lots, the railroads and landfills, the land built and rebuilt itself over and over again.

"And when you pour libations," a woman said, "each finger points me near the way I came." The woman turned to me, the face of a young girl, brown as oak beneath the silver fog around her. It covered her eyes and when she spoke, I swore I could see the pupils of more than one pair. When the mist would clear in spots, Cara appeared normal.

"What is this?" I looked out across the ledge.

"The world you are born in is just one mode of reality, but you know that, don't you? There is fate and what is predestined but who truly knows. The body is but a ritual, a series of principles and practices to reach a predestined result. We are born, live with what we can and all eventually die, to live out Eternity."

"I don't want this," I cried out. "How can I live my life when all I can see is death?"

"You'll always be reminded, even if you can't see," she said. Behind her, the land changed again; from the sprawling green came swabs of brick and stone until they sprung into towers. The woodlands and the marsh receded and rotted, tangled with metal fences and plots of landfill. I swore I could see the blood spilled throughout the eras, running under the neighborhood like a current. This was its own burial ground. "What's the difference? What is a graveyard but a place of future lives and deaths? They both commune in a place, try to cross a border or chasm that doesn't really exist. You are confronted with it every day, but it's easier to close your eyes when you are blinded by it."

My thighs, below my stomach, behind my neck, and down my spine were drenched with my sweat. There was a wind that seemed to roll in from Jamaica Bay, the first summer breeze of the year. I thought of the thousands locked in cells in towers, the lights from their windows. Who had been swallowed under this land? In this water? The decades we binged on trying to rebuild what had been destroyed long before we came around.

"Tell me," I breathed, finally, a croak in the wind. "This screaming. I hear it with my patient. She's in labor."

Cara seemed delighted. She told me: "You're more powerful than you know. The Yoruba speak of the world seen and the world unseen, the travelers that stand between the two. Children are often the easiest to wander through the cracks. They call a child cursed with such a fate an abiku, spirits who find homes in a host and are born and reborn again.

"Her elders warn her. Tell her to hang a needle or a small white stone from the edge her dress. They tell her don't go near the water. Don't go near the dumping grounds. Don't go near an intersection with three paths. Don't go to the foot of the forest, or the silk-cotton trees, or out alone at night. A spirit claims her daughter and she dies and is reborn again. Sometimes she comes back as a boy. Sometimes taller, or with the nose of the father instead of the mother's. She still comes back, the same reckless spirit, apathy for the living and their world. Finally, the mother scars the last incarnation with a sacrifice of her own. In the spirit world, she comes across the field of balboa trees. She meets the child who made space in her child, met its family. Their ribs touch and they move slowly because they are weak from hunger. The abiku come to the physical world to eat, to feed their families."

"One last thing," I said, watching the sun fade and the land cycle through time one last time. It was coming upon twilight. "Your son. Do you still hear him?"

"Yes," she said. "I can hear all of them."

WHEN A WOMAN becomes pregnant with a girl, the fetus will develop all the eggs it will ever need. This means that a mother's body can hold the possibility of three separate generations. We have always come in threes.

WHEN I KNOCKED on Treasure's door, her partner answered and hugged me. He led me into the living room, where Treasure was laid out across the couch, breathing in and out while her mother rubbed on her feet. She held her belly like a farmer held the earth, a whole world in her hand. Carrie arrived not long after me and we began to set up. The house smelled of nag champa and a bit of vanilla bark, was lit with candles and incense that smoldered in the corner. A cassette played from a stereo—Luther Vandross, "Love Won't Let Me Wait."

"Why does this feel so good?" Treasure said, hovered over the cold, porcelain toilet.

"This is how the ancient Egyptians gave birth," I told her. "In this very position. Countless indigenous women."

"Sitting on a golden toilet seat," Treasure said.

"You're royalty," I confessed.

While her mother and partner took turns rubbing her feet, I massaged her shoulders, then her lower back, pushed softly to apply some pressure. When that was done, Treasure walked around the living room and stretched near the kitchen, bent, squatted in the bathroom, did what her body needed. It told her to move about her space, to holler in the doorways, to fill the halls with laughter. All the while her partner and I filled an inflatable tub with warm water.

Carrie came back over and whispered to Treasure, "Listen, dear, you're eight centimeters. I think you can make it to ten. If the pain is too much, you call it."

"You think so?" Treasure asked, trying to breathe through a wave of crashing pain.

"You know your body."

"I do."

"That's right."

"It hurts bad."

Still, Carrie was a flower planted on the forest floor, brushing against the bark of a tree, gentle and reassuring. She cooed into the woman's ear, reminded her of the wonderful truth of the body, the womb growing a hundred times its normal size. "Isn't that remarkable," she said to Treasure. "Aren't you remarkable?"

Finally, when it was time—and she knew it was time because her body told her, her son was coming—she slid into the pool, her partner behind her.

He squeezed her hips the way I had shown him. We cheered for her, cried with her, her mother held her hand and I whispered how wonderful she was doing. Carrie crouched at the other end of the pool, her hands in the water, and I swear there was a smile, a bright spot on her typically stoic face. From her crown I could see the boy's head and I swore I heard wailing, a woman and child.

What if we are born with all of what we know when we die? What if being born and dying weren't two opposite ends of a straight line, but the same point on a never-ending path? We think of the time before birth as nothingness, as before cells and blood and a body existed, and death as the same, as after cells and blood and a body existed. Out of that nothingness, that absence of—which couldn't be an absence at all because how could something be birthed from that which contains nothing. Maybe you and I sprang from the same realm, the same well of blankness, and you went one way, my son, and I the other, on a path that will eventually lead me back to you. What if that nothingness from which we were born was the same nothingness into which we go when we die? What if it wasn't nothingness at all? What if it was full and infinite, a moment of aseity across time and nations? What if I know I will see you again in Eternity?

Treasure's baby was born in a messy bloom, out a tall mouth of fleshy petals and I wept in wonder. He was pale and violet, the boy, skin pruned from the amniotic fluid. Treasure herself cried out, sweating in the tub of warm water, caught the baby's head as he slid into water. She held her son to her belly, then her chest, dreaded the seconds where Carrie and I cleaned the boy off best we could. He wailed, soft and heavy like a bodily organ. The youngin cooed in relief, and Treasure covered her baby in tears, kissed his ear as she whispered to him. Within an hour, she breastfed her son for the first time, in her home, surrounded by her family. "Cameron," she said. The baby murmured into his mother's breast, eyes closed and hair slicked over her tiny head. Soon, he would cry into the night. He would have many mouths.

BLACK LAZARUS

COLLY (2009)

Raven told me to come and watch the next day, at the damp rec room in the back of the center. Said she'd see her aunt for the first time in years that evening. I asked if she needed me to come with her but she had her hands full. The girls were in bright green shirts in messy rows as they went through a breathing exercise. It took a while for her to calm the girls down, all of them humming with sugar and gossip. I sat near the back, half on my cell phone, half listening to her voice, tamarind in my ear. Her Sidekick lit up inside her bag every few minutes, vibrating in the chair next to me.

"All the shit from the day," she told them. "The snot-nosed boy who said you're too Black, the teacher who said you're gonna end up fast or doing nothing with your life, all that shit. It sits in your body. Makes you feel worse later. Stretch it away. Can you feel it coming undone? Now breathe in. Hold. Now breathe out. Do you feel the weight leaving you? Now shake it all away"—a dozen little people stretched and shook their limbs, couldn't control their giggling—"breathe in like you were bigger than your body. Breathe out until you are just a shell on the beach, completely still, the water pulling away from you. Remember that feeling? When the tide would pull back while your feet were in the sand? And you'd feel like you were moving backward? Remember that feeling until you feel yourself fading, floating on . . ."

She left them for a few minutes with their eyes closed, went into her bag (checked her phone, snarled) and took a CD and played it on a set of speakers. A number of songs were stitched together, all thumping bass and compressed voices. The main problem was remembering the routine. Some were offbeat by a hair but most hesitated between moves, looking at each other or Raven for guidance.

"Give me the truth," Raven said after the hour mark, and sat down next to me sweating.

"What they remembered was good," I said. One little girl stared at me, braided pigtails with neon barrettes, her mouth colored green with candy.

"And what's your name?" I asked her.

"Quay," she said.

"I'm Colly."

"Are you Miss Raven's boyfriend?"

"No," I stuttered. "Not today."

Raven didn't try to hide her smirk.

IF YOU KEPT walking down Stanley Avenue, or Wortman Avenue, past Ashford or even Barbey Street, the plastic and car plants we sometimes race our bikes down, you could still hear the electric blades cutting into steel. 857 Schenck had gates around the edge of the rooftop as protection; 797 did not. The rust-colored water tank atop of 2147 had been hit with a tag across the side, bubble letters that read FOOT across it. The land is firewood, burning until the smoke is thick enough to possess me. My nose flooded sour, the rain and sweat a haze near the curb. If I cried, would anyone notice? Even the trees perform; drop their branches in resignation, stand full-bodied and erect in sunlight. The city is the color of bones bleached dry by the sun. My snorkel felt like flowers stuffed in my arms and along my torso. Snow drifted at a slant, each flake like a whisper to the skin; there were thousands of them. The tenant association crowded my lobby while I waited for the elevator.

A note above the mailbox:

ATT: BLVD & LINDEN

THT WE DONT HAVE GROUND KEEPERS IT LOOKS LIKE WE R
GONNA HAVE TO CLEAN OUR OWN NEIGHBORHOOD

IF U HAVE BAGS IN UR BUILDING (I NOE NOBODY WANTS TO DO
THIS) WITH GARBAGE TIE THEM UP & TAKE THEM TO THE CURB

TALK TO UR NEIGHBORS ON UR FLOOR TAKE TURNS CLEAN UR
FLOORS, SWEEP, MOP & ANYTHING ELSE UNTIL WE CAN GET
SOME WORKERS

LETS TRY A PROJECT CLEAN UP DAY LETS PICK ONE DAY OUT OF
THE WEEK & CLEAN OUR OWN

LETS TAKE BACK OUR HOOD

"What's going on?" I asked Miss Moore.

"Housing employees just up and walked out," she said. "They're not getting paid like they should. For a while now, Housing won't send somebody to fix a thing. Hardly anything gets repaired and now they can't even keep up the upkeep."

"NYCHA has no money," Miss Morales explained. "That same call you put in? Thousands of 'em. Backlogged. The repair companies they contract are gonna to sue."

"Why?" I was lost.

"NYCHA won't pay them either."

"So we're starting a lil' community beautification group," Miss Moore said. "Clean up our neighborhood. Fix it up some, too."

"I usually sweep out in the hallway on my floor anyway."

"We need young folk to take the trash out to the road."

"Sure," I lied. "Let me put my stuff down."

"All right, dear," Miss Moore said. "You know where to find us."

ACROSS THE COURTYARD, Tristan, his younger cousin, and Zaire stood under his building. Brick the color of burned cork, obelisk rooted in earth. Tristan had grown taller, stout since he got me kicked out of school. His cousin had his grill wired shut, broke his jaw off the recoil of a .45 his brother let him shoot one night, off the roof of their building. They lurked under its rusted awning, spoke with their hands in their waistbands. Zaire was in workout gloves. I expected Zaire to side with me against Tristan. He tried at first, but it was hard to avoid people when you saw them everyday, when everyone was a friend of a friend and knew each other since pre-school. When Tristan spotted me he stared, his brow tight and jaw hanging open as if he wanted to say something. I ignored him, walked my ass inside.

Upstairs, I slid out of my backpack and coat in one motion, dropped a stack of mail on the computer desk. Bills for my father, credit card offers, college brochures addressed to me. The paint bubbling up along the ceiling in the living room was getting worse; a leak from the roof. I made my second call to Housing in two weeks, got through to some poor lady who sounded exhausted. "We'll send someone out as soon as we can," she said, just as a similarly exhausted man had told me a week ago. I went to turn the flame on, ended up in that middle phase where gas was supposed to catch. The stove ticked away. I breathed in and could taste the fumes of the burning cooker behind my throat. The sound reminded me of Christmas morning, when I would wake you at the first sight of sun and you'd put a pot on the stove for coffee. Holidays were the toughest. I usually went with Pop to my great-aunt's for dinner and spent the rest of the time at Nana's.

I tell anyone, straight-up. You were never, or had ever been: (1) Boo Boo the Fool, (2) one to play with, or, of course, (3) one of my little friends. Weeks before Christmas, I'd try to sneak into your closet when you were held up in the kitchen or had closed the door to the bathroom. I'd find nothing but dolls for my niece or some clothes from Old Navy for my cousins. "How do you like your gifts?" you would ask. I was upset with the bullshit in that bag, but I wasn't ready to admit I went snooping and lacked self-control. You enjoyed watching this play across my face, laughed even as I denied it. You brushed my hair down with your hand.

You took us to see the city this time of year, sun falling, as red as the sumac growing along the brush. Then it would grow dark, the streetlight spilling over our feet. We'd look down at the ice rink on Fifty-Third Street, watch kids and their parents or couples carve the ice with their skates. From above it looked like a carousel, everyone skating along the bronze railing for balance in one big rotating oval. The brave ventured out into the center, slid backward, or skated with one foot.

The tree had to be at least sixty feet, a husky pine draped in velvet and lights. I couldn't see the bottom because there were so many people. All I could do was look up, the spruce the city probably got from upstate or somewhere in Canada, one of those tall forests and all the trees seem to grow from the sky. Now it lived in a different forest, one of reinforced concrete and steel, dwarfed by the Rockefeller building. In the Toys "R" Us half a mile south on Seventh Avenue, you picked up everything we could point out to you. We didn't take advantage; Toya and I had planned out what we wanted for Christmas months ago. One time, you bought me a brand new Nintendo and I lost my shit. The year before, I had thought we'd never be able to afford anything nice again. That year, you were anxious as we threaded the aisles in search of our gifts. The lines were long behind us. A woman seemed to get her kids every color American Girl doll and various outfits. I couldn't see her face behind the boxes she held and they could hardly fit in what space was left in her cart.

"Thank you for shopping with us today," the cashier let out. "Will that be all?"

You nodded and handed her a card, let Toya measure her foot next to your own, her furry boot small next to your own all-weather shoe. I decided to squeeze in somehow, my own foot shoved between you both.

The register let out a squeal and the cashier handed you your card back. Her eyes went down toward Toya and me, then back to you.

"I'm sorry," she said. "This card declined."

"That must be the wrong card," you said, rummaged frantically through your purse. The woman with the boxes sighed behind us, shifting her weight from one side to the other. I watched your whole body clench, tighten like you filled every muscle you could with blood. The register pinged in approval and you took your card and our bags and shuttled us out as quick as you could, back into the cold. I took a drag from my fake cigarette, blew out steam into the night. On the train ride we were all quiet, pressed and leaning against each other in the row we took up. Toya mashed the buttons on her Gameboy.

I tossed and turned all night waiting until a little after six in the morning. Then I'd harass you until you rose from your bed to show me which gifts were mine. I couldn't wait to hear BeBe and CeCe Winans hit "Silver Bells," or those Christmas albums with Tom Petty and Run DMC that Interscope did. We would eat the rotisserie chicken you bought from the supermarket, some collard greens cooked with pork neck bones, rice and black beans, and some sweet potatoes that made the whole house smell like maple. You and Auntie Genesis would hold out, let me spend the day thinking I hadn't gotten what I asked for. Then you'd ambush me with a tall bag full of everything

I asked for. Toya and I would compare hauls and then retreat to our corners with our chosen things until Auntie picked up and left.

The ticking of the gaslight brought me back and I looked down at my hand. It was a foreign, pronged thing pulsing below me. After a moment it moved, twisted the knob, and turned the stove off. I was light-headed. I looked around. The room looked as if it had been washed in brine and I realized no one scrubbed the walls or the floors, waxed the tile to make the house look less shabby. I couldn't take care of a thing. Can anyone ever change? People who were here long before I was given the promise that time could get away from you, roll on and on like a hungry field. Endless horizon. I must love the end of all things.

I needed answers so I went to my parents. I'd go to you. I went to your bookshelf. I tore through the pages, flung them aside when I saw they were empty. I looked under the shelf and behind it, dust hanging and falling into my eyes. I went to your closet. Disturbed the clothes that remained from what Toya had taken, shook the bins full of things you saved, the file cabinet near the back. The order of service from the day of your funeral was tucked away with insurance claims. A bible that opened to Psalms 27. Two fifty-dollar bills lay faded against the page. In your obituary, someone wrote things like "caring and loving spirit" and "through sacrifice and perseverance." I only glanced at it the day of your funeral. When everyone got a chance to look at you, to pay his or her respects, I kept staring until I burned it into my memory. I couldn't understand it. Your small body was filled out like a doll, and I wanted to stand there the whole morning and try to breathe but I kept moving toward my place, with the grieving family.

I sat with words, the paragraphs that mapped your life so neatly. I found a marker in a mug on a kitchen shelf and blacked out what I couldn't recognize. More and more you became familiar.

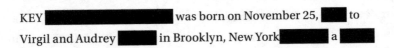

KEY ███████████████ was born on November 25, ███ to Virgil and Audrey ██████ in Brooklyn, New York ██████ a ████

devoted

community

Upon

pursuit   She

sought   the world

tirelessly

and

with colors

her own

blues

Ella   and Mahalia   a choir

humor

Her laugh   a room.

sacrifice,

in death

struggling for

home

ancestral   is

to be with the Lord ███████████████████████
███████████████████████

I kept rummaging through my parents' closet, flipped boxes upside down until the floor was covered in scattered things. I found my father's gun behind the headboard of his bed, the bed my mother died in. It fell one day, heavy against the fake hardwood. It was gleaming under the bed, flaring under the moonlight, worn silver with a scraped handle. I picked it up with two hands, afraid to hold it with anything less than a skin-breaking grip. Tighter. I aimed it across the hall.

In your photo album, I saw you at seven or eight years old, the same percipient look I've always known you to have. You were with your father, Virgil. Had to be eight or nine, two braided ponytails with barrettes. Smile with a bottom tooth missing. You couldn't know it, then. You'd never know peace, wouldn't make it to the other side of a wound, when the bleeding stopped and the new, translucent skin bubbled under. It would never grow rough and unnoticeable, only to become a marker of what your body was before the cut or break.

Perhaps my grandfather got the two of you snow cones after the photo and y'all ate them by the cool mist of the pond. The ice would melt through the paper cones, leave your thumbs and wrists sticky with red or blue syrup. Near the end of the bank, a row of ducks cooed amongst themselves, riding the gentle current. I didn't know if the wind I felt then, and now, was from this moment in the photograph or the time you and I had spent, slurping our snow cones by the pond, trying to keep sugar off our thumbs. I couldn't tell the difference between what I could taste, could feel so presently, and what you might've experienced. To me, they were one and the same.

Bright photos of you at community events; food drives, church fundraisers, movie nights at the center, a rally in what looked like the old post office on Pennsylvania Avenue. One photo of you with some important looking women, posing outside the library on New Lots. On the back you had written "African Burial Ground." The more I squinted at the old photo the more I noticed. Behind you were people talking amongst each other, including a face I recognized. He was on all those posters asking folk to vote for him this November. How did you know these people?

I would never know you, wouldn't grow older with you. I couldn't know you as my best friend, my confidante. You'll never know me as my own man, my own whatever, all I've learned being in the world, the call of it, the terror. I'll never know who I could be without you to show me; I could've been someone different. I can hardly make do. You had to leave something behind if you knew I would be without you. You should have known, made a plan for this exact moment.

This was when you had me. I was in your arms and Toya, a toddler, crawled up your leg. You were next to Auntie Genesis and another woman. Next to her was a little boy, lips pouting and eyes staring directly into the camera, or something slightly ahead. He didn't smile. They were in a green clearing down south, perhaps Auntie's house in Georgia. When I called Genesis, she was talking over the dishwasher and her favorite show, *Flavor of Love*. Why do you watch that stuff? I asked. Said she couldn't stand how the network portrayed Flavor Flav. Chuck D, the man who once said *"What we need is awareness, we can't get careless,"* was somewhere punching air. Still, the show was treacherous and she loved it.

"Anyway, why you calling so late?"

"I'm just looking through my mother's stuff. I needed to ask you about this picture I found." I tried to describe to her what I saw.

"Oh, that's Treasure. Her and your mom actually stopped speaking to each other. That's probably why you don't remember Cameron."

"Why'd they fall out?" I asked. There was silence on the line. I heard Auntie turn down her television, shift the phone from one side of her neck to the other.

"Key was . . . She put a lot of pressure on herself. I don't think she really knew some things are just out of our hands. She sort of took the blame for Cameron's death and it wasn't her fault."

"Wait, that kid is dead?"

"Oh, child, be respectful. That's my friend's son."

"I'm sorry. Why would Ma take the blame for a terrible thing like that?"

"She knew. She knew it would happen and it did. And don't ask me how she knew because I don't know. I never understood."

"Auntie, this not making sense."

"Listen—"

"Can you give me Treasure's number?"

"No, Colly. That's not a good idea. She's moved on. Look, I'll come up soon, baby. We'll talk."

She hung up. A car alarm went off from outside, the sound pressed up against the windows like it wanted to be let in. I got up from the mess I made of my parents' closet, sat down in the living room and turned on the desktop, the blue hum of the desktop washed over me. My eyes felt raw, dried out as they buried themselves into the screen. Can anyone ever change?

WE WERE TOO loud on the train. Raven animated a scene from some movie, yelling over the tumble of wheels. The grating screech of metal made my back tooth hurt, along with the cold. I picked at my hair matted down at the top. It was spring—the sun was beginning to dip and the streetlamps sprung to life in unison. Raven typed furiously on her Sidekick. When I glanced over, I saw Zaire's name. A homeless man sang out, competing with our voices that seemed to fill the cabin.

He bounced the paper cup of coins in his hand, against his leg, a tambourine he bore, moving through the train with a limp, a walk that was what I imagined a drawl to look like.

We got off the train at Court Street, loafed around Fulton Street in front of the boutiques and store fronts, the sidewalks bright with department store windows. Vendors set up tables along the sidewalks, sold natural scents and crystals, books published in someone's home or local print shop, stones and jewelry made from wire or silver, full racks of dresses and scarves with floral or kente print. The night made me light-headed with music, floated me through the incense and bus exhaust.

We ended up at the promenade overlooking the East River, slicked black oil under the white moon. Underneath us, an expressway drowned out any sound of water. I sat a few yards from the boardwalk, crowded the benches for a spot to sit. Raven had wandered to the railing alone and stared out across the river to the shore, Manhattan like hills and hills of lights and mirrors atop one another.

"My aunt reached out," Raven told me. "Wanna see me. You know she put me in foster care. I don't know if I can look at her."

She had always told me about her time in the shelter. Her brother had about seven or eight years on us, cleaned tunnels for the MTA. Their father was in Elmira and their mother had passed when Raven was six. After a few years with their aunt, the two of them were with Child Services. Their mother's sister didn't see herself fit to raise any children at the time, had her own demons. Raven felt outright abandoned by her aunt. Foster care was a dice roll and anything was better than the shelter. Her earliest memory, she had told me once, was something she didn't know to be real. It was her mother singing to her, a song she couldn't remember, and rain pouring outside.

"Maybe you do it," I said. "Put it behind you."

"The first time I tried I never even knocked on her door"—she meant her aunt—"I waited in the lobby for thirty minutes but I couldn't go up there. I kept thinking about the day I didn't see her anymore, and this lady who smelled like tree oil who took me away."

"You'll be ready someday. However long you need."

"What if I'm never ready?"

"Then you'll be old and stressed out," I said, half joking. She laughed; the song hitched in the wind, flew out over traffic, flew out over the waves and crashed. It tipped her over, made her steady herself in my arms. She looked up at me. My body was hot and I could smell my underarms, a sweetness that was swept up in the wind from the river. She stood in the light of

the descending sun, serene, looking out at the twinkling ferries, the Brooklyn Bridge.

BACK IN FRONT of the courtyard, we stood with Styrofoam cups from
the bodega. We mixed C&C Cola with liquor from plastic bottles her brother
bought and it always felt like a sugar rush, dripping slowly like a sticky syrup
or batter that warmed my face and the tips of my fingers. There were voices
bouncing from window to window, echoing above us. We followed the sound.
Everyone we saw ambled toward the park, heard in the air or ether or a
friend of a friend. Must've been a couple dozen people. A half-court scrim-
mage had unraveled into a cussing match. There was an anxious energy in
general—half-glances across the way, laughter mixed with hushed tones,
anxious waiting. Tristan was near the center of it, seated on a bench while
his cousin paced in front of him.

I let Raven sit on the only open bench, watched the playground crawl
and shape itself. There were high school girls in the middle of a step, pieced
together a routine from memory and what they could find on YouTube. Two
women held a conversation behind the parked hoods of their babies' strollers, watched as an older girl pushed a little one in a swing seat. Near the
pickup game, away from Tristan and his chorus, were folk playing HORSE
for money. There was a kid my age who was stocky, tattoos drawn in a backroom somewhere carved into his forearm and chest. His face was round, an
open vegetable you read. He walked toward the park exit, crossed the field
with his ear to a bulky Nokia phone. A car alarm went off.

I saw that Zaire watched from across the park among the wind nudging
the linden trees, the purring cicadas. Atop his head was a Ghostface mask,
which he pulled down as he walked toward us. When he walked up to the
boy, the one with the tattoos, he did so with his torso tearing back, caught
his victim with a fist to his face and it spilled open like a river. Wet snap, almost broke the jaw in two. The kid folded, blood mixing with dirt. Zaire got

low to the ground, struck the kid again. His hand was beating a drum, pounding the blood out of his head. For a moment he didn't budge, a still life of plum and flesh. The boys erupted in riot, eyes were red from the malt and cursing the sky. Tristan shouted from the other side and the set shouted back to him. They closed in on Zaire, hollered his name in victory. He was sinking into the crowd, grabbed from every which way. Still, Zaire broke away. They let him go, grew boisterous and went after the fleeing opps, raced out the gate and around the corner. By that time Zaire had already disappeared, toward the steelmakers and warehouses. I took off just the same.

THE EDGE OF the world. Across from the movie theater, east of the high-rises and abandoned train depot, was a series of roads with no sidewalks. I crossed the eight-lane boulevard and crept through the mouth of the street. There was a steep incline, the path leading, I thought, somewhere down below, underneath the dirt and concrete. Picketed fence ran along the grass, graffiti bombed and torn, rusted gates uprooted from brush and lopsided trees. I heard footfalls behind me and jumped, straining over my shoulder. Horses. Two cowboys, Black as hell, looked at me as they passed. The horses strolled beside the highway divider, each the color of red dirt.

There were houses that were once white, now with browned edges, others there were faded peach-colors and washed out violets. Some looked completely abandoned, foliage curling from under boarded windows and doors. There were homes that were gone, leaving only a concrete foundation in the middle of knots of old grass. Weeds and shrubs and thorny brambles crept through steel gates. Flocks of birds flew from the cypress trees to telephone wires, their songs echoing through the dead air. The sidewalks disappeared, leaving only the asphalt from the street and the wild brush that grew from the fronts of abandoned houses. The ones folk lived in had gardens or shrubs full of daisies. On a far corner there seemed to be a home that doubled as a daycare. Kids filed out toward their parents, rode tricycles in uneven circles

The Hole was a neighborhood close to the water table, practically under sea level. It held water like a bowl and flooded every chance it could. Families lived here until they couldn't, often going months without safe water or sewage. They packed their belongings and fled somewhere else outside the grid. The city didn't know which way to carve it and couldn't decide if it was a part of Queens or Brooklyn, if it was in Lindenwood, Ozone Park, or East New York. Most likely, no one wanted the blame of upkeep, wanted the guilt of this massive failure to its citizens.

Large tracts of corn-flowered reeds. Lost in a pit of both was a gray Lincoln with no windows. Above it stood a spreading willow tree, green tendrils reaching out every which way. I walked up to the porch of a sinking house. It still felt damp, mold pulling and pushing at the insulation inside the walls, the corners of the ceiling, the floorboards. Wasps stirred above, nests somewhere nearby. Moved from the foyer into a living room with what seemed to be a kitchen straight ahead and a set of stairs that were split down the middle. I peeked up, over the cracked railing, into a dark landing that seemed to be incomplete. Shadows hurried across the wall. I heard footsteps. I imagined I was invading someone's privacy, quiet as it was. Someone I couldn't see, a moment from long ago that I was now a part of.

This time, the footsteps were real. I turned and left the house, out to the porch and found Zaire. He stared at my feet, smoke coming from his knuckles, pulled at a cherry of fire that blinked and turned to ash.

"Nice place," I said.

"Thought about seeing a movie. Came down here. My family used to go see the horses every now and then. I never really liked the smell." He passed me the blunt, the smell heavy and sweet. "Cops don't come down here. No one comes down here. Everyone acts like it doesn't exist. They bury bodies back here. The mob. Gangs. Cops. In the landfills, around the shores. This whole place is a giant plot. A burial. What can live in that?"

The smoke was hot in my mouth, my throat, made me cough from somewhere deep in my gut. Blood rushed to my head.

"He said they could help." Zaire took a pull. He meant Tristan. "My dad needs it."

"So that was initiation?"

He didn't answer. I looked across at him, his eyes like black glass and I could see lights in them, maybe a light from the houses or the diner across the six-lane. An airplane seared the sky, headed to JFK down the road, it's engine breaking the air like thunder.

GRIEF HAD A presence about it. It was messy. Big planet-sized grief, a moon and the stars anchored above, rounding the sun to keep it in place. Zaire and I watched *Juice* and *Paid in Full* for about the fiftieth time, wiped the bootlegged DVDs down in rubbing alcohol when they skipped. He slept on the sofa, soon as his head rolled back. The shelves rattled when someone out in the hall slammed their door shut and pounded the floor like a troop barreling out of the building. My stomach called out. I closed my eyes, tried to ignore it. At my center, my very empty center, was a hole that didn't lead out to the other side but into nothing. The way the hole made me notice my body and its lack, made me realize I hardly noticed it at all. It brought me to a mirror, took my hands under my shirt, led them across my stomach, my ribs a shell or like the receivers on those old microphones Sinatra would use. My belly groaned again, this time a spring under the earth. The hole led no-where, the cracked core of a planet. On my desktop, I went through the links on Naima's page. Her blog was gallery shots and essays:

> Adrian Piper, in her essay "The Logic of Modernism," states
> there are four interconnected properties of European/Western
> art: appropriative nature, self-awareness, social awareness,
> and formalism. She asserts that formalism, more specifically
> Greenbergian formalism, doesn't seek to usurp the other properties
> until it reaches the cultural climate of twentieth-century

postwar America, where it becomes the underpinning of an argument that wishes to limit social function in visual culture, an extremely powerful medium, through methods of devaluing and differentiating. It becomes the theoretical appendage for "art for art's sake," in its obsession with its formal qualities and composition. A binary is formed between what is valued as high art and low art.

Formalism, as Piper describes, "is a direct consequence of its appropriative character," since value is placed around content that seems more abstract, disinterested, and detached—free of meaning. The formal properties became content, rather than the value being derived from what the formal properties represented. However, this conscious deflection of meaning presupposes that our "primary cognitive concern as human beings, regardless of cultural context, is to discern meaning." Most of what we think we are defining or gaining meaning from is already organized within an institutionalized structure complete with inherent goals and practices.

This is the reason the works of the diaspora are often neglected by the canon, because of its presumed social agenda and is therefore seen as propaganda, or not art at all. The rationalization that political content was incompatible with the "higher purpose of art" acted as a form of self-censorship among artists. This acts as a political program that hinders "the most powerful instrument of social change—visual culture . . ." reminiscent of McCarthyism and the discourse of the era from which Piper was writing in, which was the 1980s to the early . . .

I heard sirens from outside, a wail that only grew closer until it was all around me. Then it was gone. The television cast a muggy blue. It was harsh, felt like aluminum, watered my eyes in the dark. CW was on, the evening news. It used to be UPN—UPickANigga news, my dad would joke. Channel 9 was said to be for Black people. Tonight, community groups in the Bronx were fighting a private developer who bought up Kingsbridge Armory. Rising oil prices. The Democratic Party was broke. In California, a three-judge panel could address overcrowded jails, releasing tens of thousands of people, mostly likely Black and Hispanic. Miss Moore always went on about how the public school system was corrupt, in cahoots with private prisons. She said the number of prison cots were tied to and predicated on fourth-grade standardized test scores. I didn't know prisons could be private.

Someone upstairs didn't catch their door and your shelf rattled again. I slid a book from the middle, wiped it of dust and wood flakes with my hand. I folded it open, read *The Salt Eaters* again in the light of your favorite reading lamp. Across the ceiling the shadows took on shapes I couldn't recognize. I grew cold again, face slick with salt and I could tell you were near. I couldn't tell where so I searched the apartment, peering through your bedroom door. Nothing. Back in the living room, I stuck my hands out to find my way through the dark. When I walked past a mirror there was a flicker of silver. When I looked toward the light, there was no one there. Except Zaire. From the pullout sofa he stared at me, wide-eyed and yawning before lying back down, fully clothed under his blanket.

ON BOULEVARD DAY, that first Saturday in August, they cut off Van Siclen Avenue from Ashford to Stanley Avenues, police cars and roadblocks with beat cops working the corners. Nearly everyone would barbecue that day, and between the tenant association and the community center, or Zaire and his dad or the dozens of families who grilled in front their stone porches, on sidewalks, behind the gates in the school playground, a fog of smoke and spice hovered in the air above us all.

Zaire had left in the morning and returned at midday and beat down my door, to come from inside. He stayed at my house more often. He suddenly had money to give his folks, told them he'd gotten a job after school to help out. He kept a scale here, came with bundles of weed in the waistband of his boxers. We'd stay up all hours of the night, the apartment hazy from smoldering fronto leaf, watching movies or telling stories or looking at girls on Myspace and this new thing called Facebook. Every now and then he'd answer his flip phone and get up in the dark, his face wide and full of shadows in the blue light, slide out the door for what could be hours. I waited for what other violence would come, what could break the day open. The kids were on bikes, or ran after each other, weaving in and out of their parents' sights. They pet horses brought from the ranch less than a mile down Linden by the theater, where the land became swamp and marshlike, Black cowboys who kept it green and owned about six or seven horses. The slightly older children dived into the large, inflatable bouncy house that rocked from side to side as they launched themselves as high as they could. It was brought by Mr. Magic, who had a commercial on local TV, which made him semifamous to the kids who got their faces painted, or laughed at his balloon tricks. Us older kids gathered around benches along the sidewalks, around the courts, near the smoke from the grills. Those who could drive stood by their parked cars, cycling through stations or mixtapes they'd been handed near Jamaica Ave. or Broadway. Later they'd end up in someone's tiny apartment with all the furniture shoved into the backroom. People would walk in and out just to bum loosies under the tilted moon. I hadn't caught sight of Raven throughout the day. About an hour before her girls were to perform, Raven told me she was anxious. She wasn't sure the routine was good enough, or if the girls had learned it all the way through.

It was time—the girls swayed and jittered as Raven tried to wrangle them. When it seemed impossible, she told them to breathe with her, in and out until the music began and they began their count. It was a dance where their bodies became like butterflies and became bulls, spoke to the blueness of rivers, signaled to skies, bounced in harmony. Some of the girls forgot their moves but kept time, prepared for the next. Raven smiled at them, the ones who looked to her expectantly, some in their zones and staring down the crowd, Quay with her eyes closed like she was alone in her room. At the end everyone applauded, whistled and hollered as the kids smiled with triumph, swayed shyly with their hands behind their back. Quay bowed as if she had been used to such things, and rightfully. The kids all ran to their parents and Raven went off to speak to the head of the center. I stood around until she was finished. Somehow Zaire disappeared from my side, probably found someone familiar near the edge of the crowd.

DEVIL DON'T
NEED NO HELP

KEY (1991)

Nabokov wrote down his dreams, woke up every morning for years and jot-
ted them down in a journal or whatever he could find. He wanted to track
them out for days and days, watch the patterns, how they manifested themselves in reality, all the contradictions. He dreamed of sleeping with his sister, so I'm not sure what that said about his patterns, but dreams could be
a patchwork of memory and precognition, a prolepsis in time, could throw
what was up against what is and what will be. Time didn't move in one direction but was looping, the spool of a cassette tape being wound up with a
pen cap, recursive. Florensky talked about "the two worlds—visible and invisible," how "the border of their contact arises inevitably. It divides them
whilst also uniting them."

That day I saw myself doing the things I normally did: shit for work, shit for Mama and her fast-approaching game night at the center, running water over dishes, the safe jazz over the phone while I waited to speak to Medicaid about my premium this month. Couldn't feel the thump of the vein in my calf after climbing the steps to the elevated tracks. I only heard the train pass through a bottle, behind the air clogged in my nose and ears. There were pieces missing, moments that didn't seem connected but I was there anyhow, my body a bridge between the instances. I don't remember the ride uptown but I remember getting off the train at Van Siclen station. I don't remember speaking to a representative over the phone but I remember the music and hanging up and the dishes being clean. I wondered where those lost spaces went, if they belonged to me. What if it took me elsewhere and left my body to fend for itself, to fishtail toward my fate?

I ran errands to clear my head, hair tied up and in my running shoes. I got off the train a few stops early at Rockaway Avenue station just to walk down Pitkin Avenue. I hopped between store fronts. Girls who wore their names around their neck and ears in tiny diamonds, who shopped for Guess brand jeans and tattooed their mother's or daughter's name on their upper back, their necks. There were boys from up the block, deep into Brownsville, who kept two beepers at a time, who wore bulky Avirex leathers and sold freebase out their uncle or tía house. At the corner, the only credit union I knew of for miles. The street turned into a market, food carts and vendors that populated the wide avenue's sidewalks. Strangers could share moments at the booths, agree on bootleg cassettes or cologne boosted straight from the truck. They congregated, or walked by in stunning blue New York Rangers sweatshirts, Ralph Lauren rugbies, Jets snapbacks, messenger hats, Kangol hats, suede knee-high skirts, velour suits or just the pants set with one cuffed rolled up to the ankle. Simple overcoats or sweats, floral silk blouses or turtlenecks that stopped a hair below the jawline. Penny Hardaways or all-white Filas. The Pippens with the AIR on the side, or the Griffeys with the bubble at the bottom. Between the old players in Lincolns, the union members in dull Hyundais, the laborers in their Fords, were Range Rovers and boxy 4Runners with young guys hanging out the sides. The exhaust of the B13 blew in a fuss, spiraled along the leaning sidewalks. The Q8 could be heard from far away, a grumble from two corners down.

I figured I'd surprise my beloved a bit earlier than we'd planned. I picked up a few things from the supermarket, would make a meal for us. Couldn't go wrong with greens and whatever the nice man at the counter was cutting that day, weighed out by the pound. Today was flank steak. I needed to be anywhere but inside my head and sorting through a recipe was meticulous and painfully alluring. It better not spoil him, let him think he could just get a meal out of me whenever. He left me with a key not too long ago and I hardly took advantage. When I opened the door, I dropped the groceries I had picked out just for us.

Dante is dying on the couch in front of me, the folded limbs of a cricket stretching out recklessly. I see him retching, trying to speak, but all that can come out is the warble of fluid, a fevered drowning in the depths of a cenote or a pit down in the deepest cave. I stand for what feels like a long time. My mouth dries, tightening at its floor like a hitch or a knot. I force his name out of me, cough it up like dust. Water spring from the tender parts of this body; under my arms, down my spine, the corners of my mouth. Young and dying so fast, all a mess pooling around the wound, blood and flesh on everything. His jowls are shredded on one side, the long jaw I kissed and ran my finger-tips along now crooked, caked with salt and fresh blood, still running down his face, his neck, my hands, seeping through his rumpled shirt. The molars in the back of his mouth had exploded. What remained were pieces—dregs stained rust, flashed a gummy wince if I touched him wrong. Sweat and tears made his face a slick mask, mingled with the dark red dripping from his goatee. I stare at the breaks in the skin, the one in his shoulder and one below his collar, the size of a dime. My throat is dry but all I keep saying is his name again and again, no one around to keep me steady. Try to soothe his moaning, look at his pink-rimmed eyes, the tears running along the fis-sures where his skin would fold and smooth. The tears join the blood like a slick leather muzzle. A siren catches behind the window and brings me to the phone. It couldn't stay put in my hands, sliding from the bone, the cradle of my cheek and shoulder slick with sweat. I jab the key tones, smear them with blood. "Hello, 911? I have, I need, could you? 897 Schenck. Victim? Yes, he's—" I turn to him.

Nothing. The couch was empty, the air undisturbed. I clawed at the spot that was suddenly dry and plain, bereft of the actual, failing body I felt covered in. The phone filled the room with faraway cries until it went dead, felt useless grazing my leg, slipping from my palm.

I threw up in the toilet. A soupy bile collapsed me, kept me close to the porcelain, not a thing to hold to, recoiling from the tremors rolling through me. Violent hiccups knotted my stomach and ribs. When the last of it seemed to jump from me, floated around the bowl with its pale color, I lay on the rug sweating and cold. I couldn't open the door, couldn't risk seeing him there as real as moments ago, a wrecked body, the twisted joints of an arthritic hand. I was terrified. I lay next to the toilet curled up, half on the plush rug, the other on the cold bathroom tile, angled stiffly beneath the sink.

TWO WHITE GUYS walk into a bar, one German and one French. It'd probably be more like an auditorium or large hall, but a bar works better for the joke. They talk about time. They bicker. The German believes there is time the way our bodies recognize: our calendars, the excited plans we make on the weekends, the alarm clock we beat into submission every morning. Then there's time as it exists in our heads. Why getting out of work on a Friday feels like the day holding on kicking and screaming. How a train ride from Brooklyn to Harlem could be instant, so much so that you're racing out the closing doors when you realize it's your stop. How a night could shrink and expand at the same time like a dying star. The French guy didn't take this well. He thought it strained time of its nuance, its inherent connection to us. We were a part of its very definition.

Dante must've found me in the bathroom and carried me to his bed. It doesn't go away. Some days, deep in the tightness of my stomach, the anxious rush of blood to my ears, I felt life sitting outside my body. I was removed from it. I could just throw the whole thing away. I woke up on blue days and gray ones, felt it wasn't worth getting out of bed; there was nothing I wanted to do beside lay naked and sprawled, thinking only of the static murmuring from the radio.

I asked Ms. Pat, veneration of saints, to come and guide me, explain what was going on with me.

"Oh Lord," she said, "this child. What are you doing down there?"

"I don't know what's happening to me." I told her what I saw but I didn't need to. If time worked the way I suspected it did for her, which was that it didn't work and all the events were laid out in no sequential order, she may have already known this would come.

"So maybe he kicks the bucket soon," she responded. "Maybe."

"I wonder how I'm supposed to know."

"Some things you don't bother with."

"I shouldn't bother with none of this," I fussed. "What if I dump him and just wait it out? Meet an office scrub. Or a nice respiratory therapist."

"If that's what you want."

"You know it's not," I confessed.

"You can see those who have died through the years, at any time. What made you think you would never see ahead?"

"I should talk to the Oyster Woman."

"Cara? All she do is talk in riddles," she complained. "I don't got the time."

"I think you got plenty time, sis."

Dante was out in the living room, on the phone flipping through his vinyl collection. Prince's "Adore" was playing. I plodded in wrapped in his bedsheet, still a bit light-headed, hungrier than anything. He wore a loud Sergio Tacchini windbreaker with the track pants to match. Said he had to go check Unique on Elton Street. In and out. I said I should go with him.

"I just found you passed out on the bathroom floor," he told me and I looked at my bare feet. "You should take it easy."

"You said you'd be quick."

"It's gon' be crowded, Key."

"I could be around people. I just want you in my sight."

"Do you want to tell me what happened?"

"I just felt dizzy, that's all."

"There's something you're not telling me."

"You don't have to worry about me, I promise." I told him. *You should worry about yourself,* I thought.

ON THE DRIVE over we were silent. He could tell I was hiding things from him, blatantly now, and I could tell he didn't want to push. Maybe cause he didn't want to be pushed when it came his time to hide things. We didn't talk about what we were moonlighting as, the abrupt departures, our beepers crying out all types of night. He didn't ask about whatever the hell I was doing and I didn't ask about the second beeper, the hushed phone calls, the bizarre errands he ran around the borough. But I should ask him. And I should make him ask me. How else would either of us get closer to the truth about one another? How else could we get to the truth of us?

Unique was out back, behind a two-family row house. The backyard offered us mangos and yellow watermelon, hands outreached, baiting us, welcoming. They offered us cocoa bread and wild rice, spoke to us in a tongue we've known forever, a music that changed with saltwater, across the Atlantic. Stopped in many places. Became an artifact, a map of no origin, only belonged to us and never belonged to us. The music playing farther behind the house could share in a pulse, a drum that changed with saltwater, with the swell Atlantic. Stopped in many places. Like our language, it belonged to us and never belonged to us. Some said they heard it from the bottom of the ocean, from shipmates who beat the same drum of insurrection. They leapt from aboard the ship in collective suicide while the overseers looked on. An uprising broke open this strange threshold, this vessel for capture and torture upended by self-destruction. Death and resistance become linked in what is the unthinkable of Middle Passage, the nadir of America, the sixties, crack and AIDS in my lifetime. The music becomes dangerous, is that same insurrection, and might be the same collective suicide in how we leap, how it desires to be, would rather self-destruct than be killed, over and over again. The music is a pulse out of a dance hall, the deejay who talks fly over the drum, over the bluesman, sugar on high. It rattled the project walls, the frame of the Jeeps and MPVs, whispered to us from blocks away, made us search for the park it came from, the block party it made alive.

Raina in Southside Jamaica, Queens, who had the flyest sleeveless mink coat I'd seen, thrown over her leather trench and two or three rings shoved on each finger. She had the first name bracelet I'd seen, usually reserved for a necklace or a ring. Jackie Rowe had Fendi purses for days of the week. Seen her with Shabba Ranks at Love Peoples or the Q-Club in Queens, dance halls where many a night I was the only Yankee girl. Denese and Miss Dolly were both from Guyana and wore matching fits when they went out, either tight dresses with plunging backs or bodysuits under fur coats. Denese was from Vanderveer Projects and Miss Dolly came up on weekends from DC. They each had gold caps on their teeth and matching gold bangles around their arms. I loved Miss Dolly because of her accent, a DMW brogue, telling me about the scene down there while her cousin popped fly behind her. Ana was the first chick I saw get busy on a motorbike, right down Franklin Ave. Sometimes she'd tie a Panamanian flag on the right-hand grip. She'd tear up Ebbets Field, wore a huge gold piece on a Cuban link that dangled out her jacket. Nelly G, a fellow booster, they'd say, kept a pair of bamboo earrings, pyramid-shaped pendants, and diamond-encrusted rings. The best who ever done it, did it, I don't know. She lifted pieces and sold them at a slight discount. Her favorites she took up to Harlem, to Dapper Dan in his storefront, had him cover them in Fendi or Gucci monograms. There were the Amazons: Evelyn, Mama, Lady Outlaw, Lollipop and her sister, Callita—the Lady Homicides. They were an arm of the Crazy Homicides, started out in Coney in the eighties, giving women, but very dangerous. The Outlaws had factions spread across the city, mainly in Coney and the East, with influence in Park Slope and Sunset Park.

Dante knew Unique but I knew his wife, Deb. They never worked together, Nique the purveyor of the blocks between New Jersey Ave and Dumont, his domain of thin row homes and brick walk-ups, but would exchange stories, trade secrets even, talk up themselves and their dead and each other. Deb and I needed a drink, tall wine coolers or daiquiris, traded stories we'd heard or seen around. There were girls who got caught up, in over their heads, ended up holding the short end of the brick, their doors kicked in and rooms overturned, then chained and jailed, or their children taken away and thrust into group homes, pulled from their leases with NYCHA and forced into their mother's homes, into shelters, out of state. All 'cause they were swept up in a man and what he had going, swept in his orbit, colliding with forces one can't ever control. People walked in and out, their skin streaked and sweating, heaving for air. Everyone was bumming loosies, rolling chocolate or arie in brittle tree wrap. The floor was stained with beer and cigar guts. When I stepped back inside a crowd had gathered near the back. I could hear the series of conversations over Lady Saw, over the smoke, angry with malt. We swayed our hips. I had looked over the divide, begging to be recognized. Then, like a hole poked in an airless room, the music gathered us up and we sang along.

We bare the histories of violence like a skin. We wear it on us, put it on like a slip, and wear it for all to see. Sara Ahmed talks of a history that is still. The moment before the wind gusts and sends the leaves to scatter beneath our Adidas or Doc Martens. Our foremothers had their bodies marked for violence, were reminders of toil and burden, but also resilience and delight. I felt connected to them, saw them clear as the woman next to me, the experience of violence across space-time that bonded us all. It was embodied, the moment ineluctably connected to this flimsy state of present, to other moments, the other times, other worlds.

I am invigorated by them, brought alive by the sound and by the heat and how the body can shine under the moon if you sweat enough. It all seemed too fragile. I walked down a narrow hallway, back over to Dante. Over the music, he asked me what's wrong.

"I can't do this," I told him.

"We can leave."

"No, I mean this. You and me."

He stared at me for a long time, perhaps replaying my voice in his head, the collection of tones that made up language, just to be sure of what he had heard.

"We should go home," he said eventually.

IT WAS UNFAIR to question Dante about a dream, about something that may or may not even exist, stalking my mind with him in actions that may or may not occur. I confronted him anyway. "No, Key," he told me. "I don't know what you saying at all." He reminds me of my mother. It's the stubbornness, the way he breathed in his sleep, the presence of his shadow. He sat back down, next to me and I could feel the heat of him, trapped in his shirt and beneath his belt.

"Where's this coming from?" Dante asked.

"I don't know how to tell you."

"Be honest."

I didn't know how to organize it at first. I told him about the shore and Ms. Pat and her son. I told him about Treasure's baby and how he would be dead in a few years and Stephanie's mother and whatever else poured out. I told him about my dreams, the reach and scope of them, how I fell between the timelines and could see life every which way. He just sat there, staring at me, then his knees the whole time. I put this on all him and I knew he thought I was crazy or making excuses. I was just another paranoid girlfriend he'd realize and march out the door. He'd tell his homeboys how crazy I was, how I woke him in the middle of the night because I had a dream of him gone. *These broads, man*, one would say before a collective sigh. It was really harmless. We might wake a man up in the black of night, go through his contacts and pager, key his car or melt his sneakers, but that was harmless. A jealous man might keep his woman at home, threaten her. Women who were killed are usually victims of their boyfriends or husbands in a fit of rage or jealousy. I told him about the vision I'd had hours ago.

"It wasn't like I just seen you dying. I was there," I said, couldn't mask how it shook me. I made to get up but he touched my hand before I could.

"A ghost?" he asked, a whisper in his empty apartment.

"It's more than that."

"What does it feel like?" He asked.

"It's like I exist all at once, but I can't keep up."

"It's not about you keeping up. You're not living your own life. Otherwise, what does any of it matter?"

"You must be afraid of me."

"Why would I be scared?"

"People fear what they can't explain."

"That's not my future," he said. He was sure. He leaned toward me and kissed me, delicate at first. Then he pulled me on top of him. "I'm supposed to live in this life with you," he breathed into my neck.

I learned to make a home from my mother. I fill it with the things I know, what is familiar. What she showed me. Cabinets of laminate made to look like white walnut, filled with cans of red beans and black beans and corn stacked in rows, concentrated milk with pull tabs, Cream of Wheat in nearly collapsed boxes, sacks of brown rice, the stove with iron grills and rust creeping up the bottom. The fridge was white but marked with fingerprints. Inside wasn't full, wheat bread and cold cuts and a watermelon cut open and in saran wrap scattered, jars of relish and cucumbers and bulbs of garlic. The tomatoes were left out on the bottom shelf until they began to wither and dry. There were stalks of spinach and green onions. Mama always kept her eggs in the refrigerator so I do the same. In the freezer there were fruit I'd thrown in just before they softened, in freezer bags, tubs of almond butter ice cream, stacks of raw meat with blood frozen and hardened around the edges of their separate containers.

Would you still accept it, if you knew how love would end? If you went forward in time somehow and saw the length of your lives together. Every bit of goodness, every bit of ache. Would you watch in a grainy stupor, gum-stuck tongue dry in your mouth, your lover and the worst of themselves come alive like a monster you don't recognize because you, not the future you, but the present you, haven't known this part of them? Would you peer at the rawest parts of you? The red and pink slop, your messiest, your most vulnerable. Would you refuse to unsee, to know everything, no matter how dangerous it could be? Would you shake from the warm violence of being here, and there, in every moment, aware of every moment, for however long this thing, this could-be relationship lasted? Eight months? Three years? A lifetime? Could you carry eternity with you, heavy and writhing and pulling you with it?

I know he'll depart. We are kindred. He is a wanderer who searches for a home in many places. When that place is no longer home, he packs his things and leaves. But he won't physically leave. He'll leave in all the ways that matter. That can be worse. He'll hold on to our laughter under the fire-light, the shapes we made in the dark of our bedrooms. He'll want to feel that again, want it back in the middle of a war.

It will be a night where the rain is pounding. He will leave me in bed for the fog outside, downstairs where I can't see him. And I will hear it. An exchange, a scuffle, and finally the report of a rusted piece. I'd hear him stumble through the door, hear the sofa legs scrape against linoleum when he lands. But I am prepared. I will come out and see him as I've seen him before, my beloved, a bleeding heart soaked in rain.

'96 FLEETWOOD

COLLY (2010)

My dad and I are bound together by a terrible secret. What he did isn't much
of a secret. Ma, I'm sure you knew; I'll tell it, to absolve myself of never saying a word. It's more of an unspeakable thing, would cause more harm than
good, wasn't my place to say, a whole host of reasons I've come up with. Keeping a secret implies some allegiance to the person one is keeping it for. It had
been three years since you passed, since we had all been cast apart. We now
circled each other from afar, nebulous, floating to far corners of a galaxy,
star systems light and years away. Toya would call and tell me to come stay
at Nana's every two weeks, or I'd stop by and give them money from Pop.
Some days after school he'd show up out front, or even let me walk all the
way to the subway entrance before he'd holler my name, tell me to pay attention to what was around me.

We were cursed from the beginning.

Nana lived all the way down Flatlands, past the car wash, the baseball field, the mega church (which seemed like Mecca, in the middle of a barren sand that went for yards and yards), down East 108th, in Breukelen Houses, the housing project named for our borough's very first name in the nineteenth century, a Dutch term meaning "broken land." You can't make this stuff up. My great-aunt Joyce had her own room; Toya shared with Nana for the time being, ever since Joyce's daughter, Fabienne, had moved in with her two children, and I was on the couch. Fabienne kept all of them in the backroom with her and her boyfriend, Dude. Both cousins terrorized the narrow three-bedroom, often spilled out into the hall and into the small playground out front. Today, I woke up to Dude hovering over me, eating cereal from a Tupperware container.

"Can I help you?" I asked him. Dude said nothing and made his way into the kitchen. Needless to say, it was way too crowded.

The blue morning was becoming hot. In the kitchen, Nana's voice rose above running water and the scrape of pans. Long-legged rays of light stumbled through the curtains of the apartment. When I finally rose, she was setting plates. I missed the crackle of grease in a pan, the haze it cast throughout the kitchen. It reminded me of mornings we'd spent together, before you rushed us to school and you caught the 7:13 bus to Rockaway Parkway. We'd toss the house on its side, scatter our clothes and shoes, crossed each other in the bathroom, ran pomade through each other's curls until we decided to rub it in ourselves. The morning radio stations played under the morning news and I would bang on the bathroom every morning for Toya to finish up. When we were young, I'd walk in sometimes, brush my teeth while she showered under steaming water. She claimed one of the very few perks of living in housing was "they couldn't charge mama for hot water." Then, in that fishbowl of our kitchen, the sunlight cast through smoke from fried eggs and meats, everything was cast out and you would sit down with us, speak to us in that steady voice that made me lean against every word. Your words drew me out, made me present, as not to rush over the meaning of what you just said, what you would say. I wanted that back, that moment, collected in particles, dust in the light. I wanted you back. Nothing could be the same without you, Ma.

"She's inviting that so-called father of yours," Nana informed me. Toya's graduation was a few days out, a frenzy that capped off her string of college acceptance letters and her subsequent decision to go to SUNY Buffalo in the fall. I'd be a junior in September and Nana was already giving me Toya's old college brochures.

"You never really liked him, did you?" I asked. It was less of a question, an observation I'd have to be blind to miss.

"How could anyone? Leaving you kids there at the worst time. Doesn't matter if it's work. He hasn't been a father in years."

"Even before all that. You never really liked him."

"Some people just make the wrong choices."

"Yeah, but don't people make mistakes?" I asked, and Nana whipped around to me.

"Some people choose to," she said. "Over and over again until the people around them . . ."

"What's going on in here?" Toya said from the archway of the kitchen. Nana was scraping eggs from a pan onto separate plates, stirring in the bits that browned at the edges; I looked at Nana, feigned a baby's look of confused apology, and she grinned, shook her head, and asked Toya if she was excited for tomorrow.

"Am I? I started packing a week ago." She still had another two or three months in Brooklyn.

"A college girl. Your mother only did a semester or two at City, that's about it."

"What did she study?"

"I don't think she knew. She didn't really want to be there."

"Did you ever think about going to college, Nana?" Toya asked.

"No one really told me I should go," said Nana, taking a pot of grits off the stove top and pouring some in our bowls. "Different times. We never got the colorful pamphlets from schools when I was young. You should be excited, my love."

"I am," Toya sighed. Looked around the kitchen. There were crooked plant beds and vinyl cabinets that didn't close. The fridge was peeling at the edges and the washing machine was stuffed in the corner, flooded the sink sometimes. "I just hate leaving you here. And Lord knows what Colly is up to. I know he won't visit you."

"I'll be here all the time," I said.

"What if something happens and I can't be here for you?" Toya asked, ignoring me.

"I'll be fine." Nana was old. Older than I remember as a child, but I wasn't really a child anymore. Now, I could see the lines buried deep in her face, how slow she moved about the kitchen.

"Then I worry about you in this building. Who are those boys who are always coming in and out? All hours of the night."

"Those young men are the sweetest. Why don't you stay here, Colly?" asked Nana. She cut her waffle as if it was a passing thought.

"Here?" I asked, answered *where else* in my head.

"Stay with me and Joyce. These folk'll be out of here in the next few months. You won't be by yourself in that apartment. I'll teach you how to play spades. I'll cook for you and you won't fade away before our very eyes."

"I'll think about it" was all I told her.

OUTSIDE, TOYA AND I marched up Flatlands, past the bus stop on the corner. The day had turned to wet dust, hot enough already and wanting rain. The sun tried to light the pavement, was covered by clouds and haze, a closed fist—inescapable. We walked through the gray, empty stretch of industrial park, across the old train tracks toward the new ones.

"You're so annoying," she pouted. I looked at her, confused. "Why would you upset Nana like that?"

"What do you mean?"

"'You never really liked him, did you,'" she imitated, deepening her voice and sticking out her jaw.

"Am I wrong for wanting to know why?"

"No," Toya said. "There's other ways to go about it. He was never the best husband."

"But we were in that house. They loved each other."

"Love is different for everybody. If I learn to love over here, and you learn to love over there, who's to say our love will be the same at all? What if my love needs something yours doesn't?" By extension I suddenly felt as if my love was ugly, a messy storm that could only destroy.

"Both of you sound bitter," I said.

"You're just like him." She sucked her teeth. Just like Pop. That's who she meant. I wanted to say I wasn't, and then I wanted to ask how. Instead, we just stared at one another, around each other. Then looked away. My eyes skipped down to my sneakers. Her bus was rounding its final bend.

"Junior's later?" she huffed.

"Yeah," I said begrudgingly. "Whatever."

"You're buying the cheesecake," she yelled from behind the exhaust of the bus.

On the train, I watched the neighborhood unravel, reach out to the rest of the island we were on. I watched the creases of green in those hills of brick and gray slab. There was lead everywhere; in the tap, in the smoke that billowed from giant chimneys. My mouth was becoming a trap full of things I couldn't hold on to.

WHEN I CLOSED my eyes, I often thought of what life could be beyond the city. I thought about a great blue sky, me rolling through the hills, the pastures, the cliffs of Appalachia, and the chilly dust bowls of the Midwest. I flew over the homes, the twinkle of hearths and televisions through the blue dusk. I followed above the interstates, old scabs or flowing veins carving the ecosystems that grew from it, around it. Gas stations and dollar generals, malls with empty parking lots and hotel chains. Mornings where the sun is winding through the mountains of the northwest, the colors of the pines a vibrant contrast to the gray overcast. The Pacific Ocean would open up, not like the muddy slosh around New York, but an intense blue.

I longed to be in that car, my father's burning headquarters, where the sun made it hard for my bare legs to touch the leather seats of his 1996 Cadillac Fleetwood. The sun crumpled his face up into lines and rolls, gleamed off his bare head. It led the way for winding highways that he promised led somewhere, roads that only seemed to finish when his cassette tapes came to an end and I had to listen to him rewind them. The sun would sink lower, behind the trees and gas stations and signs that read BALTIMORE and RICHMOND. It would chase my backseat window. Then it set and took all the light with it. A shard of dull light and the curve of my mother's hip. A rush of anxiety came to me but I didn't move. Instead I began to understand a few things. I was lying on a bed with sheets, which meant I was in someone's home. The music around me wasn't coming from the Cadillac's stereo. It was a warm, deep, lush sound.

I don't remember anything more: whose house I was in or what state we'd stopped in. Pop was running his hand over the outline of my mother's hip. I remember hearing a woman with a deep voice who spoke with a thick drawl. It wasn't my mother. She and my dad would laugh in hushed tones, as if what they were laughing about was a secret to the world, low and dull, the fuzzy stuff you hear in an old record. It wasn't you.

MY DAD NEVER tilled a field, or came into an acre or so of land and built a house from the pines and oak around him. Never did he wake up at the break of dawn if he didn't have to, or ride into town with crop to sell. He did work with his hands. My uncle owned a company that hired workers and outsourced them to different construction projects. I went with him to fill his prescription. Every third Saturday of each month, I would ride with him; Broadway was full of life, Haitian cafes, and Dominican diners lined the street for blocks on end, the smoke of paella and tortas, the air tinged with grilled lamb from the halal trucks. Flags hung out the windows of Romanesque row houses and a few Beaux Arts brownstones. The doctor's office was a parlor on the first floor of an apartment building, the nice kind, under a lush green awning with the street name in script, where the intercom worked and everyone's last name sat neatly beside their bell. I'd wait in the car because he had parked in a NO STANDING zone and he didn't want to get a ticket.

The wheel would shrink in his big hands, his limbs heavy as burlap sacks of flour or sugar. It was hard to locate who my father was today, how the map I had of him spread entirely too wide and I could be lost in the rainforests of South America, or the bush somewhere in Africa. I thought he held some truth, something from his days as a cowboy, his frontier slate and narrow streets and subsidized housing. In the rumble of his voice, which I felt from the bottom of my seat, there was something he kept there that I would need. So I listened in the front seat of his Fleetwood, the inside the smell of gas station fresheners and distressed leather. I'm not sure I had the desire to live up to his expectations. Most of us, boys and girls without our parents, had written them off, cast them out of our heads with a brick or concrete seal, thought them intolerable or abusive or worse, broke. We couldn't mourn behind the bars of our windows, couldn't shoot around the courts or the yard in a breathless longing for ghosts to emerge from abandoned buildings or county or the very earth itself. Who could mourn when survival meant pushing through?

"You smoke cigarettes?" I shook my head and Pop pulled a lighter from his pocket. "Good."

"They're bad for you," I told him.

"You're right. Somehow my uncle smoked Basics his whole life and lived eighty-five years."

"You're supposed to tell me it can kill me."

"Do you need me to tell you what you already know?" He was teaching me a lesson in his own right, one of independence and self-efficiency. Still, I could hear Zaire's mom beating a dead horse, telling him more than once exactly what she thought.

"You could sometimes."

"My dad made us figure it out," he said, taking a long pull from his Newport, "let us bump around until we found the light switch. He ran a numbers ring half the time, him and a crew near Cityline, all down Pitkin Avenue, from Brownsville to damn near every corner of East New York. He'd go door-to-door, jotting numbers on anything—his hand, his sleeve, newspapers. He did rounds through the chess games in the park, yelled through the gates of the courts. He'd get crumpled up bills through the fence. He cleaned out the laundromats. He even hit the churches Sunday morning before service. Get 'em before they give they money to Jesus, he'd say. The old ladies at the senior center loved when he visited. He'd talk them out of their domino money."

I almost smiled, the thought of my grandfather putting on a charm to pull folk into his con. I saw it with Pop in flashes, wondered how it ran dry and skipped me.

"Then the laws kicked in and the state wanted their cut. He came home after some time. Started dealing heroin." These were things my father would begin to say but then wink at, hesitate and tell me "when you're older." He kept his eyes ahead. My grandfather died long before I was born and I had only color-burned photos in an album and moments like this one to imagine him.

"Any girls I should know about?" Pop asked, glanced at me this time.

"Nothing serious."

"And you're using protection?"

"I am."

"Did you need me to walk you through it?" He asked, and I scrunched my face up, shook my head. "All right, then."

We ate chicken from a soul food counter and I watched him, flakes of gold falling from a drum into his plate, let his slice of white bread soak in hot sauce. We drove down Remsen Avenue, behind school buses and cabs. He was telling me about how easy this generation had it, chewed his food with his mouth open. He spent most of his time now explaining himself to me. I didn't know why. It wasn't like I judged him any worse than Toya or Nana.

The dollar vans were their own fleet except they were their own entities. They took home what they took home at the end of the day, did laps from one end of Flatbush to the other, yet they all worked together. If one driver was full, they'd kindly hook up their friend not far behind. They yelled, slowing their vans, but never really stopping—hovering around a spot, an acute eye for street signs and parking regulations. They drove Chevrolet Express vans or Ford E-150s. They kept a string on the handle of the door, pulling it closed as soon as the passenger got both feet out the door. One van pulled up behind us with Capleton turned up so loud it rattled the frame; "*Sense did a giveaway like dem never get a pence.*" A man got out of the driver's side and walked to our window. Keith wore a necklace weaved blue, yellow, and black, the Bajan flag, under a gold one. He was the color of a coconut shell, shirt unbuttoned with a ring of sweat around the collar. He spoke with his cheeks sunken and lips forward like he was hitting a cigar.

"Dante, what's the word?"

"Blessed, blessed. How you?"

"Ah, you know. Tryna keep the business right. These yellow taxis would never even take you across the bridge, now they're all down the parkway."

"Maybe it's the arena they're building," my father wondered.

"By Atlantic yard? They been claiming that for years. Ain't building no stadium in Brooklyn."

"I'd love to be on that job. Steady work for at least two years."

"And make this borough more expensive." Keith sucked his teeth. "I had to raise my prices the other day."

"So a dollar van ain't a dollar no more?" My father asked.

"It's one fifty now," Keith signed, shaking his head. "Just don't have the same ring to it."

"This is my son, Colly."

"How are you, young man?" He reached inside the car, across my dad, and shook my hand with a sweaty hand. "You got your dad's shoulders. You a ball player?"

"Not really, sir."

"He's always reading. Or on that computer."

My father got out, followed Keith to his Ford. I turned the radio up and flooded the car with music, the low ends charged with static. Realized the pills were gone, stuffed in Pop's jean jacket at the last minute. Was he sharing them with Keith? Did he sell them? Ms. Betty had told me about him back in the day but I couldn't see it. I thought everything was right there on the surface. Pop was entirely consistent, only one setting on a dial, an oven that could only simmer. I remember a couple years back, under the train station and its elevated tracks, a few older boys from across the boulevard jumped me on my way home, took my money and an iPod I won at a raffle at the church on a random youth night. My father and I drove around for almost an hour, his friend in the backseat who I mostly saw during their weekly spades game. When we found the boys, still haunting the streets, my father and his partner got out and swung their lead pipes until they cornered a couple of them. That night, hand wrapped around a weapon, scaring those boys half to death, I saw there was an entire well within him that I couldn't see down. He wouldn't let me.

As soon as Pop slid back into the driver's seat, Keith sped off. He turned the radio down before putting the Caddy in drive and pulling away from the curb.

"Don't you need those pills for your back?"

"I'm not in much pain these days."

"What about Keith?"

"He's not in pain either," he said, "or maybe he is. He knows people who are."

"People who can't get a prescription."

"Yes."

"So you're helping them?"

"It's not about that," my father said. "It's about taking care of you. And your sister."

"Are we broke?"

"Broke is money not being where it's supposed to be and they're taking it out of your account at midnight," he said, and laughed, peeled about a hundred dollars from the wad of bills, and handed it to me. He peeled another couple hundred and showed it to me. "Bills," he said. "With the rest, why don't we get Toya something nice?" We'd pick something out at a jewelry kiosk at the mall, a gold necklace with a nameplate. Pop held on to the little black box, said I shouldn't tell my sister about today and that it would be a surprise. She'd appreciate the gesture more. I had a responsibility to protect what could be cherished, our moments with each other, however small. This would be one of the many days I wouldn't mention to my sister. It was as if part of being a man was keeping secrets.

TOYA HAD SPENT hours in the salon the day before, hours of waiting, getting her hair washed and set. She got a pedicure, got new semilong acrylic nails that were white at the tips. Weeks before she had dragged Nana out of the house to pick out a dress and matching heels. The morning of graduation, she spent the better part of the morning in the bathroom, paced the house from end to end in her bathrobe and bonnet. Through the door, I heard Nana and the crackle and steam from the other side of the door, the mouth of a hot comb eating at grease, heard Toya hiss when it got near her neck or her edges.

Nana took a flurry of pictures, put Toya in a cab so she wouldn't be late for the dress rehearsal. The old woman took this time to oil herself, her elbows and forearms that looked firm enough to crack the shell of a walnut, combing her new wig. She got out one of her better wigs, a jet-black piece that stopped at the middle of her neck. I combed my hair out, let the coils snap and fall on my shoulders. I wiped them clean and then put on a suit I had picked out for a school dance. Nana had to take in the hem of the pants, a needle between her teeth with my leg in her lap. She couldn't bend or lean forward too much so I laid my foot across her lap.

"You ready?" she asked, walking out of her room in her Sunday best, a white-and-blue floral dress. Smelled of sandalwood and mango. I took a bit of Dude's cologne, sprayed the inside of my wrists, and rubbed them on my neck just as I'd seen him do.

"Yes, Nana."

Downstairs, my father waited with the engine off, windows open wide but his shirt damp where his skin folded.

"Hello, Dante," Nana said. "I'm surprised you made it."

"I managed to get some time off," he said with a smile. "Couldn't miss my baby's graduation."

"I bet." Her skepticism felt like a jab. The first I foresaw of many. We got in and Pop fired up the Fleetwood, filled the air with the smell of exhaust and unleaded. He drove up Georgia to avoid Pennsylvania, probably clogged with buses and folk late for work.

"So, what have you been doing with yourself?"

"Same as the past sixteen years, Audrey." She waited for him to continue and he sighed. "Construction."

"More hours?" she asked.

"Yes," he said. "I gotta make it up. Key made a good amount."

"Or spent it the right way." Jab number two. I didn't know what Nana meant but it felt like a haymaker. At this rate, Pop didn't stand a chance with nothing short of throwing the old lady to the ground.

When we arrived at the campus, we followed the shoals of relatives all funneling into the auditorium, found some seats as close as we could to where the graduates would be. I mumbled about taking some pictures and left them for Toya. She was out in the hall, lined up with her class along the bulletin boards and trophy cases. Immediately gave me her purse to hold.

"Them two wrestle yet?" Toya asked, holding herself up as slid a finger below the strap of her heel.

"No, but I'd give it time. Dinner, before the first breadbasket."

"You forget we have to ride over there," she reminded me.

"Nervous?"

"I always think I'm gonna fall on my face when I'm on stage."

"You'll be fine. I look up to you for a reason."

"Don't get sentimental." She dug her foot deeper into her heel. Then she hugged me.

As the graduates prepared to file into the auditorium, I made my way inside and shuffled through the wooden rows and relatives claiming seats before I found Pop's mountain of a build shoved into a narrow chair at the end. He saved a seat between himself and Nana. It felt like they hadn't said not one word until I arrived. Soon, the lights began to dim and the commencement began. A pianist began a melody as the color guard swayed toward the stage, flags steady in their hands.

In the old studio Nana had kept for years. Embroidered dishrags. Shelves of jars. Plates that hung from walls with pastures and sunrises on them. Her ankles filled with water. I could hardly reach the sticky countertops. Back then, Nana hardly seemed to frown. When she would fall asleep during her stories, sometimes I would poke her awake and the folds of her face would ease, reassemble into laugh lines. She did have another expression, a look where her eyes focused on one thing and her mouth opened slightly. I was never able to place it until I was older, aware of her suffering. Let me sit on her lap even though her legs hurt constantly. I'd sink heavily into them and she'd smile with her thick arms around my waist. I used to move like a gecko, bouncing from corner to corner. I leapt onto the plastic seats of Nana's sofa, flopped around like a salmon in a stream. Grandma cooked a lot, probably hoping the food would weigh me down enough to stop moving.

Toya sat in front of the TV, probably combing the hair of a doll or reading Goosebumps. I leaned over the arm of the couch and picked up my favorite vase from the coffee table. It was the color of pearl, empty with vines engraved around it. I tumbled it in my hands, letting the dust roll onto my palms. I bounced up to walk back over to but was oddly stopped. My feet were staying in one place but the rest of my body was still going forward— then downward. I stuck my hands out to break the fall—but the vase took the place of my hands and the room erupted the color white, bright and painful to look at directly. All Toya could do was scream. Nana leapt into the room suddenly, placed my hand in a bowl of ice and some water. When it kept bleeding, she wrapped it with a towel. There was a deep cut along the base of my thumb on my right hand. I cried hard until my stomach trembled from it. When I bled through her third hand towel, she decided to call a taxi. The whole time she cursed under her breath, the lines of her face like the edge of a razor. She took me to Crookdale, where we sat in the emergency room watching *Law and Order* until someone came by and gave me stitches.

I smiled now, put my hand over Nana's, her hands wide and soft. She rubbed my scar with her thumb, a smooth impression now, something she's done since that night whenever she held my hand.

"YOU SHOULD'VE TAKEN Bedford to Atlantic," Nana said out the corner of her mouth. We crept through traffic, a pileup so far ahead I don't know why you would go all around the world to take Broadway. The sky had finally cracked open; white, a heavy static. Pop drove with his shades and my eyes tearing, everything wet from the heat. The inside of the car smelled of sweat and hot leather. "Now this damn thing. We're gonna miss our reservations."

"There's no reservations at Olive Garden, Audrey."

"Well, who knows how long it'll take to get a table," she exclaimed. Pop's hands tightened on the steering wheel, held on for dear life. Toya looked at me, smug as ever, a damn Oracle of Delphi. I pulled at my damp, salty collar the whole way.

At the restaurant, we hadn't even ordered before Pop and Nana went back and forth over who would get the bill. My grandmother ordered a glass of white wine and let Toya sneak sips of it when the hostess wasn't looking.

"What do you want to do?" Pop asked. "The sky's the limit now."

Toya looked reluctant, but still she let her eyes wander the walls behind us, thought for a moment as a waitress came by with our bread. She took each of our orders and both Pop and Nana asked a hundred questions. What was the broccoli seasoned with? Was the chicken breast breaded or grilled? Where'd they get their fish? *The fucking ocean*, I wanted to say.

"I think I would want to be an educator," Toya said.

"I think that's great," Pop assured her. "So you want to help young people?"

"I do."

"Just like your mother, wanting to help. I always thought she wasn't just a doula, but a psychologist, life coach, a damn yoga instructor."

"She wanted to help whoever she could," Nana agreed.

Toya went on about what she needed before her big day, her second in a matter of months. Nana and Pop just stared, the browns of their eyes wet and floating.

"I thought I'd take you up there," my father said.

"Dana and her mom are already driving up."

"Tell them your dad will take you," said Pop, looking at all of us as if he was surprised this was a potential obstacle. "How long is it?"

"It's a four, five-hour drive."

"That's a hop, skip, and a jump. I can check up on you like that." He snapped his fingers.

"God no."

"Colly, road trip? We'll just pull up one weekend."

"Oh yeah," I let out, stuffed with garlic bread and butter. Toya was still, fork hovering over her plate like a crane left abandoned by its operator.

"I think the point is to give her space," Nana answered. "She has to come into her own. She'll be back during the holidays."

"I don't think a visit would hurt," Pop said. He looked at Toya the whole while.

"You shouldn't make promises you can't keep, anyway," Nana told him, and we all turned to her, making sure she had said what we thought she said.

"What do you really want to say to me, Audrey?"

"Pop—" I started.

"Have I ever disrespected you?" my father asked my grandmother.

"Depends," said Nana. I looked across at Toya. Families leaned over their meals, talked across booths as waiters slipped through aisles. At a table behind her, a birthday set off a brief applause. A joke from the next table sent a woman into laughter, hand on knee and leg pounding the floor. Toya would only stare at her plate.

"You think I ruined your daughter?" Pop asked.

"You could never."

"Let it go. She did."

"What could she do? She was raising your kids."

"We were raising our kids."

"Well, you're sure as hell not anymore." Nana had gotten considerably louder. I looked across at Toya again, almost pleading with her. "Your home is in shambles, and I won't sit around and let your kids rot in your self-pity."

"And she wasn't this holy saint-person you push onto my kids."

"Excuse me?"

"She was whole and beautifully flawed and lived a life you can't narrow just for your sake."

"You're the one keeping secrets from them, Dante. Why don't you tell your children what you really put my daughter through? Your lies."

"Key had secrets, too."

Suddenly, Toya let out something like a whine and a growl.

"I can't even get you for a simple question on an application," she cried. "But you think sending Colly over to Nana's to give me money is enough. Where do you go?"

"What kind of man leaves his children when they need him most?" Nana with the follow-up.

"I'll tell you," he was standing now, looking at Toya. "Just come outside with me."

"No," Toya declared.

"Please, baby," he said, almost begging. After a moment she got up and they walked outside. When I went to follow, Nana put her hand over mine.

"They need this," she whispered.

I looked at her, confused. Then I resigned, sat in my seat, picked at the Olive Garden bread. Through the window up front, I could see Toya looking up at Pop as he spoke, dug in his pocket for something, maybe a cigarette. I felt my heart hot and thumping against my chest and ribs, up my throat like it might leap out. Lay pulsing and bleeding on my dinner plate. I tried to think back to what happened, trace where the match was lit. I wondered what secrets Pops meant. His were simple, earthly things that I could touch, could see the damage done by them. What were you hiding, Ma? This whole family hid things from each other, from me, and you wonder why I never learned different.

When Toya came back in, she was alone. Her eyes were red and protruded more than usual. She plopped down in her seat, her knife and fork sliding from her plate to the floor, sending full stalks of lettuce and splashes of dressing all over the carpet. She didn't reach to pick them up.

"What happened to Dad?" I asked.

"I told him I'd like to celebrate without him," Toya said.

"Whatever you need, baby," Nana said, stroking her granddaughter's hair. My sister didn't make a sound. A tear caught the tablecloth, bloomed in the shape of daisies. Her fist tightened around a black jewelry box.

THE HOUSE WAS festive when we returned. Dude had put ribs under the flame, the bottommost oven rack. My great-aunt brought out the big pot, cooked enough rice to feed a small orchestra and still have some left over. "We literally just ate," I groaned.

"We didn't," she said, looking me up and down. "And you gon' eat some more."

When I cornered Toya in Nana's room an hour later, I asked her why she sent Pop away. All she could do was shake her head.

"He just leaves you in that apartment. Why do you try and hold on to him like it's normal?"

"What is it, Toya? There has to be something else."

"He cheated on Ma. There it is. He did it over and over and he lived and ate next to us like the shit never happened."

"I know."

"Nana told me. Said Ma must've lived with it to keep us all together."

"I saw it."

"Saw what Colly?"

"I saw the whole thing. And I just lay there like I was sleep. I didn't say anything."

"What are you talking about?"

"I thought we were with Ma. Then I knew it wasn't."

"So you never said something?"

"I thought it was a dream," I pleaded.

"You never told her?"

"I was a kid." I reached out to her but she stepped away. Shocked by her own resolve, it settled, and she stood by the door. Waited for me to leave.

That night, when I left Toya's room, the house was quiet around one in the morning. I laid awake on the couch and let tears warm my face until my face was red with salt, dreamed of Pop. Drugs stick to his heart like syrup dried on a shelf or counter in a flat, caramel bubble. His frame like an oak tree rooted for half a century. In my dream, I'd smell the bark from such a tree when he'd lift me in the air, to his neck, tobacco leaf and a room in flames. It made me warm. He'd drive me down a winding highway, a couple of cream sodas and biscuit sandwiches from a Texaco or Double Quick between us. I remember a two-family house split down the middle. It belonged to a woman they called Mother Earth. "What a beautiful boy, Dante. I can't believe he your kin," she would say. "Believe it." She leaned down to me so her face was level with mine. "And what would you like to eat, young sir?" she would ask me. She went barefoot most of the day, cooked for hours it seemed, till the house was full of steam. I'd walk the length of my dad's back with the balls of my feet, kneading the knots with my heels and toes while he groaned in relief. I asked him why he just ain't ask Miss Mother Earth to do it. "She too big for all that," he would say. I didn't want him to tease her because she seemed nice. And that was horrific, in my mind, in that moment, because it felt like betrayal.

The next morning was quiet, like hollow ground. Toya and I avoided each other gracefully, sliding from rooms as cats might when the other entered. I wanted to say anything, apologize, laugh about yesterday and Pop's white linen outfit. She'd place me with him, though, the same kind of liar she knew him to be. I didn't know Toya would hate me for years. Months from now she'd be home for holiday and wouldn't speak directly to me, but around me, across me. Nana had to have noticed but she didn't try to intervene. I wasn't going to beg her to talk to me. I was ready to let her see my apathy up close, how cold my divestment could be. Oh, you think I didn't care about anything before? Well, I got news for you, sis. But she didn't care, couldn't have. Over the rolling of the tea kettle, I'd listen to her tell Nana about college, the maple trees and tumbling green hills, her friends and their shiny new internships, the sorority she was considering, the Black Student Union she joined in the midst of their fight for actual diversity, not just a selling points for admissions and their endless supply of pamphlets. Her new life. I'd excuse myself to Nana, hop on Dude's PlayStation or head out to Green Courts. There were things I knew Toya would only tell me. That's what hurt most. She wouldn't tell Nana what the parties were like, what the scene was, how crazy the white folk were, how exhilarating and dangerous it felt at times to be Black and a woman on that campus. But I still knew my older sister as the little girl with missing teeth and two ponytail braids. Instead of playing games like house or having fake tea parties, she had baby showers with her dolls seated around her, gifting herself toys she already had.

THE CURSE OF HAM,
WE ARE WITH YOU, DEATH
IS NOT THE END

KEY (1991/2010)

I am misplaced, lost in moments I believe to be linear. The same place, different texture; my apartment, the wax shredded by grit, the moths gorging themselves on fabric. The walls are the same, only dirtier and more worn. I anticipate the tick of the clock but it doesn't come. He is there. The boy. Sleeping. He feels familiar in a way I know as a part of me. They doubt the women who raise boys, doubt the men they become. The men they'd become would be emotional. Soft. Maybe they should be softer.

Even in sleep his brow is tight, a knot of worry and intensity. I know what could be. The kind of place you retreat into until you see no way out. It was knowing vulnerability well enough to do away with it, to keep private or amongst friends. Life in a place like this was to know too much about everything. People like you and I keep this thing going, the American project. You see the cobwebs under the stage, the gears that make the curtains open, the ropes and smoke machines. You see what this world really is, what it can do to the best of us, how it protects the worst. Eventually you open your eyes, look up at me, look through me. You are afraid and it breaks me open because I would never hurt you. Eyes crossed, gaze just beyond what is in front of him. What life did he look pass to get to me, years away in this very doorway? Or maybe, what life have I gone past to get to you?

He didn't have language for what was happening to him, could only dream and wake with me reaching across. I want to speak his name, have it break through the sodden, temporal wall between us like the hook of a rod through the bass' cheek. I want my voice to soothe him, warm seawater around the ankles, a balm for his clammy skin that turned cold when he looked at me. He fills the room with funk because he couldn't stop sweating over the chill in the room. I want to lie next to you, let you know my own funk until you recognize it as your own, until I am familiar to you.

I want you to stand in the doorway I'm in, your fingers along the corners of the frame, your eyes on me but not on me, to a place tucked far enough to seek me out. Your collar wet and rung out. The wrinkle in your face isn't affliction, but stone. You are wild. How can I hate what you can become? Like any mother, I can only fear it.

JUST AS THERE are innumerable futures, there are many possible histories.

I see you again, on the floor of my home, curling up with what seemed like a stomachache. Behind that crooked doorway is water hushed still. Now his eyes stare off, unmoving, flat plates transparent in the light from my window. Why does he punish himself? I think about all the hurt I accrued through the years, bound at the base of my neck and at the bottom of my belly, chewed me out like tobacco dip until it was wet pulp. I think of Mama, who still walks around with her hurt, brings it to church, dresses it all up in nice things only to dress it down in a faded mirror. I think of my mother and grandfather. All this hurt was passed down and it will keep go-ing, ramifications down the timeline, wood splinter in blood that would dis-solve eventually, scar the capillary.

Is that why you were pulling me here? To see where this timeline goes? To change something?

I roam the house, years from now. It is fading into the gray slate it was when I first rented and spent years cleaning, scrubbing and hiding things. Marks on the walls with frames, grime-filled corners with philodendrons and Dracaenas. In the kitchen, the shelves are no longer filled with Heart of palm, queen olives, artichoke bruschetta, baby corn, Calabrian chili pep-pers, cauliflower, whole mushrooms, chicken gnocchi soup, manzanilla ol-ives stuffed with pimento. Instead it is instant ramen, tuna, brightly colored snack food, and fried spam.

I THINK IT will be worse for you. Mama said something interesting the other day. She said the world has changed more in the last twenty, thirty years than she's ever known. It would only get worse. I had gone over to her house to help her and Joyce prepare for the church luncheon. Joyce sold personalized dinners two nights a week. Friends and neighbors called in for a menu and she'd bring a container of fried chicken or whiting, vegan lasa-gna, barbecue pulled pork, and a choice of two sides, usually buttered rice, stewed potatoes, or sweet yams. This was her first large order. I told Mama she better get in where she fit in. When my aunt stepped to the back to take a call, I confronted her.

"I can see Virgil." She froze, looked at me, her own daughter telling her about her hauntings. "And I know you can, too. Why didn't you tell me?"

"Things like that you keep to yourself."

"How long?"

"Years after he died. You musta been about eight or nine. But Virgil is my haunting. No child should have to deal with a parent's ghosts."

"It's inevitable, Mama, it all adds up. From you to Grandma Lucy, all the way back then. Even if we don't know it. You might as well be honest."

"I'm being honest about it now."

"I thought I was crazy," I said.

"That's not what I wanted to do, baby. I just never, I just, I had to let him go myself."

I listened to my mother's breathing, the bounce of her heart. She was fussy, brow damp as she layered the flattened pasta.

"I see your father," she said. "And I stare at him every day 'cause I don't know how to make him leave this time. He sits in that ugly chair and doesn't say a word to me. Guess all of it stays with us. We're a family of ghosts, of half-living. I don't know what's really there, but I know it's real to me."

I SEE YOU now, Colly, at the foot of my bed, hands holding on to something, your head down and sunk between the bony peaks of your shoulders. I wish you knew I was here at this moment, in all the moments. It hurts to know I will leave you someday. I don't mean to. I only ever meant to love you, protect you as much as I could from a world I tried to make over, make better. As much as I could. That's all we can strive to do. But I decided this wouldn't be your world. These six blocks, this land of stone and burning metal, all the way down to the bedrock. I come to you, but little do you know you came to me.

And suddenly you are falling, pendant—then falling—into kingdom. Into a basin of diaspora, edging out of physicality, you feel everything. You look at your feet and your hands but what is seeing? What you have seen, we have seen and wept. And something tells you that you can see what we have seen if you really look. You are where we have always existed. Where *I* falls away from *You* and the welling you've felt all along, all from living, spills out. You are home, and we are with you. My hands reach for you, years from now, like always. I teach you to walk. They clam up, the hands given to me.

How else can I hold the heads of my children as they weep into me? They were given to me by my ancestors and the sea that claimed them somewhere between what is known as Africa and the Americas. I'd lost their names centuries ago until I named them myself. The building of empires made us into orphans. Not the product of a place, but a process of history, an inadequacy to cope with time as much as resources. Our origin is wrapped up in the mapping of what became the New World. The only thing that can be passed down is loss. The church will tell you your God can't look like you, can't see you beyond the curse of Ham, can't hear the water beneath the desert lines in your hands. The news will tell you that it is your culture that is depraved, lacking—and we are all waiting for the damn thing to implode. It is your habits, the attitudes of the women who gave you quarters out their purse, the skewed values of the men who bought you hoagies when you got them cigarettes. It is simply who you are. Governments will rinse the blood from their hands by night. By morning: the natives died from weakness, not genocide, and you sold your own into chattel slavery. The ivory tower will mock the mortals you raised to sainthood yet worship their own. They will worship what is rational as the only true thing, as an artifact of their brilliance, as shining examples of acuity. All they have given the world. To us. Weighing down the heavens with his vows, writes Virgil. Have me in the Kingdom of the Dead, carving out the rocky flanks of Cumae, through that cold, enormous cavern pierced by a hundred tunnels, a hundred mouths with as many voices rushing out. No golden branch or doves to guide me to you. I didn't want to have to go down to those mourning fields and come get you.

You'll be given a city emptied, cracked in half—the air will be full of lead and settle at the bottom of your lungs, pulling you down as you move through the world. You are living every moment of a place, every pain and joy. Being from a community means contending with the history of a space; it reflects every move, every choice you believe to exist in a vacuum. Every institution fails us until, finally, the land will too. Being a family just means we can't fail each other.

I have lived a life where you died in my arms. You reached out to me and I held you on the way down. You mustn't. When you reach across space and time I can only watch, inch away and hope you can let go.

I have lived all the lives so I could know what is possible.

I will meet you near the debris of the wrack line, kelp tangled around plastic bottles and glass. I will wait by an anxious tide, under a pale sky. The water is resinous, polluted from the soot of the steam plant near the coast. You feel like you don't have anything in this world, like it won't miss you back. But you understand the fire I put in you, a furnace you've fit your grief in. I want to tell you that you'll come out of this. You'll find something you love enough to make you get out of bed each day, something that will make you feel good enough to take care of yourself. You just have to find your way.

There is no celebration, no exalting of the children who return. Along our shore we await a home that hardly is ours anymore. Sometimes I feel as if we'll never leave this shore. Are we waiting for a sign? Are we afraid? It could be we know how. Maybe we belonged here, in America, deserved nothing more than to be exiled to this far corner of the world. Halfway living and halfway dying. Even in death we could not part with this place. We are a haunting.

I will wait for you by the shore, follow you into the dark to the end.

PART
THREE

OUR SCHOOL AT
SUNSHINE'S GROCERY

COLLY (2018)

Along New Lots and Schenck, across African Burial Ground Square. Across from the library, the repainted playground, and the old church with its ragged cemetery. I went to work on the garden in the mornings, at sunrise, before it became too dangerous to labor in the heat. I braced myself against the pile of compost with a foot sinking into the steaming heap and began turning the shovel. After a while, I flung what had accumulated to the side, shaking loose a banana peel. Then scraped more of the humus from the pile until it curdled, stuck to the dulled spade. Wet leaves stuck to the bottom of my sweatpants. As the heat from the mountain of rotten food wafted up to my face and neck, I swore the massive heap was breathing.

The garden was beside a house painted pink and blue and purple, a yellow sunflower painted on the side. In the back of the house was a shed covered in kudzu. Each floor seemed positioned differently, as if someone couldn't be bothered to straighten them. The whole thing looked as if it may tilt over for good. A litter of Dobermans played in the gentle stream of a hose. There were rows and rows of plants and vegetables, wire cages with a mother hen. I was in the back with the steaming heap of wood and rotten fruit. I wouldn't be here if it wasn't for Blue's soft spot for the place. Flies and mosquitoes buzzed merrily around the sweet haze that fell over the property.

The house took things. First, I thought it was the cats, strays the owner found and cleaned and now loped around the land. Whole, entire heads of greens vanished, along with tools, folders, smartphones, a host of other shit. And then there was Sunshine, who put me on edge. She owned the property and let Coop, the resident drunk, stay in exchange for his hands, sold her produce at farmers markets around the neighborhood during the week. The rest of the time the older woman sulked around, looked at us with discernment while she murmured sweetly to her plants. She took a liking to Blue, though. She read her palms, suggested roots to her she could put in her tea or when she took a bath.

Today, the East was dry and empty. It felt like everyone had up and moved, which wasn't too far from the truth. Around noon the heat was blistering; no amount of sunscreen could calm the skin. After pulling weeds, Coop's shoulder was a violent red, his skin cracking like jagged state lines along his tank top. Bumps full of pus grew from the skin until Sunshine took a safety pin, heated the tip with her lighter, and popped each one. I must've looked stricken. Something hit the chain-metal fence, causing me to flinch. Two boys. One dug a football out the bramble.

"You're from that weird house over there," one said. He had hair that was blown out on one side and braided on the other. Someone finished half the job.

"Yes."

"Everyone there smells pretty bad."

"If you saw the bathroom situation you'd understand," I said. They stared at me blankly. "How old are you two?"

"Eleven." They said in unison.

"Y'all go to school around here?" I asked them, and they nodded, suddenly disinterested. "Which one?"

"There's only one," the shorter of the two said. He threw the ball with a high arching spin. "We were headed to the store."

"I'll walk you."

There was hardly food for miles. Besides fast food. Every chain you could think of. A lot of what poverty is remains an assault on the body. One's right to exist. The right to access to healthy food. A lot of our problems came long before any storm. The grocery was bright, sticky with sweets and snacks, stalks of beef jerky and cans of whatever you could think of. There was milk, eggs, beer, and soda behind the sliding panels, beside a freezer full with ice cream and chocolate bars. I bought bacon and cream cheese on toast, a couple of Arizona iced teas for the boys, and walked out.

"I had a taste for chocolate," Blue said when she crossed the street. We stood in front of the shop, watching the white wash of the sun behind clouds, hot against the street, the store awnings, the blossoming red maple and honey locusts.

Nikayla Blue ran for councilwoman of the Forty-Second District about two years back. She was in her late thirties and had been an organizer before owning a nonprofit in the middle of the neighborhood, on the corner of Stanley and Schenck Avenues. The day I ended up working for her, the sky was the color of boiling milk. Thumbs of mist rolled in and shined the tops of cars and slicked the roads. A dust head named Billy hopped from awning to awning, stood underneath while people rushed by him. He'd sway and turn, showing the white scurf that bore down the sides of his mouth. The copier hummed, spat out paper on one side as Blue looked through them. She was the color of knot wood, sharp eyes under heavy brows and lines, hair cut close to her scalp. The collar and edges of her checkered shirt was wet from her own perspiring, a habit I'd notice a week in.

"Your grandmother tells me you're a writer."

"I'm trying, at least," I confessed.

"Well, I have this grant request I can't seem to get through. You can do it, if you want. It's for a project I'm thinking of."

"I'd be happy to."

"Yeah, we'll see how it goes," she said, glancing at her tablet screen. Outside, it had started to trickle, runnels down the fogged glass of the campaign office. "A lot has changed since I grew up here. Crime is down, but there's more work out there. Or so they say."

"Why not run again?"

"Not in the cards right now. It's expensive to run a successful campaign yourself. I mean, the community's supportive. Pastor's a good man. But everyone has their allegiances."

"Noble?" I asked.

"His wife," she told me. Charles Noble and his wife, Inez, rotated the position, nepotism I admired even if it became unproductive. "So I don't get the same backing or the eight-hour fundraiser one Sunday. We make do."

Blue led pop-up giveaways for school supplies at neighborhood parks and gymnasiums. She made her rounds to all the tournaments (basketball, football, cricket), showed her face but not in the curated way most officials did. She helped organize coat drives at the community centers or school gymnasiums, in church recreation rooms or near park entrances. She made it a habit to visit the seniors at Linden Plaza, bringing flowers when she remembered their birthdays. She listened to the elders talk, heard their concerns, their cries for decency with what little time they had left in this life. She routinely went live on Facebook and Instagram to bring awareness to a leak in Penn-Wortman Houses or a garbage pileup in front of P.S. 306.

"Linden Plaza needs our help," she'd say, her concern visible through the crackle of pixels. "The elevator has been out since eight a.m. yesterday. Senior and disabled residents are in distress. We need your help, Mayor De-Blasio!"

She and Congressman Hakeem Jeffries would speak at the Eid Mubarak ceremony at Belmont and Euclid, would pray and be still among dozens of

Black Muslims in burkas. After the murder of Eric Garner, the two led a rally out front One Police Plaza, demanded the arrest of Officer Pantaleo. They roared their demands into megaphones, laid on their backs in the middle of the sidewalk to block the entryways. The two were arrested, along with several other protesters, for trespassing and loitering and spent a few hours in the hollows of the precinct.

I started doing rounds with her to get a feel of the work she did.

"You following me?" I asked now, and bit into my bagel.

"Yeah," she said bluntly. "Errands to run."

We walked back around the block, watched Coop as he unloaded a rusting work van.

"Got something picked out for tonight?" Blue asked, and I shrugged. Charity mixer at the public library, the main branch across from the triumphal arch on Grand Army Plaza, defenders of the Union enshrined. Blue would go to network, drag me along as a wingman, but she would stay in hopes of seeking out Inez Noble. She needed funding for the land we were on, wanted the space to be more than a farm, but the house to be repurposed into a community venue. A few offices. Maybe some classrooms. She couldn't get through to Inez's husband, and although they had been fierce opponents, Blue knew Inez was capable of being the most impartial. I saw the project as nothing but beneficial.

"I'll pick you up later but I won't stay, I'm not much for fancy talk," Coop said. Blue pulled open the back doors.

"You're shitting me," I said. They had gutted the damn thing. Behind the driver and passenger seats, where rows of seats would usually be, was just empty space with about an inch of plywood and carpet on the ground.

"It's more space," Blue said. "Better for equipment."

"Space? Where the hell am I supposed to sit?" I asked.

We tumbled through the narrow streets in that van, toward Boulevard, the expanse of government complexes and warehouse space, the soft light from behind the approaching overcast dancing atop the gray hood of the van. I slid around the back, managed to hang on to handles, then seatbelts, then finally knelt between Coop and Blue up front, clung to their headrests for dear life. The brickyard was like a shantytown, droves of people, Black people, stacked atop one another. We went upstairs to an apartment in a familiar building while Coop was double-parked. Inside a two-bedroom, the paint had shriveled and had crumbled to pieces, rotted away from water damage. All that was left was a discolored bubble, a yellow and rust-colored bruise that made the house smell like wet must. Miss Moore was older but still full-blooded, dark and glowing in the natural light.

"I done been through this before," she told us. "I'm sick and tired of it."

"I hear you, Deb," Blue said.

"These damn buildings made outta cardboard."

Blue had gone live on her Instagram; she held her phone like a mirror and stood in front the wall. Miss Moore looked at Blue, then at me, and tilted her head. I shrugged. I stayed out of the camera, leaned forward on the balls of my feet, looked at the mold rising between the cracks of paint. I swallowed the heavy smell, traced the damage with my fingers.

"We missed you at Stephanie's funeral," Miss Moore said to me. "You know, Miss Morales. It was a beautiful service. Everyone got all dressed up, even the young guys. That boy you'd always run around with? Zaire was there."

"I'm sorry I missed it." I said. Blue gave the phone to me, told me to keep recording. I watched her distilled through the screen. Black trauma was consumed, shared, and exploited by people who had never truly lost anything. These weren't concepts or ideas, but our families and friends. Why shouldn't she use it to show gross neglect by the state, upload it to the internet, post it on social media for all to see?

When we left Miss Moore's apartment, I looked up at her window as we crossed the courtyard. The outsides of the tenements were shredded, discolored, and marked with wear. With the steel support exposed and the brick finished weakened, I feared the whole place would crumble at any moment.

"It used to be so loud," Blue said once we pulled off. "Everyone out front, in the courtyard, music. Kids in the street, old folk out in their lawn chairs. Smoke from food, so much food. But you know this. Nowadays, it's a damn ghost town."

"What made you want to help out, old-timer?" I asked Coop. The ward seemed the color of mud. Soon there was an odd mix of one-story homes, city blocks, and dirt roads. Full commercial strips turned to swaths of green and concrete and river edge.

"Huh?"

"Coop's got a bit of a hearing problem," Blue told me.

"What made you want to help out?" I repeated, louder.

"I had a van," the old man said. "I ain't really have a home. "

"Cooper here saved a bunch of lives when Sandy came around," Blue said.

"Lindenwood was flooded, the entire bay. Not like Far Rockaway but still terrible. I must've made about twenty trips back and forth between here and the shelters. Loads of people in this here van. Smelled to high heaven. But each one of those families wouldn't have had shit else."

"What'd you do before that?" I asked. "For a living?"

"Huh?" Coop asked.

"Cooper was in the army for about twenty years," Blue told me.

"I wasn't much a nothing for a while until Sunshine saw me out here wandering around," Cooper said. "She gave me a job doing what I do best. I been out the army for years and couldn't get much help. I knew Blue for all of two weeks before she give me a job, too. Ain't that something?"

We drove on, winding toward the aqueduct like a rusted quadriga drawn by steel. Coop kept the radio just audible, Patti LaBelle a fuzzy murmur I could hardly make out. There were the blurs of green patches and the horse ranch, whole fields of green and lemongrass behind miles of chicken wire and wooden posts. We passed a couple gas stations and houses with boarded windows. Trees lined the sidewalks. There was an enclave of trailers on blocks, some with wheels hitched on the back of a van. Occasionally they would come across a few houses up on stalks and beams, feet above the ground. There was a flea market along the ranch-style center, a combination of cold and warm food. Rows of whiting still on ice. Blackened pots. Grills blew out dark smoke into the air, the sea, embers dancing off into the horizon. Bright fruits and produce in straw baskets. A woman behind a cauldron stared at us from a few stalls away, locked eyes with me through the wandering bodies. There were stalls that sold all kinds of material like copper wire, fabric by the yard, down to cheap clothes, off-brand shoes, fake Prada or Louis Vuitton purses, bootlegged games and movies, unauthorized electronics like Apple chargers or wireless headphones, hacked Roku and firesticks, car stereos and matte wrap by the roll, climbing rigs, bike parts, everything one could think of.

We slid even deeper into the neighborhood, through more abandoned homes, into a short field of yellow-green grass and unfinished road. Toward the end was a gray wall, a stone horizon under the blue overcast. A treatment plant. It seemed to shut us in, wrap around them from one infinite to another. More construction. A yellowed crane reached upward, out of the moat below. On the other side, farther out was the brand new part of the mall. If I somehow forgot what was directly behind me, I could be somewhere in the suburbs. A couple acres of flat, commercial space atop a landfill. We curved west, passed some modern two-, three-story green homes on short stilts. They were all new and polished, clusters of powder blues and canary-yellow outsides that almost glowed from the solar panels.

"The city and some private real estate group built these," Blue told me. "Pretty nice, ain't it?"

"Are they affordable?" I asked, hand up to my face as a sliver of sun beat down.

"Well, that remains to be seen."

We drove along the marsh until the land began to thin. The roads led us out near the bay, the wetland shriveled, receded toward us. On the shore where I met you all those years ago. There were miles of green, thinning into dirt as the ocean stretched on. There was a comfort, ease in the rows and rows of sameness, of yellow and green stalks shimmering in the sun-glare as the wind blew toward Jamaica Bay. Combs of grass and thick rush stuck together; dragonflies exploded through meadow and over the water like a flash of a wind-up camera. What I thought was mud slicked down licks of foliage, oil and sludge along the inlet. It was dark rust, more dark brown than the crimson it took on in the light. For the most part we wandered the shore, ears buzzing from the gnats. You used to appear to me and I knew it was real. I followed you back in time to learn how it began for you. I wasn't a body anymore, like you, just a brief phrase wrapped in histories and moments. Clouds reached for what seemed to be the length of the bay, the edges tucked behind the other side of the horizon; it had been like this for days.

RITUALS

COLLY (2018)

Sometimes I felt my dreams were peeks into another life, a life I lived out but not quite, not in this body. Six years earlier, I had left New York, and from then my life had been different, foreign to me, like I was watching myself go about the days from behind a thick glass plate. Something about California. I went to a small private college near the mountains, out by the desert edge of Los Angeles County. Funny, I had come to the desert from a place that couldn't hold water. Naima had gone to Texas A&M. I flew to her in the fall of my sophomore year, snuck away from a cocktail party her department held at its art studio before the start of the semester. In the dry heart of Texas, she told me that our skin had memories. Her skin told me that we had met lifetimes ago, just like this. I couldn't stand her friends there, who all planned to travel for a year or do Teach for America. She wasn't very different from them. Just looking for something more, she told me in her university's library. But she had it all planned out and I was jealous: for me, it could never be that simple. For me, this was the plan. Survive. Make it out somewhere beyond the five rivers then figure the rest out. I hadn't listened to you in years, Ma, and Pop continued to lift steel and concrete day in and day out. I'd only known people with curved backs and swollen feet, worked in steam mills and subway tunnels, in SNAP offices and daycares, in humid warehouses and malls. Cleaned fish, waited tables, kept watch in the lobby of a building where they wouldn't be welcomed on any other day. Stood for hours. Broke their bodies between paychecks. They worked, had jobs. These folk here—Black, white, and brown—had parents with damn professions: managers, administrators, executives, shop owners, heads of realtor groups, professors, insurance brokers, environmental specialists for big business. They lived in two-story homes with central air and a driveway with two cars. Watched their caloric intake, ate low-carb, or gluten-free, or a berry parfait with flax seed, or almond milk. Their plates were colonial destinations, scoops of avocado, saffron rice, spiced or beluga lentils, quinoa salads, any and all opportunities to get sushi, loved charcuterie spreads with jam, pickled onions, pudding with chia seeds, squash with curry or butternut.

When Naima used to visit me at school, we would make love in the grass hidden by the hills, among the dragonflies, who descended low enough for us to hear their wings. We were wrapped in a blanket across from the university's clock tower and a campus tour passed by and I thought they saw but kept on their way and we laughed. We once had so much time, days full of it. So many ways to spend our time. Bored with our time, selfish with our time, sharing our time, holding it up and saying, "You know what, there's not enough time in the day to do what I want," but most people grow old and gray before they even know if their desires truly belong to them. I could suddenly see a life beyond what was immediate. I let myself grow old and gray, what it could be like with Naima, with anyone.

But we spent parts of that time in parties, red cups knocked over, dark corners for stranger-lovers, sweating crowds burning red behind their necks and ears. The heat was thick enough to swallow whole, trying to slide through the tangle of tall sturdy guys on the baseball team, or played Division 1 water polo for as many years as it took to matriculate. There were girls that majored in psychology or international relations, tanned out on the quad, drove to Laguna or Santa Barbara every other weekend to hang out. Took bars right after class and into the night, or planned their acid trip around a rave like a bookend. Might walk into someone's dorm for a kickback and there'd be a vanity mirror smudged with soft white. Hoping they don't suddenly drop their -gs and -rs when they talk to me, or ambush me with slang they'd gotten off Twitter, slang that came from the streets anyway. Hoping they didn't ask me about a celebrity I never cared about, or yell out the n-word during the chorus of that one song, or call me out my name, the name that you gave to me.

My classmates expected choreography but not a stereotype because that wouldn't be interesting. Perhaps they wanted me to leave them with something, like Atticus in *To Kill a Mockingbird*, like the magical Negro full of wisdom, stories of destitution and triumph to help further their own personal journey. Perhaps they wanted to confirm something they already knew.

I mulled it over for years. Did they choose not to know me? It could only be a choice. The Black guy who sold nuts and soda when they came to the bus terminals, ripped tickets at the train station, at the post office, the guy who tells you to leave the lids up at dawn so he can empty the trash can easier. Just had to be. Were there no teachers? No old, Black librarian with thick bifocals who made ginger snaps for her job, just to keep those white folk smiling and off her ass? Even if there were, he or she wouldn't have noticed her in passing, didn't know any of them Black folk from a hole in a wall, and quite deliberately. Maybe they spoke only to inquire about the price to rotate her tire at the local garage, tipped the waitress extra at the diner at times. It was a hassle getting white folk to look you in the eyes at all. Perhaps it did make sense. In the East, it was normal to go days without seeing a white person.

Thing was, every encounter was formative or had a damn heaviness to it. They were the officers on the beat, our teachers, our social workers, the ones who interviewed us for jobs or bank loans, who read our applications at the leasing office when we thought we could move into a house or new apartment and told us no when we weren't approved. All of their choices had an impact on the trajectory of our lives, yet they couldn't know us, could not encounter us on their own. We were inconsequential that way, scattered leaves dried and swept up in a hurried gust of cold. The wind barreled through the tree-lined streets, much like the ones in this small college town, with no direction.

One time, Naima and I drove into the mountains, high up where the air was thin. She played Toro y Moi and Khruangbin with the windows down as we cut along the winding road toward the top. I took her picture heartbroken. San Gabriel was a range that looked out into a valley, hollowed out by the Santa Ana River. The watershed seemed to span counties, the mountain peaks pulling at the sun. We parked over a bluff and looked out, over Brie and crackers and hard cider. She cried over our picnic. This would be gone soon. The fire ants soon ran us away, back down the valley along the river and into the desert bowl, along the winding roads in my roommate's Volkswagen.

When I graduated, I stayed in LA somewhere among the freeways and strip-malls. I'd broken up with Naima and convinced myself it was mutual; too much distance in every sense. I think I was scared of being seen and opened up in the way love often calls for and nothing had changed. She wouldn't forgive me for the time and effort spent. For two years, I missed a lot and nothing at all. I paid room and board to a lovely woman from Ecuador who owned a one-story house in South LA on San Pedro Street, near Slauson Avenue. She sat in her bergère from Goodwill and watered her plants with a spray bottle. I hung out occasionally with her son who was a coder and dosed hourly with a few drops of marijuana tincture, bumped Flying Lotus until he mellowed out to the frantic pace and unease. I kept an eye on the old block, got my news from timelines and texts from home. Had just read a headline of a man killed in a stairwell by a rookie cop in Pink Houses, not far at all from the hood. A normal day for me started around five thirty in the morning to catch the bus I needed. Worked at a typical, financially strapped nonprofit. I usually went to the beach after work, stayed until the sun wore down. The Pacific was actually blue, not the gray soup that surrounded New York City. And when it was dark, I looked out across the damn thing and felt terrified, insignificant. That in itself was painfully exhilarating.

I made sure I was eating. As much government cheese as I've had in my life, I was certainly invincible. But how I prepared food became ritual. It was clerical but messy. It was monastic. It was romantic. There was music and sweat and sometimes tears. On a Tuesday I make a seared salmon with rice and a bowl of salad. I cook the salmon over green onions, red and green peppers, and garlic. From above the stove I let the heat flush out my head, felt the sensation of a clogged pipe gradually loosening. The smell woke my skin up, placed me in the world and its wild terrain. I rinse the leaves of raw spinach with cold water and lemon juice, toss it into a bowl with shaved walnut and feta.

Naima would write me underwater, across state lines, across your palm. It made me think of a moment from years ago, when she and I were home for summer break. I sat and watched a man suffocate on an island. It was because of cigarettes. She called me when the cop who choked him to death is exonerated.

"Are you watching this?" She had been crying out of pure frustration.

"Yeah," I said. "Why does this keep happening?"

"You know why."

Silence.

"I don't know what I called for," she told me.

I went to bed at two thirty that night, conjuring something. Ready to give something up to the universe, ready to fill all my spaces with gray matter. Filler. Cosmic dust. How do you do that? I heard your voice for the first time in years, tore me out of a dream so I wasn't sure of which realm your sentence began. I could hear you over the sound of a faraway tide, shouting from the other coast, calling me in for the night as the streetlamps began to glow. That's how it was in my head. In this temporary room, narrow and full of dust, the screen of my iPhone is blinding. I couldn't fall back to sleep, so I scrolled through Instagram. I thought it was informative, seeing who everyone thought they were. I looked at my own feed, wondered what version of myself I wanted folk to see: it was bare, some skylines, a few concerts, filtered photos of me looking candid or anywhere but straight ahead. The avatar I had curated was a recluse. Well, that was just untrue. Naima's social media feed told the outside world that she was fine, had moved to the emerald of the Pacific Northwest. Pictures of her classroom. Between the glossy alphabet posters and dry-erase boards were aphorisms on large butcher paper. Every student's work hung from the corkboard no matter the assignment. Gold stars were handed out with fervor, as if they would suddenly dry out, sliding off homework and spelling tests. She would write her tweets like she would a poem. *If he were real, he would be a fraud.* Our last days and nights seemed far away, nebulous and removed from me. I hardly knew what her life was like anymore, so I pictured the Naima I knew, alone but not really alone in the city she took up. I imagined her filling her apartment with books, the smell of lemon tea, waxing her snowboard when winter comes and she can go up to the mountains. I imagined her running every morning and every other evening, passing by the shops and office buildings. She would feel the tautness of her skin, red and wet under the sharpness of the cold. On the weekends she pouts, stain smear and teasing, her boyfriend gone for weeks, feels like, her heels ascending, towering over whoever may decide to talk to her. She puts on her coldest look, and because she is beautiful and knows it, her eyes feel as gaping and searching as the wind on the valley floor. She lies in bed with sugar on her teeth; nothing seems to belong to her anymore. Too much room in her bed. Where did these habits come from? Does she look for things that remind her? The rawness in her throat, the visceral beating in her chest, all of it feels familiar. Maybe she shares what she learned with the kids. She has papers to grade, readings to finish, essays to ramble through.

I just wanted to meet Naima for the first time when we're almost thirty, when I wasn't so stuck on this path that feels so inevitable. I want to meet her at some event—a workshop or a film screening through some mutual friend. On a random Saturday afternoon. I want to hear about where she went to college and why she has such distaste for it. I'll tell her about a small town in California that has the most beautiful sunsets. I'll tell her about you, my defiant mother, how you're my guardian angel, and she'll say I should come visit, and we'll spend countless afternoons laying around letting our skin touch after making love, and I'll realize that I love her on a Tuesday after a very ordinary day. And then I can love her for as long as I want because I won't have to choose and I'll have my whole future ahead of me. That life was so clear I wore it around my flesh to hide the real one. I was headed down another path. I was already back home, sitting outside in Zaire's backyard drinking beer under a falling sun until I was drunk, drunk as all fuck, wanting to set something afire, a child with their first matchbook. This pattern couldn't exist anymore. Though it often coincides, love isn't grief and grief is more than what we lose, at least that's what I convince myself. My time in Los Angeles was done, and I gave into intuition. Maybe I don't let you lead, but I let you push.

I let you guide me home.

YOU ARE IN
COMPLETE HIDING

COLLY (2018)

When I made it home in the summer, Raven had moved on and Naima wanted nothing to do with me. They wanted revenge, to be as powerful as they could; I wanted to mourn you under the heavy moon with sweet beer. Instead, I just mourned. Sweeping across the city, a land more mythical than anything, in light and stone and people than the world itself is the silver heat of summer. High in the air, below the orange slopes of sun excess, was heat, the oppressive kind that stayed in your eyes and the grooves of your mouth. Your words spilt out of my suitcase.

Dad's house smelled of Red Stripe and fried fish. I threw a party for you in the backyard and invited the friends I see. The whole hood came, and Zaire helped pull some speakers in from down the road. Pop played gin rummy at the top of the stairs with the guys on his cricket team, drinking malt till the sun slipped below the hills. Outside, the city was overcrowded. Broken windows or broken spines.

I walked by and spoke to those I knew. Stared out the windows with eyes as sad as yours. The tops of buildings vanished behind the humid night, the streets busy and winding, an asphalt river through a metal and stone canyon. I watched the clouds drift toward Jamaica Bay. Raven found me near the back, by the window, pinched my arm by the top of the elbow. When we were in elementary and middle school, she was the girl us boys wanted. She leaned in to hug me, and I heard the schoolgirls sing Miss Mary Mack with their hands smelling of Shea butter and their teeth full of tamarind. Raven would pop her bubble gum, count the number of times the jump rope hit the tar before she jumped in. The bobos tied around her hair sounded like fat raindrops.

"How you holding up?"

"Not too good," she told me over the music, over the swelling tide of people talking over one another. "He's still trying to figure out bond."

Before Tristan got picked up, he ran a fake check scam out of a two-bedroom walk-up. Turn a hundred into a thousand, except he scammed people out of most their money. It was easy when people were desperate. Who could afford to be poor in New York City anyway? The mother of his child would hobble in from the kitchen, armed with plates that steamed under aluminum foil. Some days I'd be there as Tristan camped out by his phone, rose to his feet when it groaned, then rummaged through shoeboxes scattered in the corner.

"Didn't you hear me calling you, stupid?" Raven would say. Tristan hardly listened. He was in the middle of an act. His daughter, Melli, rocked side to side in front the television.

"Do you blame him?" I asked Raven. Not God, but Tristan, I meant.

She looked toward the front room, the stream of folk coming and going. They bring the heat with them, a tithe for the season. "People are just people who always end up making mistakes," she said. "That's who we are."

I stayed at Raven's for weeks after they took Tristan. Fraud, identity theft, some ambiguous form of larceny. The detectives had a warrant and a dossier full of witness accounts. They claimed if he cooperated, he could have some dropped to misdemeanors. They spoke as if he had already been to trial. I rode the bus to the station that day with my stomach uneasy. At least he was alive. I saw months-long docuseries, talking heads and news pundits, colorful pamphlets handed out at Union Square: "Survive the encounter," they said.

I watched Melli during the day or Raven took her to whoever would have her. Her own mother would sour at the sight of us.

"Runnin' around like a mad woman, baby on your back, shopping bag around your neck. That boy oughta be grateful to you."

Tristan's mother had been beyond helpful. Raven could never thank her without a loss for words. "Chile, if you don't get on with that," Mama cried as she gestured for Melli, arms wide and trembling. She had one lung from smoking Newports for decades and spoke from the roof of her mouth. She remained resilient, and while gossip about her son followed her to church and the beauty salon, she opted to see the same boy who needed stitches after splitting his knee in front the community center.

Raven worked at the daycare on Belmont Avenue her cousin helped run. She was there in the mornings and left long after parents picked their children up. She'd come home in a storm of plastic bags and read with Melli until her dinner was ready. When her stamps ran out, about the same time every month, I brought food or ordered in with what little money I had.

"I'll stick by him." Raven's voice was merging with the group next to us. They nodded to us and I gestured with my drink. "I will because I'm supposed to, right?"

"Or because you really love him," I said and she looked at the floor, the faux-wood tiles already wet from tipped cups and beers. "You ever feel like talking to someone about it?"

"Like who?"

"Anyone."

"I need someone to talk to these damn bill collectors."

"Tell me about the first day," I started. "The first day you two went out."

"He was rude," she said, licking lime and salt off her lips. "I was in tenth grade and he looked at me with those bug eyes and told me my head would get bigger if I kept talking."

"I get it—talking, hot air," I said.

"Very charming," she said, and I laughed at the way she sang her words. "I wish you would've talked to him."

"You know how he is," I shrugged. Then: "How did you know you were in love with him?"

She thought for a minute, making lines in the dirt with the sole of her running shoes, "How would I not know?"

Melli had to be at Tristan's mom's place. The air was rich from someone's backyard grill, thick with jerk powder and ginger. I walked through the front room, through the hall with felled clear plastic cups. A woman stood beside two older guys in the staircase, rolling sour and grab she crumbled with her fingers into a rolling paper. I went downstairs, pressed against the heavy metal door into the outside, the night balmy and hazy. Murals stretched across dead metal, rust-covered fences and twisted wire amongst the slumped high-rises and warehouses. Streetlights burned halogen stains into the sky.

That was the thing, when you are twenty-something and wandering. It was episodic and spontaneous. You covered dinner even though you have just met these people. Cheers to new friends, anyway. You learned the language, asking if you can bum a cigarette on line, to face the dry cold. I lit my own with a raw thumb and check my phone. Naima had left me a text.

But you are in complete hiding.

I WOKE UP the next morning in a sticky fugue from a heavy knock on the door. The sun had climbed enough to warm the cool summer dawn. My dad's house still smelled like sweet liquor and cigars, the couch I pulled out in the center of it all. I stumbled to the door and swung it open. A NYCHA serviceman with a cart stuffed with toolkits, hazard gear, an aluminum stepladder, paint buckets, and more, held out a clipboard with a request for repair made from this apartment.

"I guess." I took the work order. "Seriously? This claim is from almost ten years ago."

"Came up in the system today," he took the sheet back, hurriedly. "You want me to take a look or not?"

"Fine." I moved aside to let him wheel in his shopping cart, directed him to the wall in question. When he was settled, I rushed over to my phone I'd heard vibrating against the headboard and swiped to answer.

"You have a collect call—" An operator's automated message.

"Yeah I accept," I said. "Trist?"

"You looking after my girls?" Tristan asked.

"More like the other way around."

"Sounds like them."

"You talk to your lawyer?"

"I haven't seen that guy since I got here," he said. It had been between bail and a decent lawyer. The long game may have been to go with anything other than someone court-appointed, but I could understand bail.

"I've been here for almost a month," Tristan was saying to me, and I could tell his lips were right up against the receiver. "I need you to come through for me."

"I'm doing what I can."

"I know, it's just—this place."

"We'll get you out."

Silence. I heard chatter on the other end, a buzzing of some kind. I lit incense and walked it around the front room before shoving the nonburning end in a small hole out in the back, by the bedroom, where you had hung a frame years ago.

"Did Raven tell you about the baby?"

"She did," I said. The Housing guy looked down at me from his ladder and shrugged.

"Melli's gonna be a big sister. She'll have a little brother to take care of. I never met my dad's other children till I was older. I don't want that for her."

"She'll be great" was all I could say.

My old home felt like every moment piled up, one on top of the other, as if time had fell in on itself. There were crates and bins stacked everywhere, full of dust, on tables and counters, pushed all the way into corners. There were shelves and shelves of vinyl sleeves and boxes of cassettes, books and my old Nintendo cartridges. Pop would watch movies on his laptop placed on top of an old amp. There was a tape player, a vinyl player, and about a year's worth of Essence magazines. All the dust and clutter made the air feel heavy, something I could taste on my tongue.

My father shuffled into the room with a box of Salems. "He gon' tell me, 'You better change your tone,'" the old man was saying. "I tell him: 'First of all, this my house. I'll change my tone when I get outside.'"

"Pop, it's only gin rummy," I said. He looked up and I realized he was on the phone.

"Not when you putting money up." He plopped down in his chair and lit a cigarette, still cradling the phone between his neck and jaw. "How's work?"

"It's going."

"You talk to Tristan?" Pops' asked.

"I went up there last week. We're trying to get bail together."

"How much?"

"Damn near three thousand," I said, I reached into my pocket and sought my phone. "I need to borrow your car."

"Ain't no gas in that thing." He handed me the key.

"I'll fill her up."

The serviceman had collected his things and said he'd need to come back the next day because the wall was worse than he thought. The local news played as ambience while Pop talked to whoever was on the line. Could be one of the guys on the cricket team from up the road, who always had oil on their hands, their skin the dark color of tree bark. It could be his friend, the one he refused to tell me he was seeing, who left a pair of house shoes and a few outfits in his overflowing closet. I couldn't hear the report but I read the headline. A boy hung himself out of his mother's window, after being left for years on an island. He had been on Rikers Island for something he didn't do. They kept showing a splintered window frame surrounded by bramble.

The Q144 went up there, from the stretch of Queensbridge and Astoria, along the murky channel of the East River. If downtown filled up where Tristan was being held, or he went to trial months from now and lost, Raven would have to ride it toward the peak of the city, across a far-off bridge into a small island covered in stone and barbed wire. Inside was cold, but not just the air—the tables, the metal chairs, the walls. Women guards with latex gloves would search her all over, feel across her chest and between her legs. She'd talk to the father of her child through a window, a thick panel of scarred Plexiglas.

"Black boys don't commit suicide," Pop said now, to the phone he held, to me, the room in general.

The story wasn't as uncommon as the news made it out to be. Pop couldn't understand it. He thought it was weak, self-centered. I knew he knew better. When the body becomes its own heavy and terrible husk. It was to wake up every day crushed by something outside yourself, losing your breath until it becomes you, and anything outside of that cannot exist. To have every reason you are free in your lungs, at the back of your throat, only to be speechless, breathless. I thought of an island, the men who drowned or lost their breath and the boys who were lost at sea. I thought of the women who waited at the shore, like Raven, who would wait and wait and wait for the tide to come in, not knowing we had disappeared completely. It made me think: were there other conscious deaths, other ways to kill yourself? Did Tristan stumble about the holding cells like he was half-living, a ghost, dead as soon as he wasn't free, because freedom was life and to be without the former was literal death, knowing the whole time that institutions hardly care about intentions. There was me, speeding ahead with no intent—wild enough to burn out like a hot and dying star in colorless space. Was that a kind of suicide?

I looked at the old man now, his red eyes wet from the smoke of his Salem. He was a brick wall, still a solid man, spilling over the sides of his chair. He always failed to mention all of what my mother gave up. She didn't kill herself in the end, but she was killing herself. He turned to me with a face I recognized once, when I was a boy and he'd come tumbling into the apartment in the middle of the night, looking at me as the sole witness. Now, he dove into another story on the phone and I stayed and listened to the news for another half an hour, hearing nothing else. Finally, I patted him on the shoulder and left. It had been like this for years now.

RAVEN HAD TIME to cook that night, which was a rarity. There was steam from the white rice soaked in butter, chunks of jerk-rubbed chicken, with sautéed onions and peppers in a thick broth. Her apartment was a large room with a short hallway that led to a bedroom and bathroom. Melli came in from the bedroom dressed in what seemed like drapes.

"Look, Uncle Colly," Melli exclaimed. She spun in a circle, the bedazzled robe twirling.

"She's preparing for a play," Raven told me.

"You look beautiful," I said. "What's the play?"

"*We Are the Dream*."

"That's great, baby girl," I said to Melli, then to Raven: "At least it's in June and not just during Black History Month."

"They still cover the same three pages in Melli's class as we did and somehow that makes it through the month. We were slaves and Harriet freed some of us, then Lincoln freed all of us, and at some point, Martin Luther King took us to a mountaintop."

"Come February, they couldn't wait to wheel in that dusty, old ass TV. They used to make us watch *Eyes on the Prize* like fifty times."

"Wait now, I love *Eyes on the Prize*."

"I do, too."

Raven used to light incense, the wood panels of her shelves and end tables still hinting of nag champa. She would light candles from the 99-cent store, the tall ones with white Jesus surrounded by vines or roses and whatever baroque imagery had been set behind him. Since Melli, the house had become the baby's room, the carpet littered with dolls and mats and toys that lit up seemingly at random. We ate, laughing until Melli fell asleep on the couch. I carried her to bed, Raven's bed, and helped straighten up the kitchen. I turned out the front lights and let the commercials on the TV play on mute.

"She says some of the girls at school tease her," she said over the soft murmur of the television.

"Tell her to knock the biggest one out."

She smiled for a moment before letting out another sigh. Nothing was fair, she said. How was she supposed to do anything? She couldn't even dress her child properly. Couldn't afford an attorney.

"I never had time to just be me and see what works," she said. "What doesn't."

"There's always time."

"Never enough." She leaned her head on my shoulder. "Sometimes I wonder what you're even doing back. You have a degree, you have options."

"I don't feel like I belong anywhere."

"Who belongs here? This place is just an in-between. I'd leave and never come back."

"That's the problem, no one ever comes back."

Raven sat up suddenly. She didn't say a thing. Instead, she slipped into her room, careful not to wake Melli. I couldn't tell if she believed me or not. When she came back out, it was with her sorority paddle. It was pink and bedazzled and draped in ribbon, a heavy panel of wood she brandished in my direction.

"Back when I used to stroll." Suddenly, her face was wet from the heat or her eyes were welling. The night played out in shadows across the walls. Music reached across the boulevard, through the car alarms and scattered voices. Raven sighed as she sat next to me on the sofa, head on my shoulder. Her hair was up, wrapped in a silk scarf that she smoothed along the edges every once in a while. She was losing weight and her sullen brown eyes looked too big compared to how small she seemed in my arms.

SOME DAYS I could do nothing more than think of you. I had put money on Tristan's books, what I could offer from my savings until he was out. I holed up in my father's house, appearing only to give Raven and Tristan's mother the money we took for bond. I picked Melli up from camp, her knotted pigtails hovering slightly over the crowd of little people. The counselors were in bright yellow shirts with sweat pulling their collars, kids my age who were waiting for something better.

"I think your mom is picking you up from now on," I said to Melli.

"How come?"

"Your mom wants all the fun."

"Will you still visit?" She asked.

"Of course."

"Mommy says Daddy can't come to my play because he's not coming home."

"He should be home soon, baby girl," I told her.

"I don't know if I want him to come home."

"Why not?"

"Mommy doesn't cry as much. I miss him, but . . ."

The street was like a black channel, a world beneath it humming, bleeding under our feet. We sat on the stone porch of my father's walk-up, waited for Raven to walk by on her way from work, watching kids ride their bikes through the hard mist of fire hydrants, their mothers calling after them.

Men under store awnings looked wet and sluggish from malt. Their wives and girlfriends were at work or gone completely, living across town with the children they made. They complained about child support, how their license was suspended and workers checks broken into. Somewhere, the chimes of a far-off ice cream truck were like relics of church bells. A gash ran down the side of Tristan's old building and when the wind pushed ahead from the shore, it blew away the tarp that tried to plug the holes. Windows were boarded, abandoned by families who couldn't take the flooding anymore, the vermin, the deteriorating of the home around them. My stomach is a sour burn like the white sun above. I had the sudden urge to go to Naima, to empty my savings and fly, or take Pop's old Fleetwood that he wasn't sure would make it too far out of Jersey. Instead, the summer is a heavy wound I'm nursing. It is red and bottomless like the sunset, violent as the parkway that carved the neighborhood into divides. I didn't hear from Naima, but I liked to daydream about what she'd say, where I'd be when my phone would open up my only line to her, across thousands of miles. There are versions where she doesn't call or write and I think about those too. She'll meet somebody, maybe on the patio of a bar or at the gym after work, through a chasm of lights, empty posts about the show or reading she caught that night. And most days she'll truly be without me. She will go to the mountains, feel herself most when the air is thinnest, hiking through the pine and the cottonwood trees. There is a trail along a row of alders, past the juniper trees that drop berries onto the rocky foothills, to a bluff covered in tumble grass. Goldenrod grows from the cracks between the jagged rocks.

DODGE CITY

COLLY (2018)

I always had a hard time feeling normal at these things. Gala events—white tablecloths, chinaware sets, words like capacity building and leveraging funds. Sustainability. Access. It also didn't help that I was helplessly drunk. Coop had been kind enough to drop me off at the house so I could get ready for the evening. Around seven, I took an Uber toward the Grand Army, arriving in front of the glass face of the Brooklyn Museum. The room was cavernous, made prominent by the walls that could've reached high enough to fade completely. I had made a break for the bar. At the head of the room, in front of the dais and its row of speakers, the night staff hurried to take tips and dessert orders. I was struck by how nimble they were, moving between the large tables. Among the laminated name tags and placards were donors and community leaders and professionals who knew helping folk didn't mean working for free. Everyone sat on some board or worked for some foundation or taught at some university. A woman from the 92nd Street Y was my RA in college. A few others I knew in passing roamed the aisles, all spread between United Way, the ACLU, or Margaret's Place. Near the very front were the big guys, auxiliaries from the Annenberg Foundation, some city officials, wielding money I could only dream about. I nursed a glass of red wine. Everyone mingled, sought out people for their networks, their ideas, their money.

Smiles full of white teeth. I wore the suit I bought myself for graduation.

Blue worked the room, allowed herself to smile ingenuously, to plot and steer a conversation toward the verge of discovery. We both were out of place, and she was sweating freely beneath her suit. She would take off her jacket and roll up her shirt sleeves at any moment, rather be at the Center preparing school supplies for a drive, laying out talking points on her livestream.

"I see you need saving," I said.

"Good lord," she exhaled. We sat at the bar. "I should walk around with my goddamn personal statement on a name tag."

I suddenly felt the need to update her on the grant I was supposed to be writing. She paid me no mind. Instead, she stared past me and I turned to see Inez Noble stalking toward us. Her husband had been the councilman for the Forty-Second District for nearly a decade. By no means was she undeserving. She had represented East New York as a member of the state's assembly, taking over after Diane Gordon, who promised a contractor a multimillion-dollar parcel of land if he built her a house. Caught ole girl on tape talking about how she wants mahogany or burgundy wood doors for her office, too. And you better keep your mouth shut, she had said, damn near. What a queen. In her defense she tried to rectify the situation, gave the money back she received for bribes. Can't put toothpaste back in the tube, the district attorney said to reporters.

So Noble left office and Inez took his place, similar world views that white folk found polarizing, same "colorful" remarks, as the papers liked to put it. In turn, he took her place at the assembly. The unemployment, Blue had mentioned often. The homeless shelters that won't stop popping up. They've done so much good but a lot of this is on them. What they allow in East New York in exchange for the "greater good" for all of us. "See, I got families in apartments that are falling apart from under them. Kids with no backpacks or notebooks for the first day of school. How do we survive day to day? What structural change can we help to make someone's life a little better for tomorrow?"

Inez had beaten Blue last year, but it wasn't the whooping that the papers claimed. People liked Blue and her anti-poverty campaign. Shit, I liked it. She'd done way better than anyone in recent memory against the Nobles. Yet Blue wouldn't run again, was content with the nonprofit and the work it did for kids and seniors.

When the councilwoman walked up, Blue was genuine. Inez was kind to us. I felt grounded, eased by the vibration of an inner wisdom. In the write-up of her I read in the *Village Voice*, it was mentioned she was a teacher and a principal before entering politics. I could see myself being in her class, how the boys and I would usually disrupt a class and catch fire and end up getting soothed into learning by the soon-to-be councilwoman.

"So good to see you," Blue said. "I meant to congratulate you on the Senior Interagency Council. I've been saying we need to pay more attention to our seniors. How's the, what is it, the library program you raised money for last year?"

"It's being defunded," Inez sighed.

"Are they shutting you down?"

"Who knows how long we got."

"Those kids," I said, exasperated. Shook my head for good measure.

"I mean, why cut these programs?" Blue asked. It was rhetorical; there were a million different truths that could have existed and we understood them all.

"No one bats an eye when our taxes are dumped into God knows where,"

Mrs. Noble said, throwing her manicured hands up to the sky in fatigue. "But education, arts. This administration, I swear."

"Infuriating. I wanted to talk to you about just that. Colly, could you give us—?"

I couldn't even sit at the bar alone. A debate had broken out around the ways to properly support communities, how to empower rather than lead the conversation. I felt the room tense, threatening to turn on itself. Every initiative was entirely "community-based" or "community-driven," something I found hard to believe. The community didn't have the vol-au-vents this evening. It was a world that didn't include Nana, or Miss Moore, or Tristan—didn't include anyone from above Central Park, or too far down Atlantic Avenue. Everyone was keeping up appearances, enjoying the circumstance that gathered them all for causes beyond them. I had a creeping fear that none of this would help. I felt more like a visitor, tagging along intermittently, stumbling toward the desert sun like a pariah. I needed to excuse myself, to break character, to go into the bathroom stall and breathe.

Blue ambled back over. A light sweat had returned and now ran down the nape of her neck, slicked down her lush edges.

"What happened?" I asked her, bourbon sweet on my tongue.

"Difference in opinion" was all she said.

IT WAS DARK as we rode from the museum, through the dim side blocks, Coop switching through radio stations like he wouldn't eventually settle on WBLS. He'd picked us up in something with seats this time, an old town car that looked like the ones from the cab service on Livonia. When we pulled up to headquarters, Sunshine was home and sitting by the dark smoke of a firepit and plates of roasted greens. One of the chickens stuck its nose through the gate, chirping at the commotion. Mosquitoes nipped at our ankles when one strayed too far from the smoke. Coop brought out about a dozen Wild Horses and I looked at Blue in disgust. She shrugged and tossed one to me before snapping the lid on one of her own, toasted us as we all sat around the fire.

"My mamma, God rest her soul, lost everything in Katrina," Coop said. "We was out a few miles from the river. It didn't kill her then but she couldn't stand what came with it. Straight from hell. The mosquitos festering over this mess. It was like a soup, with dead things and half-alive. We were flooded for days, weeks. Ninety degrees all day every day. You can't imagine. They say that land is cursed."

"Do you think so?" Blue asked him.

"Maybe the water is," Sunshine cut in. "Maybe the water is cursed. All that blood spilled. Millions of people. I imagine, much like any grave, it's haunted."

"I pray," Blue cried. "I pray it washes everything away. We can rebuild. Sometimes I think that's the only way. I fear for the lives of the women around me, their safety. Their minds. I only wanted to find a place for us, to live as safe and free as we could imagine. I wanted to take something back."

"Where would you find a place like that?" I asked her.

"I don't know. But maybe I'm not looking in the right place. Maybe it doesn't exist yet."

We finished Coop's pack of Wild Horses as the fire eventually burned out. I fell sleep under the sound of the fire, thinking it was a dream but would wake as if he was still submerged in some vastness. I dreamed of a place in between that felt like the South. Behind one of those houses out by the bayou. We broiled crawfish, buckets full left to sit in a bag of seasoning for hours, sucked at the meat beneath the shells. Everyone was out by the lake in two inflated boats. Tristan, Raven, and Blue were trying to flip Coop and Zaire. Naima squawked from behind Zaire as they curled around their aggressors. I closed my eyes, as if a cool wind from the ocean swept sand into my hair. When I opened them, I watched as the horses stood with impatience, in groups spread across the dappled pasture.

I heard a scream that pushed me out of my dream. It was just before dawn—Coop was fussing across from me. Blue, who had fallen asleep too, began to stir.

"He's cursed!" he yelled, looking straight at me.

"What?" I asked.

"This has to stop, Coop," Blue told him.

"Who is she?" The old man turned to me now. "Why does it follow you?"

"All right, enough. Up you go." She took Coop by the shoulder, let him fuss some more as he led her upstairs. *"I know what I done seen . . ."* he carried on.

Soon the yard was silent and I was reminded it was morning. In the kitchen, the faucet leaked into the basin of a metal sink. A starling busied itself near the window, rehearsed its song and disturbed the light that came through the blinds. I reached for a fresh coffee filter, a few left stained beside a pot that cooled.

WENT AWAY, TURNED COLD (2019)

They saw each other at Key's grave every year, around her birthday in November. Audrey managed to take a shaky cell phone picture and send it to family. Flat headstone with a bronze marker. Flowers she bought to give to her daughter, dahlias and lilies and chrysanthemums. Farmingdale was almost an hour out, and when they all finally came across the plot it had become hard to breathe, hard to ever fully catch their breath. Toya was there, set a picture frame behind a fresh bundle of roses. Inside the frame was a poem she wanted Key to hear, had read it aloud before it was time to go. In a burial ground, death becomes a constant realm—it becomes the everyday. The cemetery is exceptional and separated from everyday regularities and yet, at the same time, remains a domestic and ordinary space. It was a plane that defied time and space, connecting past lives and future deaths, rejecting our urge to move forward, something we mistook for living.

Colly helped Audrey onto the paratransit, the bus lowering itself for her walker. The driver called himself Mister, just Mister, though his last name was printed across a laminate on his dashboard. Audrey stuck her head out her bus window brightly, toasted the passing cars with her pomegranate juice and sea moss. On the way home, her grandchildren hardly spoke, or hardly spoke to each other. They looked out of place in their mother's childhood home, tight and narrow. Light strained through blinds and moving shadows across apartment walls. The sun lit Audrey's whole place, from the east, still low but sitting behind a steam plant that blew dark smoke into the air.

"Those girls talked my ear off today," Audrey said, journeying about the room to sit in her wheelchair. She spent the morning at the senior center, a bit of physical therapy for her legs before she spent lunchtime arguing over a few games of spades. "Whole bunch a nothing. I like the soap talk, but one lady talked about her bladder condition for a half an hour, at least. Toya dear, can you wash that spinach for me? I'll tell you. I look at them and say to myself, 'I can't be as old as they are.'"

Toya rinsed the greens in the sink, had spent most of her time with her mother on her mind, bumped around rooms like she would, trying some of her words out; the things Key told her. Somehow, her granddaughter had become more of herself, a self she always envisioned but, also, put together on the fly. Audrey didn't know much about what she did, but she was proud. Toya worked in education but couldn't stand the politics, and for some reason, had a somewhat contentious relationship with an academic institution that paid her bills consistently.

Colly made some coffee but she couldn't have any because of her blood sugar. Audrey rolled her neck to stretch out the tightness knotted there. She had begun to doze off, could fall asleep anywhere but more often than not it was confined to her wheelchair, slumped to either side and snoring occasionally. She kept hearing hushed voices and the pulling of drawers, the slamming of cabinets, the creak of closet shelves and floors.

"I know I seem like I'm being extra and I know it's convenient for you to pop up when you please but you need to be here more," Toya said. "I can't do all this by myself. Nana's getting old, Colly. You think there's someone coming to save us. There's no one coming.

"I'm sorry I was away," Colly said, "but you act like you've been here the whole time. You left, too."

"You're just like Pop." Toya pursed her lips so hard they turned pale. "The two of you won't ever change. Why do you pretend to care about anyone else?"

When Audrey finally got her bearings, Toya up and slammed the bedroom door behind her.

WHEN AUDREY'S PREGNANT belly had grown at first, she couldn't keep anything down yet craved the strangest things, soda floats from the ice cream shop run by the only Italian family left in the neighborhood, or dozens of red Swedish Fish from the corner store on Ashford Street. She was swept up in Virgil, all so fast, his voice that was a rumbling that came from his core, his joyful gait as he filled a room, made others shrink to him, willingly, beautiful as a young Coley Wallace. When her daughter was born, it was a gray and rainy Wednesday in April 1970. Key was seven pounds and six ounces. Audrey held the slithering thing in her arms, protective and firm, looking for some recognition of what she had grown in her body. Joyce looked elated, splashing big tears everywhere from what she could see of the labor room. She realized, as her womb bled and the sweat became cold on her face, that she had always been afraid to be alone. Virgil knew his way around the waiting rooms, around the machines and curtains and the bed as they let him see Audrey, see his daughter, holding her knowingly with a hand relaxed but firm behind Key's head and neck. When Audrey felt the fog, saw her own hands from far away, through silver coin binoculars atop the Empire State, reminded her that he was there, knew a little something but was still learning, and they would get it together with time. She had made her choice that first time she encountered Virgil on the street, eyeing the wedding band on his finger as he slid his hands in his pockets. It wasn't an issue before, she swore, made sure within herself that she wouldn't bring up the ex-wife in an ultimatum, and didn't allow it to become an issue for her until it was too late. How else could it turn out? He had other obligations, another woman with a child who was also his. Audrey expected him to be there for Key, why would a mother only a few neighborhoods over want anything different for their child? She had eventually learned to glue everything out and could sit for hours without a thought, Key pulling at her breast for milk, listening through the thin walls of her studio, could retreat into this new world, one where her daughter became her anchor. Something her mother would say. Strange how we women know when a man leaves us—even when he's still with us.

Audrey had told him to be gone before the sun rose.

She had stormed out in her pajamas and rain boots, a warm spring night that swelled from the coming summer. Behind the building, in the center of a courtyard that split open toward the street, was a large plot of dirt covered with bottles, scraps of newspapers, and plastic wrappings. Audrey wanted to dissolve into the earth, crumble between the soil like sand in a riverbed. She raked her fingers into the ground in frustration, as if trying to climb her way inside.

AROUND FIVE IN the afternoon the light had moved to the other side of the apartment and Toya was preparing leftovers from last night. Ari Lennox's "Night Drive" played from her laptop and she grooved along with it, mouthing the words. A Third World Women's Alliance sticker took up a corner of Toya's MacBook, a USB keychain of the Hanged Man her girlfriend must've gotten her.

The scene reminded Audrey of being a child on Sundays before church. They'd be asleep and Lucille would bang on the door of the room, Cream of

Wheat wafting in from the kitchen. Nat King Cole crooned from the vinyl player as the old woman hustled them into the washroom.

Audrey asked her granddaughter how everything was.

"Fine," Toya said. "Just tired."

"Are you sleeping?"

"It's admissions season."

"So not much."

"Yeah, well," she fussed with an overcrowded drawer beside the stove. "Someone's gotta do it."

"Will you and your brother be okay?"

"It's not him," Toya sighed. She looked at her fingernails before she continued, "I let my father come see me at school one year. Colly had already left and Pop was alone in that house. I showed him around campus. Took a drive to the Walmart in town to get me some computer stuff. I bought a laptop with my refund check. He wanted to use my name for a credit card. I told him tough luck because I already burned through two of 'em. I think that was the most honest we'd been in years. I said I was unhappy and it was his fault. And that wasn't true, but how can you say 'I miss the other parent more'? I feel like I made up stories about all of our lives to make me feel better. Now I'm not sure what's true or not."

Audrey always considered Toya's loss but didn't know how the girl dealt with it, assumed it was healthier than whatever boy was doing. Audrey never thought her granddaughter felt the urge to seal herself away.

"Do you ever hear her voice?" Audrey asked her, desperately. She meant Key. Toya looked confused; perhaps Key didn't present herself to Toya in the same way. Audrey tried to smile, putting her hand on Toya's arm, then turned on the TV, a dusty Panasonic from 2005 with a VCR slot. On the news, Puerto Rico was still without power after a deadly hurricane that hit months ago. In Sacramento, a young man is shot in the back by the SPD.

"If I ever tell Ma anything," Toya said to Audrey, "I know she can still listen better than anybody."

• • •

VIRGIL SAW KEY as often as she'd let him. Everyone struggled to find work and after he got fired from the docks, he ran a numbers ring with a crew near Cityline. He would go door-to-door, jotting numbers on anything—his hand, his sleeve, on the corners of newspapers. He'd pick up his daughter, great bronze knobs he'd shove in his trouser pockets, mumble how he liked what Audrey had done with the place. She'd make a noise, a grunt that couldn't be folded into words. He'd tell Key he was taking her to see the chimps at the Bronx Zoo.

"You sure?" Audrey had asked. "Or is that Toyota on its last mile?"

"It was on its last mile when I met you."

"Huh," she snorted. They'd let the past sneak its way into the room, lift them all up in possibility.

"Can we go, Daddy," Key pleaded, bouncing on the balls of her feet. "The chimps might get cold and go inside and we'll miss them." Audrey feared her daughter had only learned to play both sides, to mediate, to say the right thing or stretch the truth, whatever the cost. Feared she internalized her parent's love language, a brogue thick with yearning and resentment. She knew her daughter was a familiar soul, an old one she knew back in Warren, a bit of Lucy souring at the sight of any attempts to settle.

Key had fought her way into her windbreaker and was pulling at Virgil's leg. He checked for crust in her eyes, pulled softly and caressed her face, teased her about boogers that weren't there. Audrey had looked on, swallowing what could jump out of her, anger or adoration or just regular-ass disappointment. Possibility, when it was all over and the thing was splayed out and bleeding, was simply regret. Years passed; the bass guitar Virgil had bought, the Fender, his most prized possession, was pawned off to a shop. He needed another high, another mouth of a well to gaze up at. When he died, suddenly, without warning, Key was only twelve years old. Audrey remembered how she felt: numb, regretful of the mess they made. She missed those days in the cornfields, his jaw in the sun and how it made the bottom of her belly jump up, flutter like the wings of a Violetear. How she could still hear his breathing when she woke up in the middle of the night, still could measure his soft padding toward the bathroom as he tried not to wake her. But she was awake and would lie on his side until he returned, burying his face in her neck as he slid beside her, cradling her with his long body like ripe corn in its husk.

IT WAS ALWAYS about what she was left with, even after she sent Virgil away. Audrey had felt emptied out, all the water in her eyes no longer fell, but stayed there, until it threatened to drown her, to carve out a voice to resemble what seemed like her own. Now, instead of a fish restaurant, she was above an organic mini-market. Around the corner was every food you could think of and it wasn't too far from the park. Most train lines were nearby and she even saw a gallery open up a couple blocks down. The renovations to the building itself were supposed to be a reward for the tenants who remained over the years, but now they were the reason she was getting priced out. She glared at Virgil, who was still mumbling something to himself through clenched jaws.

"I oughta leave you here so they can put you out again," she said, shaking her head. Audrey opened a bottle of cheap zinfandel and sat by her bedroom window, regarding her face among the jaundiced light from the street. She was losing weight in her face, sullen brown eyes that looked big compared to how small she seemed. What if she moved back to Warren? Went back for the farm, still in her and Joyce's name. She remembered the old supply store in town, the stretch of roads that led to the swamps, the chapel on the hill that filled the air with the sound of bells at dusk. She wasn't sure, however, after all these years, it would feel like home. If so, how could she feel she ever belonged anywhere?

Audrey limped out toward the kitchen but saw a cold light by the dining table. Her grandson was behind the silver screen of his sister's laptop.

"You're still here," Audrey said, shuffled toward the seat across from him.

"I'm looking at apartments," Colly told her. "I can't stay in that house, Pop is getting too loose."

"I can imagine."

"Funny," he said, but didn't laugh. "I used to think I'd kill for him to be in that house all day. Now I hate it." It was like it dawned on him that he hadn't considered that place home in years. Audrey could relate. He asked Audrey if she thought Toya would ever speak to their father again. Of course, Audrey said, he just had to find out who she was again, and that she could still use his help and his gambling money.

"Will you and your sister be okay?"

"We'll be fine," he said. What Colly meant was that *he'd* be fine. He didn't want to leave anyone with the task, the burden, of learning him. He didn't want his survival, or rather, more gravely, their survival, to depend on the labor of people who loved him. Colly was determined, however blindly, to do that labor himself.

He got them two glasses and the water pitcher in the fridge. He steadied his grandmother's hand when she held out her cup and he poured. She pushed herself toward the living room window. When it is nighttime there is no typography of stars, just the moon and the chemical burn of the city. She went to put down her cup, only to find a box made from red cedar, filled with gravel and fresh soil.

"What's this?"

"I built you a little planter's box," Colly said. "For your succulents."

An explosion out of darkness pushed us across millions of years. Audrey would shake her head, saying God made all of it in a matter of days, rested only after he had finished his work. Key would interject. *Why couldn't both be true?* she would challenge. What is a day to the immortal? How many millions of years were in a week? Audrey stretched out her hands, kneaded the soil between her fingers, cool clumps coming apart and falling to the floor. Then she leaned forward, placed her forehead against the cedar wood.

EAST BROOKLYN RESCUE AND RECLAMATION

COLLY (2020)

The wind had cut itself on the edges of buildings. It whistled as it folded into lobbies and under doors, bent against windows, fit under the awnings and scaffolding wrapped around the buildings. The facades were worn and crumbling. Above was a tattered mist, the fog smothering us under its shape. It hid the towers, smoothed their lines into blurred shapes, monsters tilted and felled by an indomitable presence. It had become worse; the scabbed brick of the tenements had burst open even wider, letting the rain and its chill into dozens of homes. The decades-old plumbing system failed entirely, leaving us with no hot water, nonstop leaks, and eventually several instances of flooding. The $30 billion deficit that NYCHA faced ensured a lack of upkeep, especially some yard in the corner of Brooklyn.

There were the beginnings of an exodus, people latching on to family with space elsewhere. Folk left behind clamored for information from community groups they heard that could speed along an emergency transfer, or rental assistance programs. Some sought lawyers, or organizations that provided legal consultation for those who couldn't typically afford it. Zaire and I stayed behind and did what we could. We attempted our own rebuild, fixed what we could, saved who we could, herded them in the right direction, the community center, or the empty apartments by the mall. Some of the units weren't even finished, half-painted with no power or heat. We began our own thing. Called it the East Brooklyn Rescue and Reclamation. Zaire would manage to swipe some equipment from his job, mostly tools and work belts and random gear. I'd talk to Blue about making it an actual nonprofit. We weren't authorized, but the lady behind the Plexiglas window at the local NYCHA office looked relieved, desk lopsided with ticket requests and invoices.

My old building was all but abandoned. Pop was in the midst of packing everything he owned, sour at the idea of being run out by forces beyond his control. I felt better that he'd move in with the lady-friend he wouldn't tell me about instead of spending his days in a rotting apartment. He had watched his friends die one by one, first in his teens and now midway through his life. Men in their fifties, young still, with fat hearts and guts that hung over the top of their shorts. They are large as tree trunks, and take my money gladly in drawn-out hands of spades. They stroke, or their big hearts go out like punctured tires. Their blood becomes mush, or their addictions catch up with them, whether it be liquor, drugs, food, or sex. The old man was worried. He played Eddie Kendricks all day, hated church folk, and would never admit that he was lonely. He was afraid he would die by himself, in the room he paid seven hundred dollars a month for. I'm afraid he has no way to deal. I'm not my dad. But if I was him, seeing my friends die all my life, learning about my own potential death, I'd probably feel as if this was borrowed time. But mostly I am afraid that, like him, I will push everyone away and there will be no one there when I am on my way out. How would I make Pops truly see me, how not all right I'd become. How complicit he is in that, in this family not working. I tried to do that already, showed him my self-harm with my body, my flesh, underfed and numb. Now was time to figure out how to demand better of him, of myself.

The elevator shaft was flooded just below the first floor so I had to take the stairs. It was filled with about an inch of water, the eternal sound of water trickling down stone. I climbed the stairs a flight up, held the railing because the treads were slick. I opened the door to the fifth floor. Some of the walls facing out toward the street had weakened and collapsed. I could see the skyline through an opening of brick and exposed rebar. I stood at the mouth of the scar, an opening of a tumbled brick cave. The wind bit at my pant cuffs. I could slip right through, a tongue through clean teeth. Brown water sloshed under my boots, came from under several apartment doors, some closed and some left ajar.

I found the one I was looking for: a door that couldn't be closed all the way. The lock had been broken long ago. When I touched the knob, my ears went in and out. From far away I could hear water, not from the pipes, but from what seemed like the ocean. I dug in my ears until they were clear. A wet musk coated the apartment, smelled like it became permanent long ago. I splashed around the endless stream. The vinyl tiling under my feet had grown soft, curled at the corners from the leak. The walls were discolored from top to bottom, a greenish bloom mapping its way up to the ceiling. Chairs and sofas were puddles, shapes that were once definable now one, amorphous. The sodden textures were damp, began to fray. The pipes were sprung from beneath the sink cabinets, along the walls. A kitchen table swayed on mangled legs. At the head was Miss Betty, a mug cupped between her unsteady hands. Skin of ochre. The inside of her hands like persimmon fruit felled in dark soil. She looked up at me, a cloudy set of eyes and a slack mouth. Quickly licked her lips.

"I came here to get you out," I said. She made a face of recognition; she was disappointed.

"Where you been all this time?" she asked, indignant.

"Away."

"You shouldn't be here," she said, but didn't look my way.

"What do you mean?"

"Sit down." She pulled the metal chair out for me, right beside her. "Tell me where you were." She had a kettle going, a mug waiting on the counter already. The water sloshed around our ankles.

IT WOULD RAIN and rain later that night—for days, the news had said. Not like Sandy had, not even remotely close. But we'd get a few inches, heavy enough to plunk around near the gutters and steep curbsides. I imagined the whole thing flooded; the shores devoured by the salt of the bay. It would swallow the land in its rolling tide, thick with debris—doors of homes and street lamps. The neighborhood would be wiped clean, a Hall of Fame if the ice melted, pillars and ruins spilled across the bedrock. Abandoned. Washed anew, as if that was the only way. Funny how public housing was meant to be temporary. We were left here, and years and years from now we will leave signage that we were here, to be dealt with toward the end of a half-life. Just shove 'em to the outskirts, the edge of the city like the tower blocks in the outskirts of Paris, the estates just outside London. A problem they'll have to deal with after we've gone. Robert Moses would sleep peacefully in his grave.

"Where's your daughter?" I asked.

"She's gone," Miss Betty said. Wouldn't elaborate. There were many outcomes, many ways you could be gone from someone. Most of them amounted to the same kind of gasping. "It's like I don't know her anymore. Sometimes I think it's me. I wonder if she hates me."

"You just want more for her." For everyone. How did I know? What did anyone want? To survive. Or was that a necessity? I wanted more for me and you. More for everyone.

"You're a sweet boy." She nodded. "I should do something special for my baby."

Somehow, I knew her daughter could never come back, and that made me feel sad for Miss Betty. In that moment, however, watching the odd way the light disrupted her, the weightlessness, my eyes watered. She was used to having to look beyond what was in front of her. Faith was trying despite immaterial possibility, because something inside had ruptured so, and a thing outside the flesh was needed to confront the way ahead. There was no way ahead.

"Now can you come with me?" I asked her again.

"I can't."

"Why not?" I could hear them; voices from a faraway shore. There was someone here that wasn't of the world anymore. I could hear them all. "Answer me."

"You know why. The people out there won't take you for your word." She said, detached suddenly. "Reason why your mother is a myth. They'll call you crazy."

Miss Betty was losing her outline in the fog pushing in through the windows. The water was cold in my shoes, sent a chill through my arms and legs that made me spring up from the table.

"Your mother," she kept on. "The KiKongo would call her a nganga. The Haitian voudon might call her mambo. The Yoruba might call her Iyaláwo. The real question is, what will you call her?"

I didn't say anything. All I know is to call you by your name. Blocks away, a train leaves from the Van Siclen Avenue station and I hear the rolling stock shuffle forward, the coil whine as it skips along the rail. The bodega serves hot soup around this time for free and I could hear a crowd gathering below. The only conceivable way to escape history's slipstream was to do away with the body completely. It was bound by nations, desire, and suffering. I had once gotten lost between other futures, a salt harbor I could walk out onto. You were there. The knot of a hundred years or a distrait summer, how I could feel all of it, close enough to measure both with the same deliberate wonder each deserved. Misremembering. Jumbled. How I house the past with my very bones. A living portal, from where and to where I did not know. I was about as sure of that as I was that Miss Betty was alive. Yet here she was. More than an artifact left behind by an immaterial realm, forgotten by the living. The voices grew louder over the gushing pipes. Maybe the only way to escape history was to not have a body at all, do away with it completely. What was it to be free of a history of state violence, unbound from a history of suffering? I could still hear the meat bees that hovered about the sand of that shore with heavy wings, darting through the cherubs. I fell among them, my body a fever that threatened to burn everything around me. But this was an emancipatory memory. It is always reproducing, therefore it is always present. You are always present.

DISCUSSION QUESTIONS

1. Colly struggles to recover from his mother's death, but not for the initial reasons given. How does Colly's grief evolve throughout the novel? How is it affected by his sense of guilt?

2. There is an element of magical realism embedded throughout the novel. How do the dead function in this book (Key, the Oyster Lady, Virgil, etc.) and how do they grant these characters a rebirth?

3. By the end of the book it is clear that Key becomes all-seeing. How is Key transformed as a seer? How do the different narrative forms and traditions in the book signal this change?

4. Family plays a central role in the novel. How does Colly's love for his older sister and father differ from his love for his mother? How does this love manifest itself amid his grief?

5. How does the primary romantic relationship—between Colly and Naima—mirror or differ from the other relationships in the novel, like Key's relationship with Dante?

6. All the personal relationships in the novel are marked by issues of identity, class, and social conditions. How is this reflected in Colly's relationship to other young people in his community, specifically his friendship with Zaire? How and when does Zaire's life pivot to a different track than Colly's? How about Raven and Tristan?

7. Tyriek White conceived of this novel in relation to Orlando Patterson's theory of social death, summarily defined as the state-sanctioned denial of citizenship for a particular group of people—particularly slavery. The novel reframes this for the modern day as those living within similar

margins of society—in poverty, within the prison industrial complex, etc. Can you speak about how the material conditions of characters in the novel relate to this theory?

8. The narrative circles around themes of grief and anxiety—and yet the novel offers a place of hope. How does the intersection of history, memory, and narrative allow for a broader view beyond Colly's negative associations?

Q&A WITH TYRIEK WHITE

Q: Why did you decide to set your novel in East New York (Brooklyn)?

A: I'm interested in how a place set on the outskirts of empire and its contemporary history of police [re: state] occupation mirrors and sometimes speaks back to the past, mainly to the legacy of slavery in America. A stretch of perhaps twenty or so blocks all the way into Jamaica Bay and the Atlantic Ocean, of marshland and landfill, informs a lot of the language and choices found in my writing.

I wanted to write a story that centered working-class, blue-collar residents who face constant discrimination in housing, education, and employment. I wanted to explore the many ways we survive (and don't survive) at the intersections of race, class, and the environment in forgotten communities.

Q: At what point in the writing process did you understand that this novel could or should not be constructed in a linear way? What was it about this particular story that resisted linear narrative?

A: People don't typically experience the world in a linear way. The experience of participating in the American project as Black people doesn't feel sensical, or linear. It is a tradition borne from Toni Morrison's *Beloved*.

Q: What were your concerns as you were writing the supernatural "seeing" elements of the book? What inspired you?

A: I hoped that readers could negotiate the very real lives of these characters with the supernatural nature of the story. I think ghosts, spirits, monsters are often the only ways we find to make sense of our realities, living in certain environments or living through particular histories. The way state violence manifests and plays a role in our everyday lives is often inexplicable. The works of Gabriel García Márquez (*One Hundred Years of Solitude*), Juan Rulfo (*Pedro Páramo*), Isabel Allende (*The House of the Spirits*), and others use elements of magical realism to tell stories of families embedded in particular social/political moments.

Q: Two thirds of the main characters in this book are women, and you've written them with such beauty and nuance. Where did you pull your inspiration for them?

A: Initially, I pulled from the women I knew. I pulled from my grandmothers, my aunties, my mother. I thought about the friendships I valued and I pulled from Barbara T. Christian and Fannie Lou Hamer. I pulled from books like *Sula* and *Fruit Punch*. I avoided ideas about all-knowing sages and indestructible black women. Through a black womanist framework, conceived and nurtured by scholars/artists such as Audre Lorde and Paule Marshall (also indirectly Toni Morrison and Gloria Naylor), the body becomes a bridge between ideas and theory. I wanted the women in the book to enter the text as embodied, bringing with them the meanings and definitions ascribed to it as it moves throughout the world.

Q: Can you speak about some of the research you did while you were writing this book? How did you navigate the academic work of research with the creative process of writing fiction?

A: Listening to my elders speak about their experiences of New York City in the 1980s informed how I wrote my way into Key's life. Channeling my own upbringing—the sight of the city, the smell of the hallways and streets, the sound of the music that played—opened up the world of this story. My research also involved searching my own family archive: obituaries, a documented family tree, photo albums, all to reflect the idiosyncrasies of an actual family. Archival work to me can be an act of summoning, a means of access to generational/ancestral spaces.

The story benefited greatly from immersive research into the structural and environmental policies that have gripped East Brooklyn from environmentalists such as Dorceta E. Taylor. I realized there was another realm to explore, the circumstances that have led to this community in the present day. This involved old *Brooklyn Eagle* articles, accounts from residents who left journals, texts on early-American/African-American lifestyles and cultures by Robert Hertz, Marcus Rediker, Frances Smith Foster, and more.

Even the spread and transformation of West African or Central African spirituality throughout the New World, due to processes of colonialism, had to be properly examined. More direct understanding of the movement of African spiritual practices involved various texts, such as a dissertation by Marcus A. Watson from the City University of New York regarding relevant anthropological information, a closer examination of the "artifact assemblage found in 1998 under the garret room floor in the attic of the Lott Farmstead" as a clue into "an extension of Kongo-descended cultural practices" in Brooklyn during slavery.

WE ARE A HAUNTING:

STUDY GUIDE

FURTHER READING

Toni Morrison—*Playing in the Dark: Whiteness and the Literary Imagination*

Imani Perry—*Prophets of the Hood: Politics and Poetics in Hip-Hop*

Saidiya Hartman—*Lose Your Mother: A Journey along the Atlantic Slave Route*

Audre Lorde—*Sister Outsider: Essays and Speeches*

Barbara Christian—*Black Feminist Criticism: Perspectives on Black Women Writers*

Meredith M. Gadsby—*Sucking Salt: Caribbean Women Writers, Migration, and Survival*

Zora Neale Hurston—*Mules and Men*

Orlando Patterson—*Slavery and Social Death: A Comparative Study*

Jimena Canales—*The Physicist and the Philosopher*

ESSAYS

Schaeffer, Felicity Amaya, "Spirit Matters: Gloria Anzaldua's Cosmic Becoming across Human/Nonhuman Borderlands," *Journal of Women in Culture and Society*, The University of Chicago, 2018, vol. 43, no. 4, pp. 1005–1029.

Watson, Marcus A. *Kongo to Kings County: African Cultural Continuities at the Lott Farmstead, Brooklyn, New York*, City University of New York, Ann Arbor, 2016. ProQuest, http://umiss.idm.oclc.org/login?url=https://search.proquest.com/docview/1793676489?accountid=14588.

"An Old Burying Ground: A Relict of the Last Century in the Dutch Settlement of New Lots," *Brooklyn Daily Eagle*, 1891, p. 15.

Johnson, Peter, "The Changing Face of the Modern Cemetery: Loudon's Design for Life and Death," 2012. Heterotopian Studies, http://www.heterotopiastudies.com.

LITERATURE THAT INSPIRED THE BOOK

Yaa Gyasi—*Homegoing*

Carmen Maria Machado—*Her Body and Other Parties*

Kiese Laymon—*Heavy*

Nafissa Thompson-Spires—*Heads of the Colored People*

Adam Johnson—*Fortune Smiles*

Garth Greenwell—*What Belongs to You*

Jesmyn Ward—*Sing, Unburied, Sing*

Juan Rulfo—*Pedro Páramo*

Virgil—*The Aeneid*

Toni Cade Bambara—*The Salt Eaters*

Toni Morrison—*Jazz*

Gloria Naylor—*Mama Day*

Zadie Smith—*NW*

James Baldwin—*Another Country*

Victor LaValle—*Big Machine*

James Baldwin—*Just above My Head*

Octavia Butler—*Wild Seed*

Jonathan Lethem—*The Fortress of Solitude*

Ralph Ellison—*Invisible Man*

Gabriel García Márquez—*One Hundred Years of Solitude*

Jhumpa Lahiri—*Interpreter of Maladies*

Isabel Allende—*The House of the Spirits*

WE ARE A HAUNTING:
THE PLAYLIST

"There's a particular lineage of Black music that runs through my debut novel, *We Are a Haunting*, artifacts of migration across regions and the resiliency of ever-expanding traditions. The book is an archive, a preservation of the journey of Black music (and arts culture in general), rooted in the blues and soul, preserved through the ancestors—Martha and the Vandellas, Harold Melvin and the Blue Notes, The Gap Band, Dionne Warwick. Then, there is the next generation—Shirley Murdock, the Mary Jane Girls, Whitney Houston, Eric. B and Rakim, A Tribe Called Quest. Music helped me shape the material lives of the characters in this story, but also the emotional resonance of their experience.

"This is the playlist I used during the process of writing *We Are a Haunting*. More specifically, these songs helped me write myself into a certain scene, moment, or character."—Tyriek White

"Be Careful" by Snoh Aalegra
"Zion Wolf Theme (Unfinished)" by Jai Paul
"Too Fast" by Sonder
"I Hope You Know" by bLAck pARty
"Nights" by Frank Ocean
"Floods" by Lucky Daye
"Sister" by Ben Howard
"Goat Head" by Brittany Howard
"Good for You" by Blood Orange, Justine Skye
"What You Wanna Do" by Faye Meana
"Make Me Cry" by Pip Millett
"Mother Maybe" by Kadhja Bonet

"Something New" (feat. Etta Bond) by SiR, Etta Bond

"Treat Me Like I'm All Yours" by Sasha Keable

"Childqueen" by Kadhja Bonet

"Spontaneous" by Flying Lotus, Little Dragon

"Dark" by Rhye

"Presence" by Brittany Howard

"Dawn Chorus" by Thom Yorke

"Joy" by Kadhja Bonet

"Due West" by Kelsey Lu

"Didn't Know" (A-Side) (feat. Joe Armon-Jones) by Jerome Thomas, Warren
     Xclnce, Joe Armon-Jones

"Tiada Akhir" by Yuna

"KINDRED II" by Kelsey Lu

"Trust" by Brent Faiyaz

"In My Dreams" by ANOHNI

"free drugs" by Ambré

"Just Bright" by Soft Glas

"Karma Plays" by McClenney, Baby Rose

"Static" by Ari Lennox

"PDLIF" by Bon Iver

"Over" by Baby Rose

"You and I" by Toro y Moi

"Lightning" by Orion Sun

MOVIES TO WATCH AFTER READING
WE ARE A HAUNTING

Daughters of the Dust (1991)

Paid in Full (2002)

Pariah (2011)

Belly (1998)

Eve's Bayou (1997)

STEP INTO THE ART OF TYRIEK WHITE'S
WE ARE A HAUNTING

Book of the Dead of the Goldworker of Amun, Sobekmose, ca. 1500–1480 B.C.E.

Jan Martense Schenck House, 1676

American Gothic, Gordon Parks, 1942

Blue Landscape, Hale Woodruff, 1968

Black Girl's Window, Betye Saar, 1969

Frontal Passage, James Turrell, 1994

How Does a Girl like You Get to Be a Girl like You?, Yinka Shonibare, 1995

Presentation, Dana Schutz, 2005

Ain't I a Woman, Mary Enoch Elizabeth Baxter, 2018/23

School Children, from the series An Ode to (You)'all, Akea Brionne, 2022

A House Called Florida, Allison Janae Hamilton, 2022

Way over There inside Me, Torkwase Dyson, 2022

ACKNOWLEDGMENTS

To my mother, Debora, for supporting me in everything. To my father, Troy Jr., who told stories all day and let me listen. My brothers, Troy III, Reese, Tory, Spank, my sister Cola, the first novelist I ever knew. My uncles gave me the world: Ernest, Bird, Al, Dennis, and more. Thank you to my aunties who are more like mothers, Yvette, Darlene, and cousin Audrey, for never-ending love and support. And to my grandmothers—Geneva, Carrie, and Lillian—who watch over us all.

I want to thank my agent PJ Mark, one of my fiercest advocates and who has steadied me throughout. I deeply appreciate Kerry-Ann Bentley, Ian Bonaparte, and the wonderful people at Janklow & Nesbit for making this all work. I can't thank my editor Danny Vazquez enough, for his remarkable insight and care. Thanks also to Rola Harb, Rachael Small, Tiffany Gonzalez, and everyone at Astra House who have poured into this book.

I do not take for granted the teachers and mentors who have forever changed me. Without them, this book couldn't have been what I hoped it could be. In Mississippi—Kiese Laymon, for giving so much for being one of our greatest living writers. I can't say how much I appreciate Tommy Franklin, Ethel Scurlock, Derrick Harriell, and Garth Greenwell for their limitless kindness and clarity. In Claremont, California—thank goodness for Jonathan Lethem and Nina Revoyr. I want to show gratitude for those who deeply informed and provided language to a living framework, Lara Harris, Theri Pickens, April Mayes, Phyllis Jackson, Rita Roberts, Sidney Lemelle, and Valorie Thomas.

I want to thank the New York Writers Institute—more urgently, the privilege to work with Dana Johnson and Christina García. I must give my appreciation to the Calalloo Creative Writing Workshop, Charles H. Rowell's vision as a whole for the opportunity to grow within an extraordinary tradition of writers, and the genius of Ravi Howard and Jacinda Townsend.

I am grateful to share in fellowship with incredible peers: Clarisse Baleja Saïdi, Toni-Ann Johnson, Courtney Moffet-Bateau, Keenan Norris, Anya Lewis-Meeks, Nafissa Thompson-Spires, Jayson Smith, and others; my classmates and friends who spent time with this project in workshop and beyond, Nadia Alexis, Julian Randall, Helene Achanzar, Latoya Faulk, Ida Harris, Laura Avery, Sadia Hassan, and Amy Lam.

I am incredibly grateful for Johnaé and Denise for being generous with their time and giving with their journeys. I learned so much about birth doulas through their stories and experiences.

I thank my friends for their endless patience. To Shiyah, Kelsey, Michael, Nabila, Nolynn, Sharod, Sahir, Rob, Kasie, David, Sarah, Jonah, all of us. I appreciate my first home for perspective. To Amir, Prince Joshua, my cousin Theresa, and many more.